ASCEND

BOOK TWO
SHADOWED VEIL SERIES

Billie Jade Kermack

ASCEND   *Billie Jade Kermack*

All characters and events in this publication other than those clearly in the public domain are fictitious, and any resemblance to actual persons, living or dead, is purely coincidental.

Copyright © 2013 Billie Jade Kermack

The right of Billie Jade Kermack to be identified as the Author of the Work has been asserted by her in accordance with the Copyright, Designs and Patents Act 1988.

Copyright and sole ownership of this book, cover photography and its contents belong to the author Billie Jade Kermack.

All rights reserved. No part of this publication may be reproduced, stored in a retrieval system, or transmitted, in any form or by any means without the prior written consent of the Author, nor to be otherwise circulated in any form of binding or cover other than that which it is published.

Contact the author at: shadowedveilseries@hotmail.com

ISBN: 9781523894376

ASCEND *Billie Jade Kermack*

To Noah, Aavie and Gumball,
with love

PREFACE
☙❦

Death is not the end. Death can never be the end.
Death is the road. Life is the traveller. The soul is the guide.

—*Sri Chinmoy*

ASCEND

Billie Jade Kermack

೮ಌ

I had travelled far and wide by air, sea and land. I kept my feet moving in an attempt to forget her, desperately seeking solace in the natural beauties the world had to offer – Paris, Brussels, Greece – but everything was tainted, a dark cloud firmly overhead. It had been months since I had been with her, yet the memory of her rosebud lips as they curled into a cute half-smile was as clear in my mind as if I had been there only yesterday to kiss them. Some things were harder to remember though, and with every day that passed I lost a little more of my Gracie. Her words were now distant and muddled. On the one hand I tried desperately to forget and move on, the pain an all-too-real accompaniment which followed me everywhere; on the other hand, the idea of forgetting her and what we had was just too emotionally and physically crippling.

Whenever I wanted to run back to her, every time I convinced myself that she needed me (even if it was only for a fleeting moment), I had to remember the pain I had caused her. I had nearly gotten her killed. I couldn't do that to her again, no matter how much her absence from my life was killing me. I had been there the day my parents had died, their last breaths a concerned whisper for my safety. With my three-year-old self carried out of the battered steel enclosure of the freak lift crash, not a mark on my body, I had taken something other than feelings of sadness and loss with me.

I was cursed that day, an orphan forced from apparently nowhere to bear a gift; a gift to see the spirits of the dead, talk to them, help them, and in some cases, banish them. I have never known normal. I have never been ordinary. The day I met Grace was a glimpse into what could have been, a life I could have had, a life with love, hopes and prospects. I had fallen head over heels for her when I should have been watching my back. It was my fault she had been hurt. I had felt compelled to tell her my secret and as each word left my mouth, my revelations becoming more unbelievable with every passing second, I could sense she was still right there with me – she had accepted me, warts and all.

Her unwavering acceptance of my gift had attracted some unwanted attention along the way. Our feelings had become a beacon to a greater evil, the spirit of a dead serial killer intent on making Grace one of his victims. I had unwittingly welcomed her into a world filled with soul-stealing Shadows, spiteful spirits and enough evil to fill the Olympic stadium ten times over.
The memory hits me again – the look on her beautiful face as I callously turned my back and walked away from her. The still present echo of the crippling heartache that vibrated in my chest as she pleaded for me to stay. The soul-destroying realisation that I would never see her again which flitted unwelcome through my mind when I stepped on to the train.
I had to protect her. I had to leave.

ASCEND   *Billie Jade Kermack*

ONE
ಸಿಂಚೆ

BEAU

I opened my wallet and pulled free the strip of black and white photo booth pictures of Grace and I, the fold-line almost worn through due to the amount of times I had looked on it fondly. Her beautiful face was a happy yet cruel reminder of the life I had left behind. I had arrived in Rome in a last ditch attempt to recapture my sanity; the bells of Basilica San Clemente, just south of the Colosseum, distracted me briefly as they rung loudly above me. Their whimsical chimes ignited smiles on the faces of those sat on twisted metal chairs in the quaint cafés that surrounded the courtyard. I stood in the centre of the marble-paved town square with my backpack secured on my back, two weeks' rent money in one pocket and an open train ticket crumpled in the other. I was standing at a crossroads in my life, each final location just out of view.

A young man with a sandy-blonde ponytail halfway down his back and a guitar slung over his shoulder bundled into

ASCEND   *Billie Jade Kermack*

me. Eyeing a petite redhead in a blue sundress who had just passed him, his concentration was elsewhere as she suggestively mirrored his playful smile. He apologised with a wave of his hand and only a brief glance of eye contact. In a split second he changed direction and caught up with the mysterious woman, his charming first line clearly a hit as she slowed to walk beside him. I envied them and those like them, people free to live in the moment, free of consequences. Something slammed down hard and fast to the dark depths in the pit of my stomach, leaving remnants of sorrow in its wake; a dull ache, my constant reminder of her absence.

I readjusted the strap of my backpack and continued to head north, the final bell ringing, signalling the end of my trip down memory lane. I made my way down an unevenly cobbled, dimly-lit street two streets over from *Mrs Rosa's B&B*, the quaint maisonette overlooking the river where I had been staying.

With its whitewashed window slats and eclectic array of window baskets filled with wildflowers, it looked idyllic. It was sandwiched between a dentist's office with sterile grey everything and a small boutique that was surprisingly still in business even though it was called *The World of Cutlery*, a shop renowned for its singular stock of – yes, you guessed it – cutlery. The garland display of handcrafted forks in the shop window and the burgundy and canary-yellow interior left me feeling depressed, but I couldn't quite single out why; it was a building that stood out for all the wrong reasons. As I turned the corner I caught sight of the neon

ASCEND

Billie Jade Kermack

blue *Mrs Ro*sa's *B&B* 'Vacant Rooms' sign, just about visible as the bulbs blinked dully in the distance.

'Nice night for it.' His voice came out of nowhere, steady and loaded with meaning as he awaited my reaction. A young dark-skinned girl and her mother passed the vendor with little regard to his presence, their faces expressionless as they continued past me. 'Would you like a sweet treat Beau, a candy cane maybe?' I turned to face the stranger who had seemingly plucked my name from thin air, eyeing him quizzically. He was a round man, his arms and legs at least three times the size of mine, even with the slimming properties of his dark slacks and black T-shirt combo. He fiddled with the short length of his perfectly-trimmed beard as he waited for me to fill the void of silence.

'How... how do you know my name?'

I realised quickly as his smile contorted into a wicked grimace that I was asking the wrong question. It didn't matter that he knew my name. The fact that he knew me at all when I was in a foreign country, hundreds of miles from home, meant that I was dealing with someone or some*thing* probably not of this world. Signalling my unease, a beaten-up radio perched on the windowsill of the coffee shop across the road began to whine. The intro to Marilyn Manson's 'Sweet Dreams' bubbled to the surface, fighting with the crackling radio for airtime; unnaturally soft and reserved at first, the pace grew in intensity as the lyrics spoke of my plight. He smoothed his hand down his red and white-striped apron and drummed his foot along to the beat, this

ASCEND   *Billie Jade Kermack*

small action thundering in my head as I tried to mentally arrange a rational thought. I considered running; my exits in the quiet, almost completely deserted street were readily available, but as he expertly played his next move I was glued to the spot.

'I see you still have that memento I left you with last time we met.' He pointed his grubby finger at my chest. I instinctively covered my heart with my hand but, beneath my T-shirt, the pale pink scar just above it radiated heat as it recognised its maker. I gritted my teeth, not wanting him to know just how painful his mere presence was to me. 'I was never one for anatomy. Two inches south and it would have ended very differently for you, my boy.' He mocked me with that same disgusting grin, lowering the music to background noise with just a flick of his fingers in the air behind him. 'You should think yourself very lucky' he laughed, prodding my chest with his stubby finger. I recoiled, but the pain vibrated up my neck as contact was made. He held his finger in mid-air; even with space between us, I was still tethered to him.

'Funny that – who would've thought getting stabbed through the chest with a bayonet sourced from the horn of the almighty Devil himself would leave a scar.' I played it down with a slapdash of sarcasm, but the memory of that moment threatened to crush me from within as the frantic beating of my heart thumped against my ribs. He lowered his finger, severing the connection between us, the pain and tension melting away with it.

ASCEND

Billie Jade Kermack

'It's amazing the things you can find on eBay, isn't it? A weapon, a Billy Ocean LP and a new pair of cargo pants, all for the amazing price of £24.99. Who would have known the bloody thing had real powers!' He beamed like a car salesman offloading the latest MG on their lot. 'On a more fitting note, I do apologise for our previous encounter, but I really can't be held accountable. I have this strange and biting urge to maim something – or in your case *someone* – when I don't get my own way. My mother always did say I was a stubborn little git.' I watched silently, gauging his expression as the memory of his mother flitted through his head: fondness? Love? 'But then I did eventually behead the witch, so I guess we're even.' He chuckled, his laugh carefree and light.

'Can we get on with why you are here?' I pushed, knowing very well that there was no answer to this question that could bring me any comfort.

'I have realised that what I have done, who I have become, is wrong; a disgusting shell with no heart, no real feelings. I want you to help me. I want you to help me save my soul... please.' He stood there wide-eyed, nervously fiddling with the pink stringy sugar left on a candyfloss stick from his cart.

'Really?' Well, this was a first. Shadows were bottom-feeders, the lowest of the low in the food chain. I was momentarily dumbstruck as I tried to ignore every bad impression I had about his kind, every terrible atrocity I had witnessed them commit. 'Really?' I asked again, as the last

ASCEND *Billie Jade Kermack*

remnants of my disbelief pulled on their welly boots and headed out the door.

'No not really, you fool. I have never had and will never have a soul, and that's the way I like it. You of all people know how I love to watch people die; preferably in fear of course, but we can't have what we want all the time, can we?' He beamed. His joker antics and wayward sense of humour had me on edge and as he licked his lips, sensing my uneasiness, I could tell I was giving him everything he desired. 'Look, enough of the games – this body is really starting to chafe. I can feel this dimwit fighting me from the inside and it's really starting to get on my nerves.' He huffed exasperatedly, pushing the candyfloss stick down the collar of his shirt to reach an itch on his lower back. 'You, my friend, are the talk of our world and I was sent a message that I thought might interest you. Although draining you would make me beyond giddy, I have been instructed to leave you in one piece – the words *sill breathing* and *with a heartbeat* were used, so I couldn't argue. Downside of my business, unfortunately; we are sticklers for orders.'

I felt sleepy, my balance shaky, his energy radiating from him in a bright red haze that was slowly suffocating me. I stumbled, steadying myself by leaning against the cart. 'I guess giving you a little headache to go home with will just have to do' he smirked, clearly enjoying the effect his presence was having on me. 'So anyway, I just *happened* to be in the area when I caught sight of Willy Wonka here'; he motioned to himself with a lopsided smile. 'Everything else was pretty much due to my boredom. Being dead does have

ASCEND *Billie Jade Kermack*

its downsides – mainly the lack of gun-toting DUIs and sacrificial murder – but hey, it also has its bonuses' he said cheerfully, his smile growing darker as the breeze tickled the hairs on my bare neck. He bowed his head and with a flicker of the streetlight above us his face contorted, the deathly-grey hollowness of his true identity now mere inches from my face. I swallowed the lump in my throat and fought my body's natural instinct to take a step back and away from the creature. To give in would only spur him on. Without the comfort of home soil and a Wiccan by my side with the ability to banish him, I would have to steady myself and see this through.

'You mentioned a message?' I whispered, my ability to speak faltering mid-sentence as fear constricted my windpipe. The lamplight pinged back to life and the Shadow once again hid beneath the guise of the innocent street vendor as it slipped effortlessly back into his body.

'Yes! Silly me, the message. Step back a little so I can channel it.' I waited silently as he closed his eyes and shook out his hands. *'The one you love – she is in trouble. When the full moon rides high in the black sky and souls once tragically lost line the streets, it will take her. Glittering diamond shards will surround her, a cool sea breeze in her hair. An evil stands tall above her. I see blood – so much blood.'* His words were even and calm, strangely filled with compassion.

Suddenly, he started coughing. Bending down to his knees, he lost the link with his vision: 'Help me, please, for the love

ASCEND   *Billie Jade Kermack*

of God, help me!' His now thickly Italian-accented voice was filled with panic and his hands shook violently as they grabbed at my thighs. A moment passed and before I could answer his pleas, he was standing upright again. It was clear the Shadow had once again taken hold of the poor man who resided, trapped, in his own body. 'Sorry about that' he said, all trace of an accent gone. 'Kind of comes with the territory. I told you he was itching to get out.'

'The message, is that it?' I pushed impatiently.

'She dies in a bloody mess unless you get there, blah, blah, blah! Now, how about that candyfloss?' he offered.

I took my phone from my pocket and grimaced at the dwindling signal bar.

9.20PM

Gwen,
When is the next full moon?

9.21PM
Tomorrow...

I ran as fast as my legs could carry me with little regard to what was happening around me. I had to get to the nearest airport... I had to save her.

TWO

ಌ

GRACE

'It wasn't supposed to end like this.'

As I lay there battered, brutalised, my muscles in knots, wondering why and how I had got myself into this mess, everything went hazy. I had met my dream man. Beau had strolled into my life and touched it with a sense of bewildering magic. He could see and talk to spirits, he could literally change lives. I loved him with a passion I didn't truly understand. But as he walked out of my life, irreparably shattering my heart and shrouding my soul in grief, I realised his gift had stained my life a murky black. I had opened up my mind to the possibility of the unearthly and unnatural existing among us; I had opened a door allowing every crazed, depraved ghost a free one-way pass into my head. He had left me with this.

I grasped at the sodden sand in clumps around my fingers, stained red with my blood. My natural ability to focus

ASCEND *Billie Jade Kermack*

dwindled with every strained breath. I struggled to make out my surroundings as flashes of bright white light from the boardwalk, emanating from the dead souls that had lined up to watch my torture, blew in quickfire succession. My head felt as though it was on fire, pressure building around the cavernous wound. I could taste the warm, rich iron nectar flowing from it as it travelled down my face.

Now I lay me down to sleep,
I pray the Lord my soul to keep.
If I die before I wake,
I pray the Lord my soul to take.

A forgotten memory pushed its way to the forefront of my mind, and I smiled; just a little one, but a smile all the same.

As delirious or insane as it may be, I felt her warmth – my Nanna, my dead father's mother, a bright shining star amidst a sea of perpetual darkness. Her wrinkled face loving, her voice tranquil and melodic as she spoke the first words slowly, urging me as she once had her own children to follow along. I only remembered snippets of my grandmother; she had died when I was four, and having her with me was comforting. I recounted each word along with her out loud but still at a whisper, harrowed by the dry, stabbing pain in my throat. Through fits of gargles, splutters and masses of built-up blood, I made it to the end of the prayer.

'Grace, Grace. It's time, sweetheart. Gracie...' Her voice trailed off into the distance as the shadows swallowed me

ASCEND   *Billie Jade Kermack*

whole and dragged me into the dusky void that would be my final resting place.

Love is hoped for, life is a trial, death is inevitable.

ఎఁ⚹

With a shuddering jolt up my spine and a blinding flash of white light, I was free. Free of the dream, the vision, free of the female stranger, free of the pain, free of I don't exactly know what. Free for now at least. The fairground music echoing from the arcades lining the seafront was now thunderous, flighty and whimsical as it mocked my experience. The dazzling multicoloured lights streamed out onto the pavement and the laughter and chatter of passers-by made me feel more alone than ever.

Why me? Who was she? Why me?

Although my skin was free of wounds, apart from the scrapes from the minor – but very real – car accident the day before, my muscles were still painfully tense. My arms ached and my head was still throbbing with pent-up pressure and conflicting emotions.

'Do you make a habit of walking barefoot in the rain?'

I knew that mesmerising voice, but praying I was right and desperately dreading I was wrong made me rigid and unable to move a muscle. I felt his hand on mine but I still couldn't move. Uncontrollable tears welled up in my eyes; I closed them tight and wiped them on my jumper sleeve, the fabric rough against my wind-beaten skin.

I'd thought about this moment for months, wished for it, yearned for it, dreamed about it. I never thought it would really happen. Beleaguered with an onslaught of thoughts and emotions that I couldn't straighten out, I finally found the will to move and as I turned my head around – there he was.

'Hiya, Miss Gracie' he drawled, as though he had seen me just last week. His mellow approach whipped my sensibility into a confused frenzy as I fought internally with what to do next. His stunning cobalt eyes fixed on mine as he beamed down at me with a set and familiar smile – *my smile,* I thought, heartfelt. He pulled me up onto my feet and we stood there in silence, exchanging looks as my mind raced. With every passing second sadness and anger equally tugged at my heart, furiously trying to repair the gaping hole he had left me with when he walked out of my life. I felt light-headed, sick, confused and overjoyed all at once at his return, which made the floor spin. My experience with the shrouded stranger who was a little too willing to throw a punch, my heartbreak at Beau deserting me. My composure slipped away. I fell back onto the sand and rested my head on my knees.

Breathe, just breathe. You can handle this, just like riding a bike. Jump back on that bike and give him hell! my Inner

ASCEND   *Billie Jade Kermack*

Bitch screamed at me, riling me up. I felt adrenaline coursing through my veins, spiking my senses, finally clearing my mind. 'Where the hell have you been?' I muttered quietly, my eyes still focused on the sand beneath me, the confidence I wanted to possess falling short.

Wow, don't get too angry, you might blow a blood vessel! My Inner Bitch reacted caustically, dumbfounded by my sheepish behaviour.

'I don't think you're going to find any answers down there... come on.' He held out his hand towards me.

'I think I deserve an answer' I demanded with a scowl that could melt ice, declining his hand.

'I had to sort some things out – what happened to your face?' he asked in a panic, taking another step towards me into the light and dropping to his knees by my side. 'I was sure I got here in time, you were meant to be all right.' I moved away sharply, feeling every little bit of progress I had made over the past few months to repair myself and survive without him dissipate into the bitter night air.

'Don't change the subject. So you had some things to sort out, that's OK then – never mind that I was worried about you!' I screamed, barely recognising my own shrill voice. I had begun to rant inaudibly; I might as well have been speaking French. I refused to make eye contact with him. I looked down at the sand and continued to rant on, fearing that if I gazed into his beautiful cerulean eyes for longer then five seconds I would be bound to him without question.

'I mean if nothing else, we could have been friends. If you didn't want to be with me that was your choice, but a simple phone call to let me know would have been nice. A call to let me know you were OK – that you were alive!' I continued curtly.

Every attempt he made to interrupt me was brutally shut down with a mixture of quickfire glares and brusque hand gestures. Beau had walked into my otherwise dull and mundane life with a gift, a power unlike any I had ever seen. He had a two-way open connection with the spirit world that had led to me nearly dying. You heard right – *dying*. If you can believe it, the fact that I was nearly made into sushi by the knife-wielding spirit of a serial killer wasn't the hardest part; losing Beau was. But I was my mother's daughter, and stubbornness was ingrained in my DNA.

'I loved you. I don't fall in love all the time and I can't believe you could be so selfish.' Like a woman possessed, months of heartache and anguish spilled onto the once-beautiful beach and rushed out with full force to engulf Beau. Feeling so close too death and so close to living at the same time, flashes of what it felt like to have my head caved in by an angry visitor and what it felt like to be back in Beau's arms confused me. For a few painfully long seconds, we were both silent. He looked vague and perplexed and deeply hurt by my words.

ASCEND

Billie Jade Kermack

'Wait a minute Grace, back up. What did you just say?' He shuffled across the sand and his warm, sweet breath caressed my cheek.

'What, the part where you didn't bother to call me to dump me, or the part where I told you that you were a selfish git?

'Neither actually, I think it was in between the two – something about you loving me?' he said with an unanswered smile, a smile that even through all my pent-up anger and spiteful words still made my knees weak.

'Yeah – so what, I said loved – think past tense!' I shouted at him defensively, not thinking or meaning it. I stood up and walked away, stifling yet more tears.

'Oh – OK, so you don't love me any more then – present tense?' he teased, knowing full well what the answer was. I didn't get far before I collapsed onto the sodden sand again with a thud.

'I told you I loved you, I SHOWED you I loved you, and you still ran.'

What's the point of running away? All I want is him, for so long all I've wanted is him! I may be tainted by the dead now, but is that an excuse to stop living?

The rain had settled a little, so I pulled down my hood and nervously ran my hands through my matted hair. I had no idea what I should do. I was a moth flying too close to the flame, completely mesmerised; although the outlook was bleak, a glimmer of hope still fluttered beneath the surface. My Prince Charming was there in front of me, solid flesh and blood in all its handsome and desirable packaging. But was that ever enough? I feared I had only touched the surface on the baggage that came along with loving Beau, with being a permanent fixture in his crazy life. *If I expect the worst, is that the same as inviting it in? Is 'happily ever after' actually a possibility?*

OK, so my stubbornness could ruin this if I let it. But how could I bypass the months of sadness and heartbreak? How could I let him back into my life knowing I could be back here again, in this crippling moment? Who would have thought that only ten minutes previously I was being attacked, beaten back and blue, the sand around me stained with my blood? He sat down and extended his legs either side of me. As he pulled my hair to one side, exposing my neck, I felt his warm lips on my skin. For the first time in a very long time I felt like a whole person; complete, outside and in. I turned to face him, my fears and my anxieties.

'I never truly believed you felt that way for me. I never let myself believe it and when everything happened and you got hurt – because of me – I just switched off. I did the only thing I knew to do. I ran. I *did* and I *do* love you Gracie, more than you could ever imagine. Leaving you was the hardest thing I have ever had to do but I just couldn't stand what I was doing to you. Hurting you is my worst nightmare; I couldn't stand by and watch you go through anything like that again. I never wanted to lose you, you are

ASCEND

Billie Jade Kermack

the best thing in my life, but I thought that by leaving you I was doing the best thing for you. I can admit when I'm wrong. To be honest, I couldn't have stayed away much longer.' He gazed deep into my eyes. In that instant my soul warmed and my heart mended with every warming word that left his mouth.

Beau placed his hand gently on the cut on my face, and his thumb lightly brushed the small open graze on my fat lip. 'I had to come back to you. I am here to protect you.'

There was no dam to stop the flood now. As the tears splashed against my coat I wiped them furiously, begging them to stop. Still, there was a welcomed smile on my face; I finally understood their presence. A wall had been knocked down, the bricks crashing with a thud around me, once again opening my still-fragile heart. In that moment I didn't know whether to laugh or cry.

It took me a few seconds but I managed to compose myself. I relaxed into his body, rested my head on his shoulder and looked up at him. 'I'm a mess! A bloody, blubbering mess. Crying uncontrollably, mascara halfway down my face...' I guessed only half of my sentence was audible as I fought to speak and breathe through the sobs.

'Not at all. I love you, Miss Gracie – tears and all' he replied tenderly, and this time I believed him. He pushed my hair behind my ear and as he pulled his hand back his fingers caressed my chin, wiping away what tears had broken free.

ASCEND   *Billie Jade Kermack*

'I shouldn't have left – I know that now. I couldn't watch you fall apart around me, *because of* me. You deserved a chance at something normal Gracie, and that meant me leaving. If I had known how difficult it was going to be, I probably would have had a rethink.'

I grabbed the now-crumpled note he had left me the day he abandoned me. I had read and re-read it probably a thousand times, and now held it mere inches from his face in protest. 'Where have you been? This is all you left me with, scribbled words on a torn piece of paper!' I was shouting now, not holding back. He would hear the pain he had caused me.

'I'm sorry, I don't know what else I can say. I didn't want to leave. I thought I was doing what was best for you, keeping you safe!' His face was solemn as he looked at me from beneath his eyelashes, his head bowed towards the sand. 'I love you Grace, more than I could ever explain. I have spent every day, every week, every month thinking of you, dreaming of you. I would give anything to get those months back. I can't change it; I can only promise from here on out that I will try every single day to make it up to you. Gracie, I promise with every inch of my heart and soul, I will never let you go again, no matter how rocky it gets. I love you.' His words sung to me, setting my body alight as the tense, invisible void between us slowly vanished in the cooling night breeze.

'Love you always, miss you always, with you always. In this life and the next.' He beamed, bringing my open hand up to

ASCEND

Billie Jade Kermack

his face and holding it there, his breath grazing my palm, his lips dangerously close and making me well up again. Loving him was easy. If I was honest, I had never truly stopped, even when my anger seemed a front-runner. He was mine, and I was his. It's just the way it was.

'I love you too, Beau – more than you could ever know. Please don't leave me again, my heart couldn't take it.' I giggled through my tears. There was a short silence, filled only by only the crashing of the sea onto the sharp, weathered rocks on the bay pier.

'I can't do this without you' I whispered as he wiped a stray tear from my cheek, his face suddenly panicked:

'Do what, Grace?'

'Survive' I protested, bleary-eyed, my head now in my hands. I felt emotionally, mentally and physically drained. My body was sore, my muscles still in knots. My vision, my experience – whatever the hell it was – had taken its toll. He put his strong arms around me and I cuddled up to him; still, even with his declarations of undying love, not as comfortably or wholeheartedly as I would have before he had left. He sensed my unease, his embrace growing tighter as it spoke of just how much he wanted me.

The rain started to fall again, heavier now, the heavens opening with a crashing of luminous thunder towards the north, its sharp white light reflecting on the waves. I didn't care. I had him with me, for now at least, and nothing was

ASCEND *Billie Jade Kermack*

going to ruin it. We pulled up our hoods and looked out onto the dead grey sea, the now crow-black starless sky.

'Thank you for these, by the way. I didn't realise I had them until I reached the south of France.' He held out the now-worn strip of photo booth pictures of the two of us from the front pocket of his jeans. I traced my finger over them fondly. I had watched him leave me that day in the train station, every inch of me crying out for him to stay. When I realised that my words could not make him stay I knew that a piece of me – however small that piece may be – had to be with him. I had slipped the pictures into his jacket pocket and watched him leave, the world around me in tatters.

He placed the photos in my palm, covering them with his hand. Whatever would happen, whatever his gift would bring, I would not leave his side. I wanted to stay there in his arms forever. As love walked back into my life the once-solemn and silent surroundings bounced back and noise, colour, joy was finally restored. But for how long? How long could I keep my secret? Would he leave me again if he found out?

ASCEND *Billie Jade Kermack*

THREE
෨෬

We climbed the wide limestone steps hand in hand in the pelting rain, broad smiles etched on our faces, eyes fixed on each other as we practically fell through the glass-fronted entrance of the hotel where I was staying. We stopped for a moment, my feet planted on the woven Chinese rug in the lobby, rushes of air escaping my lungs in quick bursts. His eyes, dark and musing, bore into me.

I didn't wait for an invitation and without warning, I figuratively grabbed the bull by the horns. I tugged at the collar of his coat; with the faux fur edging of his hood matted and drenched between my fingers I pulled him towards me, wrapping my arms around his neck. Then, there was *just us* as my lips met his. Those sweet, soft lips that I had longed to touch again, in the same breath fearing I would never again feel against mine. His hands tightly wound around my back, his hands locking together as he lifted me clear off the ground with my boots dripping rainwater on the rug below. We couldn't possibly have been any closer than we were at that moment.

ASCEND
Billie Jade Kermack

I didn't want to, but the physical need to breathe and my natural instinct to stay alive made me pull my lips free. I looked at him, his eyes still closed for a moment as he savoured our embrace. I ran my hands through his wet hair, fiddling with the shaggy brown strands that curled slightly at the nape of his neck, tracing my fingers along his jawline as I brought them around to his chin. He lowered me slowly, his brooding cerulean stare now fixed on mine.

'Wow' he said, taking a much needed, steadying breath.

'Wow yourself' I whispered, relishing the feeling.

'Lift?' We said in unison, silently struck by the same idea. I wasn't psychic but I recognised that boyish, playful look of Beau's – it didn't matter how long we had been apart.

We rushed through the marble-floored hotel, playing out our very own version of the Wacky Races where I was in the lead, but not by much. The rubber soles of my sodden Converse squeaked on the freshly waxed floors as I took the stairs two at a time. Beau swung across me, round an oval mahogany table with curved, gilded stem legs.

Atop the very expensive looking table was a pink ceramic vase which could have held a gallon of water with ease, filled high with lilies and pink chrysanthemums. His sneaky move meant that he had taken the lead and as we bundled into the hallway I grabbed for his coat, pulling him back from the lift and victory, giving into my schoolgirl temptation to cheat. He counteracted my move and pulled me into a spin, our

ASCEND

Billie Jade Kermack

combined weight bundling us into the cold granite wall behind in fits of laughter. As he pulled me up and away from the wall my eyes did not leave his; I couldn't help the fear that if I closed them, even for just a moment, he might disappear.

I stepped backward a few paces, with Beau matching my steps. His face was now mere inches from mine, our stares still locked. His hand searched into my coat and settled around my waist. With a sharp tug his soft, warm lips met mine again. As a *ding* sounded the approaching lift's arrival, he slowly pulled away. I hung there in what felt like mid-air for a moment and sighed dreamily, composing myself. The lift doors opened with a whining creak.

'What floor would you like?' said an immaculately chic brunette woman, holding a pink raincoat-clad pug puppy. She eyed us disapprovingly with a drawn-on eyebrow that now greeted her hairline as our sodden coats dripped rainwater onto her Prada pumps. 'This lift is temperamental, don't be surprised if you end up back where you started once you hit Level Three. Maybe you should take the stairs' she suggested, fiddling with her dog's crystal-encrusted collar and taking a step back away from us.

Ignoring her, I turned to Beau. 'Fifth please' I said, threading my fingers through his. The woman exited on the third floor, leaving us alone with just the stench of wet dog, the sickly sweet scent of Chanel N°5 and the surging gravitational pull between us.

ASCEND   *Billie Jade Kermack*

ಸಃಅ

The thin rain-soaked fabric of his crisp white shirt delicately graced his rippling muscles just enough to tease me and send my thoughts into a frenzy. As his soft, wet lips gently explored my naked neck my whole body began to tingle and in no time at all, I relaxed into him. I let myself go with the feeling.

Beau's hands were suddenly wrapped around me; warm, confident hands. As he lovingly kissed my neck and drew my body into his, he traced his finger along the neckline of my shirt and with one smooth movement tilted my head towards him. He lingered there for a moment or two, lost in thought. His sweet, laboured breaths caressed my neck as his hand stroked my hair, strands tickling my back. This was a perfect moment in time, a moment I would never have thought possible just a few hours ago. For a split second what I saw before me felt like a dream, a collection of my hopes and desires all wrapped up in a perfect, mind-blowing bubble.

Is it possible to be this happy? Am I still dreaming? The thought that I might be setting myself up for the biggest fall of all did cross my mind. I had taken this leap with Beau before. I had entered into something so wholeheartedly that when it was taken away, I was left in tatters; my stomach churned at the thought of how broken I had felt since Beau

ASCEND *Billie Jade Kermack*

walked out of my life. Then a warm smile broke on his face, immediately reassuring me, my fears now just an echo in the distance.

My drenched shirt grazed my shoulders as I pulled the buttons free and let it slip down my body. It floated towards the lush, thick cream carpet of the hotel room beneath my now bare feet. I shivered due to a mix of things: the rain, which felt as though it had penetrated down to the bone, the light beachront breeze floating through the open bay windows and the sheer, overwhelming excitement of the moment.

Beau's hands slowly made their way down my now almost-bare body and as his fingers tripped over the boning in my bra, I let out what can only be described as a whimper. How I'd longed to have his hands touch me again, to have his eyes fixated on me as they delved into my very soul.

The anticipation and desire to be as close as humanly possible to Beau was both daunting and uncontrollable. I pushed my palm to his chest and, one by one, slowly unbuttoned his shirt. As raindrops from my hair trickled down my forehead and across my cheek, his fingers were there to wipe them clear. I couldn't resist him – not that I wanted to. The air around us pulsed like electricity, our bodies perfectly attuned to one another. A stifled, hitched breath left my shaking lips, making him smile broadly.

Nothing had ever felt so complete, so right. The glow from the red glass bedside lamp glistened on his tanned chest as

ASCEND *Billie Jade Kermack*

it heaved with every waiting breath. My hands wandered happily along his strong, broad shoulders, slowly freeing him from his shirt.

With nothing between us but air, I traced my index finger suggestively down his chest and along his abs. Like something ripped from the pages of a Harlequin romance novel, I could feel an intense yearning to be locked in his arms forever. His balmy and inviting lips caressed mine until everything around me became blurred and obsolete.

His hands skimmed my now-bare midriff and I recoiled only half-heartedly as the sensation ignited a sinking feeling low in my body. Those many months of endless tears, utter heartache and despair without him disappeared in an instant as I opened my eyes and he was there, beaming down at me. He was no longer just a memory; he was here with me, and he was my Beau again.

My head was suddenly all over the place as I quivered beneath his roaming fingers. Under an onslaught of emotions, there was one thing I was sure of: I never wanted Beau to be anywhere else but by my side. In this moment, for the first time in what felt like an eternity, I felt complete. His burly hands nimbly roamed the contours of my back. As they nestled comfortably just above the belt of my jeans, I met his stare and a rush of all-encompassing warmth and ecstasy flowed through me. My pulse raced and my heartbeat fluttered nervously like a hummingbird's.

We embraced tightly, my feet barely touching the floor

ASCEND

Billie Jade Kermack

beneath me as he secured me in his arms. With my head resting on his shoulder, an uncontrollable tear fell down my cheek. Nestled in his arms, we moved backwards together towards the opulent, antique, four-poster bed. He lowered me down, his hand sweeping away the rogue tear, stroking my cheek as he smiled lovingly.

'I love you. I never wanted you to forget that' he said, the guilt of leaving me now present in his wide, sorrowful eyes.

'You're home now, that's all that matters' I whispered, my breathing laboured, skin sensitive as I fell into his protective grasp. Our fingers intertwined, we fell back onto the fresh, white cotton bedsheets. I wanted to stay lost in that moment with him forever, but I couldn't shake the heartbreaking, unwelcome, all-too-believable fear that one day he might again leave me.

I knew he meant what he said. The sincerity in his voice couldn't possibly be tarnished by lies. But I also knew that if my life hung in the balance, Beau would do whatever it took to keep me safe; even if it meant living unhappily ever after.

I pushed the thought aside, realising almost instantly that worrying was futile. I was his and he was mine and nothing would ever come between us again, unless I let it. My nightmare and brutal death on the beach could wait another day at least; whether it was a sign of what was to come or just a bunch of messed-up synapses still broken from my attack last year was a question which, for now, I could discard.

ASCEND Billie Jade Kermack

I will keep my secret from Beau. I have to... right?

FOUR

I awoke in a panic, sweat pooling at my clavicle, my pillow drenched. Light rain still softly pelted the windows, the morning's lighter skies holding nothing but the white glare of the still-high full moon. The vivid and unwanted memory of the previous night, before Beau had returned, the pain, the fear – it had all felt so real. But who could it have been? Was it Luan Lesney, the deranged witch who had worn Gwen's skin like a snow suit? Or maybe it was Glen again, sending another ghost to finish off his murderous plan. Whichever angle I looked at it, the answer was still the same: I had no idea who or *what* it was that had attacked me on the beach. The memory ate at me, churning round in my head, sparked into new life by my worries. I quickly banished the thought when I caught sight of Beau. His mere presence calmed me.

All is well with the world, all is well with me. A night so perfect has led me to the conclusion that, for the foreseeable future at least, all is well with Beau and I.

I recited the words as though they were a mantra, a belief

ASCEND   *Billie Jade Kermack*

that would somehow save me from my own undoing.

⁂

The burnt-orange sunrise began to creep through the white net curtains, flooding the balcony and lending the cream carpet a warm hue. I rubbed the sleep from my eyes and stretched out my arms, awoken from the best night's sleep I had had in months, lulled by his mere presence.

Beau was lying on his back next to me, still fast asleep. With his arm around me I had nestled comfortably into his side, my head resting on his chest. His smell was intoxicating, his chiselled body with all the right accents and contours. I propped myself up on my elbow to get a better look at him.

Sighing deeply and tracing my index finger along his collarbone, I had to remind myself that I wasn't dreaming, that my soulmate was in fact sleeping peacefully beside me. His bed-hair was ruffled, his lips slightly parted, his chest rising and falling in a sated, mesmerising rhythm.

You might want to wipe that silly grin off of your face and look in the mirror – just because he wakes up looking like an Adonis doesn't mean the same rule applies to all of us mere mortals. Fraggle Rock probably isn't the best look on this particular occasion, my Inner Bitch scolded with an underlying hint of joy. She was revelling in my panic. I shot up as carefully as I could without disturbing him. Every creak sounded like an earthquake.

ASCEND

Billie Jade Kermack

The ornate Victorian mirror attached to the dressing table against the far wall was the perfect height for me to quickly flatten and rearrange my hair as best as I could. 'Oh my God!' I whispered; she was right. To say I looked rough was an understatement.

I pulled at my hair, running my fingers through my unruly brown curls to dislodge the knots. The skin around the cuts and scrapes on my face was now a lavender colour, the puffiness almost completely settled. I hadn't exactly looked after myself since Beau had left me last – I blamed the heart-wrenching, soul-shattering, constant depression for that one. I had lost a fair amount of weight, weight which I hadn't stored a lot of to begin with. I prodded at my cheekbones.

If I was honest, I was grateful for the accident; my body's reaction to the trauma meant that I could hide behind the face of a size 12 when actually I had almost disintegrated into a miniscule size 8. My Nanna had often told me I would have childbearing hips and she wasn't wrong, except when I had ignored my need for food. While I fought with my feelings of abandonment, my bones had only pushed further against my thinning skin.

Pulling my hair away from my face I realised I hadn't seen that crystal shine in my big blue eyes for a while, and the rosy tint to my flawed skin added a dash of perkiness to my expression; it was welcomed. I resumed my position in the comfort of his arms and propped myself up again, strategically arranging my hair to fall around my shoulders.

ASCEND
Billie Jade Kermack

His other hand was resting across his stomach, those strong hands that I had thought would never touch me again.

I swallowed uncomfortably hard at the thought. As though he had read my mind, the arm that was wrapped around my back softly rubbed my forearm, up and down, to and fro, sensually slow. Without even knowing it, he was making every nerve in my body ignite and stand to attention.

The edge of the crisp white sheet hugged low at his waist, leaving very little to the imagination. I placed my hand on his chest and explored the trail of hair to his navel. Feeling alive and brimming with bravery, I gently traced the small white scars on his otherwise-perfect torso as he continued to sleep beneath my touch. They weren't scary or unnerving to me, but intriguing; they represented a hidden part of him, something I was yet to discover. I ran my finger gently along the thin raised scar on the tanned skin just above his heart. It looked fresher than the others – deeper too, I guessed.

'Good morning, beautiful' he murmured, running his free hand through his light-brown hair. I smiled broadly up at him, happily fixed in the moment, finally content with the direction fate in which had taken us, with him by my side. He moved his arm behind me, pulling me closer to him, his lips softly meeting the top of my head.

'How did you get these?' I asked, diverting my stare to his chest again.

'I got into a bar fight with a pixie,' he chuckled. 'Don't

ASCEND *Billie Jade Kermack*

believe the stories. One too many Cosmos and Tinkerbell's Hell's Angels streak comes out.'

'Very funny, but Tinkerbell is a fairy' I added.

'It's so cute that you know that.' He kissed me quickly and stretched out his arms.

'The ins and outs of *Never Never Land* aside, I really want to know!' I pushed, running my fingers up the ticklish spot on his side as his stretch left it exposed.

'You might want to know, but I don't fancy ruining the moment the second I open my eyes.' He clasped my hand in his, expertly subduing me as his lips grazed my knuckles, his eyes still fixed on mine.

'Was it a Ghostbusters-related incident? Did you piss off the Ghost of Christmas Past that year you had your aversion to turkey?' I asked animatedly, wide-eyed. I chuckled into my hand at my own joke (I use the term *joke* loosely), as the corners of his mouth twitched up into a smile.

'Yeah, hand me my Proton Pack. We came, we saw, we kicked some ass!' he said in his best American accent. I just gazed at him, eyebrows raised. 'You haven't seen it?' He asked, shocked. Now he was wide awake. He readjusted his posture, tutting and shaking his head disapprovingly. 'That's a slice of film history right there!'

'Chill out, it's not like you wrote the film!' I laughed, fiddling

ASCEND   *Billie Jade Kermack*

with the edge of the bedsheets.

'Its a classic, a must-see!' he argued passionately, his geeky, comic-book side leaping to the surface, his charming persona subdued in a WWF-worthy headlock.

'I thought you said a spirit had to physically touch you to leave a scar?'

'A cursed object, or one sourced from a great evil – although rare – is not impossible to find. Sometimes very easy to find, in fact... and has the power to imprint the ghost's intentions upon our flesh.' Whenever Beau spoke of his gift and its effects, it always sounded as though he had read it straight from *Magic For Dummies*; it was a part of his life he hated, one he tried really hard to push aside. Knowing I was treading on thin ice, I ignored my better judgement and pushed further.

'And these?' The pads of my fingers danced over the other small pink scars which marked his torso.

'Minor consequences of the job, not worth bothering over – a collection of stories for another time, possibly when you get me good and drunk.' His smile's sincerity didn't quite reach his eyes. He gazed at the pink scar on my cheekbone, the guilt he felt for the pain I had gone through clear on his face as he quickly changed the subject. He reached up and looked at the time on the alarm clock beside me. 'I want to show you something.'

ASCEND

Billie Jade Kermack

Before I could come back with a witty one-liner he had jumped out of bed, securing the flimsy bedsheet around his waist. Without warning he swept me up into his arms in a fireman's lift, throwing the sheepskin comforter from the end of the bed over his other shoulder.

'Hey, put me down!' There was very little conviction in my voice. I had dearly missed Beau's playful side – no sadistic spirits, no Shadows causing havoc, no imminent death of a loved one looming. Any stress that may have remained magically unaffected by his charm was swept away in the cooling breeze from the window. He made his way through the slim double-doors onto the balcony, still carrying me over his shoulder. The early morning sun splashed against my face as he lowered me onto the round, cushioned wicker sofa.

I happily sunk into his arms and enjoyed what was left of our magical night. It suddenly occurred to me that there was no need to desperately hang onto the night before; this was our life together now. With a sigh of sheer happiness and Beau's soft kiss on my forehead I realised that this was our first real sunrise, a moment perfect and unspoilt. The sun rose from beyond the endless blue shoreline and we slept, right there on the balcony, safe in each other's embrace.

ଛଠ

'I have something for you. I was going to give it to you last night, but your welcome home party was... distracting.' I blushed brightly, arranging the blanket around me, his

ASCEND   *Billie Jade Kermack*

words tickling my modesty.

Arching his back, he grabbed his coat which was slumped over the wicker sofa just inside the room and pulled out a small, red-ribboned box from the inside pocket. My eyes lightened and my heart lifted without warning. A whirl of images flashed through my mind, memories I had yet to experience. Our summer beach wedding, our first home, the birth of our kids, one boy, one girl... suddenly, a Nicholas Sparks sensory overload of romantic happily-ever-afters swamped my otherwise sane train of thought.

'Oh no, it's not what you think! I mean one day, sure, in the future, just not now!' he panicked, clearly reading my mind with a stressed-out smile that trembled at the corners, awaiting my response. I smiled back at him, but mine lacked conviction. I felt something twitching inside me, a feeling that I couldn't quite make out – a Frankenstein concoction, a hybrid emotion hovering over me. Disappointment, rejection, contentment, relief?

What on earth did I want him to say? Of course it's a crazy idea. I'm only eighteen years old. I don't even know if that's what I want.

Who am I kidding? I want commitment – hell, I want it all!

But, for the time being, I was happy to keep that thought to myself. As I opened the box I realised that what lay inside meant everything, said everything that Beau was feeling. Any commitment that I wanted was there staring me in the

ASCEND *Billie Jade Kermack*

face, and it wasn't ring-shaped.

'It was my mother's. I want you to have it.' He held his breath, gauging my reaction. Secured with a pin inside the cushioned box was the necklace that usually hung around Beau's tattered childhood teddy on his 'memory shelf' at home. Or, at least, what used to be his home.

Is he planning on going back to live with his foster mother, Gwen? Had he started a new life when he left me? Has he met someone else?

The pendant was stunning. It was made of gold and platinum and hanging from the snake-like chain was half a heart-shaped locket with different coloured gems, two hanging either side of the pendant. Inscribed on the back with the word 'Reinca' in swirling letters. After the untimely death of Beau's parents, his mother's necklace was the only thing besides a crumpled old photograph that he had been able to keep hold of.

'Beau, it was your mother's. I can't take it.'

'You can and you will.' He pulled back my hair and draped the soft metal around my neck, fiddling with the clasp. 'She would want you to have it, Grace. I want you to know that I'm never going to leave you again.'

Any doubts I had faded, my desire for a marriage proposal along with them. From all the words in the English language, I could only muster two: 'Thank you.' His fingers

ASCEND

traced round from the base of my neck to my jawline, never losing contact with my skin.

'One day, I will marry you. One day we'll have the house, and one day – in the *future*,' he emphasised, 'we will have our own little squad of Ghostbusters.' I was sure that Beau's gift of seeing and communing with the dead wasn't his only talent. It wasn't the first, second or even the third instance he had appeared to read my mind.

'I...' he pushed his index finger to my already-pursed lips to silence me.

'For now, you get me. If you still want me, of course.' His expression lightened as I naturally began twiddling the necklace between my fingers.

'I want nothing else but you. And some peanut butter on toast, if you're offering.'

'That can be arranged,' he chuckled. I pulled him into the blanket. The warm, wet kiss that followed was drenched in yearning and desire and my heart leapt into my throat. I fiddled with the pendant, my heart swelling with the gesture it carried.

'Do you know what it means, the word on the back?' I asked.

'No. Never have; but it looks like only half a word, for half a necklace.'

ASCEND   *Billie Jade Kermack*

'Do you remember her – your mother?'

'Not really. I remember the idea of her. As time has passed, my memories have dwindled into an amalgamation of shapes and colours, thoughts and feelings that could very well be torn from the pages of a storybook. I don't know if they're even my own any more; probably more likely a mixture of *Brady Bunch* TV specials and a Wes Craven box set' he chuckled, sadness still present in his glazed blue eyes. 'I didn't know what a mother was until I met Gwen. Something about her just felt right. The moment I saw her I knew instantly that she would protect me, love me without question, accept me and my gifts. She is my mother.'

The phone rang loudly and we both jumped, our conversation finished, for now at least. Beau ran into the room, holding the bedsheet tightly around his waist. I hugged the blanket greedily, smiling at the sea as it crashed forcefully against the nearby cliffs. He picked up the receiver, sat on the edge of the bed and pushed the flashing button.

'Hello sir, I am just calling to give you your wake-up call.' The receptionist's voice flooded through the speakerphone, ringing with an air of distaste.

'OK, I didn't know I had asked for one. You know this isn't my room right?' Beau replied, confused.

'If these walls could talk, *sir'* she purred, then lightly cleared her throat. 'I really hope I wasn't interrupting anything. I just wanted to let you know that if there is anything, absolutely anything at all that I can do for you, please don't hesitate to call. I'm Millie, by the way.'

Beau's attention was now fixed on me, draped in the blanket, leaning against the glass panelling of the balcony doors. 'Sir? Sir, I am at your disposal.' Her soft chimes were a definite come-on; I would have had to be deaf and dumb not to have heard it. To Beau she was just being polite, but I knew better. In girl-world, you fight fire with fire.

'OK, thanks Tilly' I mumbled, as I sauntered towards him. Our eyes were locked; my fingertips grazed the dark hair on his forearm, across his knuckles that gripped the receiver, tickling his hand into submission as it followed my unspoken command. I could hear Millie's frustrated little voice dwindling as Beau hung up the phone, fumbling to switch off the speakerphone button. His attention never wavered from me as he placed his free hand around my waist.

Knock, knock. We eyed each other quizzically, each gauging the other's response to a stranger on the other side of the door. We both just shrugged.

'Grace, I know you're in there so open up!' The voice was stern, uncompromising – *parental*.

'It's my mum! We've been rumbled!' I whispered with an awkward half-grimace, half-grin.

ASCEND

Billie Jade Kermack

'This doesn't feel like one of those laughter-appropriate situations' he hissed, panicking.

'Well, I don't know about that' I beamed, pointing to the underwear he had just grabbed off of the floor.

'OK, so these definitely aren't mine.' He threw my pink lace panties at me with a raised eyebrow and only a hint of a smirk, as another knock came from my mother beyond the door. All I could seem to do was giggle as we scrambled for our clothes. Beau went for his jeans, strewn across the floor by the bathroom door – as he ran to retrieve them he fell over one of his boots, hitting the floor with a *thud* and losing control of the bedsheet covering his manhood. My giggles were now a full-pelt laugh as he danced into his jeans. Seeing his bare bum again was a joy, just not one I wanted to share with my mother. There was yet another knock, this time softer.

'Look, I'm not a fool and I'm not angry. I know you're eighteen and an adult now, I just wanted to pop by and see if you wanted to go to lunch?'

I ran for the door, attempting to flatten my obvious bed hair and re-wrap the bedsheet to cover myself properly. I opened the door a smidgen to my surprisingly chipper-looking mother.

'I'm assuming you had a good night then?' She smiled suggestively. I couldn't help but beam back at her, my cheeks flushing crimson.

ASCEND
Billie Jade Kermack

'Yes, thank you' I replied, still unable to break my ecstatic composure. OK, so I wasn't expecting this.

'Hi Beau!' my mum yelled, standing on tiptoe to see past me into the room. I pulled the door open a little further and there was Beau in just jeans, only one boot on with the laces undone and his crumpled shirt in his hands.

'Hi, Mrs O'Callaghan' he blushed, running a hand sheepishly through his hair. Unlike mine, his bed hair needed no alterations; he was one of those people who just fell out of bed looking good.

'Call me Louise!' With the corner of her mouth twitching north, I could sense just how much she was enjoying the situation. 'W-O-W' she silently mouthed, wide-eyed.

'Mum, really? Inappropriate!' I chastised, pulling the sheet around me, very aware that it was the only thing other than air between us.

'I was only coming by because one of the hotel receptionists, Macey, or Millie, I think her name was? Anyway, she told me that my daughter came into the hotel late last night acting very unladylike with a dangerous-looking young man. After she described *every* detail of this brooding stranger, right down to the sparkle in his eye... well, knowing how responsible you are and assuming the effect Beau must have on women...' I could see her train of thought wander, her expression familiar. I had seen many woman do the same

ASCEND   *Billie Jade Kermack*

when the image of Beau crossed their minds.

'Mum!'

'Sorry, lost myself for a second, anyway, where was I? Right, I assumed that it wasn't too late, you were not acting unladylike and that dangerous-looking young man was in fact Beau. I'm guessing by your achingly happy expression that you're delighted and I wanted you to know that I am happy for you, so go get dressed, meet me downstairs in an hour and we can all go get some lunch.' She eyed the necklace that now hung around my neck and smiled. I would tell her all about it later; for now, I had an hour to be with Beau before the Inquisition started.

'Sounds great mum, I'll see you downstairs in a bit. Oh, mum!' I called out as she turned to leave.

'Yes, sweetheart?' she smiled.

'Thanks.'

'My pleasure... it's nice to see that smile again. You deserve all the happiness in the world.' She ran her fingers across my cheek and pushed a strand of loose hair behind my ear.

I waved her off and pushed the door closed with a sigh of relief; no, not relief, more like contentment. After years of muddling through, never quite on the same page, my mother and I had finally come to an understanding. In the briefest of moments I realised that she trusted my choices,

ASCEND *Billie Jade Kermack*

she wanted nothing but happiness for me, she respected the person I was growing into. *So this is what it feels like to be an adult* I thought, striding back into the room.

Beau was still half-naked, which I was way too happy about, a spanking new hotel toothbrush hanging from his mouth. We both looked towards the mess that was the bed: *One, two...* I thought, reading his expression perfectly, knowing the numbers danced too in the forefront of his mind. We raced towards the bed, falling onto the mattress in each other's arms. As long as I remembered my mum was expecting us in an hour, everything would be fine.

Forty-five minutes later, the yellow noon sun blazed in through the balcony onto the carpet beneath my feet. Beau placed a chaste kiss on my bare neck and bundled into the bathroom, turning on the tap to fill the sink. I gathered up the bedsheets, vaguely attempting to recreate the artistic arrangement we had found them in. He walked back into the room, now dressed in a white T-shirt and skinny jeans, which was lucky; I couldn't promise I could keep my hands off of him if I saw his bare chest again. He tuned in the radio as I packed the last decorative cushions onto the bed, cranking up the volume once he had found a station that wasn't playing early-90s pop.

Within seconds of a melody starting Beau was behind me, his fingers in the belt loops of my jeans, holding me in place against him. He swayed his hips, guiding mine in sync with his to the rhythm of the song. As the words started to flow through the speakers, he sang along perfectly to Marvin

ASCEND

Billie Jade Kermack

Gaye's 'Ain't No Mountain High Enough'.

Releasing me in a spin and holding me at arm's-length, he shimmied towards me with a glint in his eye as I playfully retreated to the bed. Swinging round one of the bed poles, biceps flexing as they held his weight, he landed back on the carpet gracefully. He could dance – nothing surprised me with Beau any more. Never one to back down from a sing-off (or usually a mime-off in my case), I grabbed my hairbrush from the dresser.

With every ounce of diva I had in me, I threw caution to the wind and belted out the words; yes, I knew them, and yes, I went for it. We pranced around as though we were stuck in an episode of *Glee*, giggling like teenagers until the song finished. With the final note still ringing in our ears we slumped back onto the bed and kissed warmly, fits of laughter still rolling in.

'Hey Miss Gracie, I think your mum is probably waiting for us downstairs' he laughed, glancing over my shoulder at the alarm clock on the bedside table.

I grabbed my coat, and as Beau laced up his boots I attempted for the second time this morning to re-make the bed. I gave up halfway through and Beau pulled me towards the door with a playful smile, which is when I caught a glimpse of myself in the mirror on the wall.

'Beau, I seriously think I need to do something with my hair. How about you go downstairs and I'll meet you there in five

ASCEND

minutes?' If I was being perfectly honest my hair was fine – at least, I had seen it in worse states – but I desperately needed a moment or two to collect my thoughts. I needed to pinch myself, stop for a moment and take one real breath. I needed an instant not clouded by the golden hue of his affection. The suffocating fear that it *could* all be a dream was fleeting as he placed his arm around my shoulders.

'You look beautiful' he mused, pulling me out of my reverie and gazing at my reflection as he stroked my hair and leant in to kiss my cheek. 'But you know best, and I know better than to argue' he laughed, raising his hands in defeat.

I walked him to the door. As I shut it behind him, I glanced into the peep hole and there was Beau, with his very own congratulatory dance: 'Hammer Time' was back with a vengeance. My giggle was obviously louder than I had expected.

'You can see me, can't you?' he yelled from the other side of the door, all the blood in his face rushing to his cheeks.

'Yes I can Mr. Milner, and I have to say, you have some serious style' I mocked, a smile widening on my face. 'Shake that ass, show me what you got!' I sang at the door with a little 70s jig of my own, my gaze still fixed through the peep hole.

'Ha, ha, ha. Thanks. I think I'm gonna go now' Beau said with an embarrassed grin etched uncomfortably on his face.

ASCEND
Billie Jade Kermack

'Hey, I really did love the dance.' I continued to torture him; to be honest, it was fun! OK so he wasn't wearing a silly pair of kangaroo slippers, but it did feel like a little part of karma had come to pay him a visit after he had laughed so hard at my *Fame* ordeal.

He waved at me and danced out of view, jazz hands at the ready. I leant against the door and for the first time in fourteen hours inhaled a settling, warm breath of air. My mind, still a fuzzy midsummer-night's dream concoction of adoration and love, refused to budge – reality was overrated anyway.

FIVE
ೀಾ

'Grace, Grace —
it wasn't meant to end like this, it wasn't meant to end like this, it wasn't meant to...'

I woke up suddenly, headbutting the window as our cab jumped a little too enthusiastically over a speed bump. The Great British weather softly pelted against the glass, and the once-bright blue skies were now swamped by murky grey clouds. All I could see for miles ahead in every direction were rows of endless, towering green trees.

It took a sobering moment or two to remember her whispered words, slathered with fear and intensity. Whether the attack on the beach that night was a blurred reality or my overactive imagination, I was certain of one thing: someone (or something) had followed me there that night, and had a warning for me. There was something they needed me to know. But what was it?

Get thinking, Grace. Either you find out what this is all about or you risk going completely insane! And by the way, talking to yourself, even if it is in your head, screams

ASCEND

Billie Jade Kermack

'nutjob'! My thoughts werent as calming as I might have hoped.

Beau had covered me with his green parka, and the faux fur trim on the hood tickled my nose and made me sneeze. I turned onto my other side, scooting over the black vinyl seats and snuggling into his chest. Although he was napping, he cuddled closer to me in response. I pulled his jacket up to my chin and closed my eyes, the calming rhythm of Beau's heartbeat helping me fall back to sleep.

'End of the line!' the greying taxi driver hollered through the small perspex window.

We had slept nearly the whole way home. The sky had begun to clear, and now strobes of warm sunlight kissed my face as baby-blue skies poked out from behind white foam clouds. I rubbed my eyes sleepily.

'Tired, are we, Miss Gracie?'

'Well *someone* kept me up all night.'

'What's the coined term – it takes two to tango?' He made his point by rounding off with a big yawn.

'And may I just say what a mighty fine dancer you are, Mr. Milner!' I added a jig that mocked his little floor-show from the hotel hallway, making him beam.

'Sleep's overrated' he said, leaning down to kiss the top of

ASCEND *Billie Jade Kermack*

my head. I could still feel his cheeks warming me.

'Welcome back to reality, Grace' I said under my breath, as the driver held open my door. I paid the man and made my way round to the back of the taxi.

'I was thinking, maybe I should go get us some lunch from Mason's Deli. We could spend the weekend in our PJs – no excursions, no visitors, just you and me!' I proposed, imagining Beau sockless, shirtless and in just a pair of low-waisted sweatpants.

'Sounds like a plan, maybe I can cook you dinner tonight?' Beau said as he unpacked the boot of the cab. My candy-pink rucksack hung on one of Beau's shoulders, his military style green holdall on the other.

'I'd say yes, but I've got a scary suspicion that your idea of dinner is beans on toast with a packet of Skittles for dessert.'

'Hey, what's wrong with that? I promise you can have all the red and purple ones this time,' he proposed.

'OK Mr. Milner you have a deal. Except how about we change that beans on toast for a 15-inch Vegetable Supreme from Domino's, your treat!'

We walked through Gwen's ornate, magically sculpted, *Alice in Wonderland*-style front garden and Beau dumped our bags on the newly built, pristinely whitewashed front porch.

ASCEND *Billie Jade Kermack*

Gwen, Beau's foster mother and town psychic, was a force to be reckoned with. Yes she was incredibly sweet and yes, she had a heart of gold, but she also had unmeasurable powers... powers I'd only ever read about in comic books. Trying to decieve her was pointless: she was a walking, talking lie-detector. She could see things that us mere mortals couldn't comprehend in our wildest dreams. But she was Gwen, and I loved her; she had also saved my life on more than one occasion, which made me love her that little bit more. A pang of guilt hit me. I hadn't been to see Gwen since Beau had left me – since he left *us*. I should have been there for her.

'Well Miss Gracie, you are on. I will even treat you to a Friday Night Special: two pots of Ben & Jerry's finest and two, yes I said *two*, films from Blockbuster. That's four little packages of pure happiness. Am I good, or am – I – GOOD?' he asked, a bold, boyish grin on his face. I made my way to the lemon-painted porch swing which matched the daisy filled window boxes. I relaxed into the swaying motion, my feet grazing the wooden slats as Beau searched in his jeans for the door keys.

'This deal seems to be getting better and better! I'm not silly you know, I've realised that when you want to get on my good side you charm me with that stunning smile of yours.' As soon as the words left my mouth that beautiful smile of his that I was talking about floored me, yet again! That smile was *my* smile.

With the front door ajar, turning his back to me, Beau knelt

ASCEND   *Billie Jade Kermack*

down to his hefty duffel bag.

Interesting! I thought.

Beau was no Batfink – he had about as much stealth ability as Mr. Blobby. He pulled something from the front zip-pocket of his bag and slid it into the waistband of his jeans.

'What are you hiding?' *Oh God, I sound like my mother. Scary!*

Beau pulled out a giant, family-sized packet of Skittles and waved them at me. Taunting me with sweets was evil, even for him; Skittles were to me what a five-pound kipper was to a cat.

'I think these deserve a little action. Shuffle that cute butt over here and give me a kiss!'

'Beau, bribery – really?' He answered with a simple nod. 'OK, but only because you asked so nicely.' I fell into his arms. He tilted me back and rested his sweet-filled hand on my back. His lips had barely grazed mine when I made my move and grabbed for the gold.

'I hope you've learnt your lesson Beau, bribery is wrong!' I giggled. I ripped open the bag, pulled out a handful and greedily threw them in my mouth.

'Hey, that's stealing! I'm pretty sure that trumps bribery on the wrong list. I deserved at least a minute.'

ASCEND

Billie Jade Kermack

'Sorry, I'm eating, I guess you'll just have to wait', I teased. 'That cute-boy stare will not break me, Mr. Milner – I'm stronger than you think!' Judging by the heated expression on Beau's face, I could tell our great evening was going to jump off-schedule and start early. And so began the water fight; or not so much a water fight as an all-out water war. Luckily for me, I was nearest the hose. The one-sided drenching didn't last long. Before I knew it I had been backed into a mud bath that was due to be a newly-installed fish pond, with the hose that was once my trusted ally directed right at me.

In a mix of mud, water and Gwen's pile of freshly-cut grass he settled me beneath her willow tree, basking in the low afternoon sun with very little care to how we looked. The conversation was great, the weather lovely and the kissing – absolutely perfect.

'So, do you think I need a shower?' I giggled, trying and failing to keep a straight face.

'Not at all, Miss Gracie! I think the mud mask, grass-infused hairdo and water-drenched sun dress combo is an absolute winner. How are you not on the cover of *Vogue*?' He mocked.

'Ha-ha funny man, you crack me right up.'

I went in for the kill, Beau's ultimate weakness: the ticklish spot under his arm and down the side of his torso. I gripped on like a monkey as he tried to shake me off, and we ended up rolling around in the mud with little concern to the gloopy sludge that was again smothering us. I picked up a pile of the brown stuff and taunted Beau with it.

'All's fair in love and war, baby' I mused. With a flash of my teeth (the only thing not covered in mud) and a flick of my hair (now a bunch of sodden rat-tails), I flung it at him. He beamed at me, taking the mud like a man, paying me back with a rugby tackle me to the floor. But hey, horizontal worked for me!

'Hey kids, looks like I missed a party.'

'Hey, Gwen!' I was both surprised and elated as I jumped up, fruitlessly brushing myself off. The mud had dried in the afternoon sun and the embedded grass and gunk in my hair was not the best of looks. My mum would have had a fit; as a hairdresser, she didn't approve of my hair at the best of times.

'Now sweetheart, I would hug you but I really don't want to – that's more than enough mud on you and in this case I really don't want you to share. Though if you fancy throwing a bowlful of those Skittles in your pocket my way, I won't refuse! I think it's about time you two washed up. I'm heading up to Lincoln to visit the grandkids, and I know you and Beau will probably have a nice romantic evening planned.'

I glanced back at Beau with his hands in his jeans; even

ASCEND
Billie Jade Kermack

beneath the caked on mud on his face I could see the flush of crimson in his cheeks. Thankfully I side-stepped the embarrassment by completely blocking out my thoughts – using a church-worthy inner gauge of 'appropriateness', I succesfully censored my otherwise roaming imagination.

'There are sandwiches from Mason's on the counter and fresh orange juice in the fridge, so enjoy, and for God's sake do not sit on my couch in that mess,' she chuckled. I should have seen that coming; her gifts were as sharp as I remembered. *Saves me a trip into town.*

'It's nice to see you around again, Grace. Are you ready to start work with me at the hospital next week?'

'Always,' I replied.

'That eagerness will disappear eventually Grace, I'm not going to lie. Sorting old patient files isn't the most fun you could be having, but it beats being poor!' she smiled.

I was actually looking forward to jumping back into work – my last job had unexpectedly been cut short. Having a boyfriend who could sense that my ex-boss's wife Claudette was dying of a brain tumor and couldn't be saved had put a depressing twist on the whole employer/employee relationship. After Claudette passed away Mr. Luigi sold the restaurant, and I was out of a job. Enter Gwen and a pregnant college graduate on maternity leave. The job was there, and I had a woman on the inside. Gwen pulled me in close and kissed the part of my cheek that didn't have dirt

ASCEND *Billie Jade Kermack*

on it. 'You bring a whole new light into his eyes and I've missed that... I've missed *you*, sweetheart' she whispered into my ear lovingly.

'It's good to be back', I beamed.

SIX
୨୦ॣୠ

'Film?' I chirped.

'Check.' Beau held up the selection of DVD cases branded with the Blockbuster logo.

'Skittles?' My tone was serious, as would be expected when it came to my favourite sugary treat.

'Check!' he chuckled as he dropped a couple into his mouth.

'Ben & Jerry's?'

'Freezing.'

'Pizza?'

'En route' he mused, pulling a crumpled twenty-pound note from his jeans pocket and slapping it down on the table.

'Well then, I think we're ready.'

We settled onto the sofa, my finger on *Pause*, ready for the

ASCEND
Billie Jade Kermack

latest slasher flick in the DVD player to start. I was the horror buff and Beau was into the oldies; a copy of *Rebel Without a Cause* starring his favourite actor James Dean was propped up against the flatscreen, waiting for its turn in the machine. We had discussed whose choice should be viewed first. I use the term 'discussed' loosely – as usual, when it came to important issues such as these, I won.

Waiting for the pizza, we used our time like responsible adults with a game of Skittle Dunk. I'd like to stress that we are adults and have on occasion been known to be mature, but this game was a hell of a lot of fun, except of course when someone misfired and got a Skittle in the eye. I, as usual, beat Beau ten to four. He was pretty useless when it came to aiming sweets at my mouth; either that or he just enjoyed throwing them at my face.

ဆဝ

So the film was OK; actually thinking about it, OK is basically the only word to describe it. After the crusts of the pizza lay lonely in the box, all the red and purple Skittles had been stripped from the bag and we had gorged on a hell of a lot of ice cream, I felt like a major fatty. A cuddle as I rested my head on Beau's chest was perfect; no big movements, that was key!

'So! Fancy playing a game, Miss Gracie?'

'You really want to go up against me? I am the reigning champion of Skittle Dunk, and I don't want to embarrass

ASCEND

Billie Jade Kermack

you' I teased with a mocking grin, throwing a Skittle up in the air and catching it in my mouth like a show-off.

'Wow, I think it's time to take you down a peg or two, little lady!' he laughed, nudging me on the shoulder.

'OK, what's your game?'

'Pictionary?' he suggested, holding up a pencil.

'You know I can't draw to save my life – what else you got in mind?'

'OK, what about Scrabble?' he replied, with one outstreched arm already deep beneath the sofa. I thought it was an odd choice, but I agreed all the same.

സ⃰ശ

'I would pretty much stake my life on the fact that you didn't come up with that word on your own, Beau. Where are you hiding the dictionary?' I lunged at him like a lioness at her prey and patted him down. It had suddenly occurred to me what was going on; after half an hour of playing with words like *abased, sabres* and *Tenedos* laid out in front of me, the penny had finally dropped.

'Who's been helping you?' I accused.

'I'll have you know every one of the words I used are 100% real. Don't give me that look, I read books!' he chuckled,

ASCEND *Billie Jade Kermack*

beads of sweat – the telltale sign of a lie – creeping over his hairline.

'I can't remember the last time I saw Spiderman described as *affable* in a Marvel comic.' I raised an eyebrow and waited for his response. His silence spoke volumes.

'This game is so much easier when my opponents don't know about my gift...' Beau muttered under his breath.

Having a boyfriend who could see and talk to the dead certainly put a new spin on cheating.

'Beau, dish it!'

'I don't know what you're implying' he laughed, in a well-to-do posh accent.

'Ha-ha Beau, I know you have an ace up your sleeve, who is it?' I pointed an accusing finger at him and gestured towards the ticklish spot under his arm.

'Don't even think about it!' Beau said, edging back towards the sofa.

'A girl's gotta do what a girl's gotta do, now 'fess up!' I barely touched him with my fingertip and he caved.

'Ruth Booth' he admitted, without making eye contact with me. There was a short silence as I wracked my memory to add a face to the name. Once again, the penny dropped with

ASCEND

Billie Jade Kermack

a resounding *thud*.

'Are you talking about Mrs Booth, from Nickel Street? Liked a tangerine-sunset twist perm?' Beau was silent but his grin bore a window into his soul, and it was screaming *big, fat cheater!*

'Mrs Booth, the 2003 - 2008 winner of the British National Word Games Championship? Mrs Booth who died from heart failure last year?' I added.

'The very same' he laughed, glancing towards the cream 18th century-style armchair next to the burning fire.

'I could have sworn that I'd heard whispering most of the night, I knew I wasn't crazy! So how bloody long has the lovely Mrs Booth been helping you lie?'

I glanced inquisitively between Beau and the invisible Mrs Booth.

'Not that long... only the past forty minutes or so. If you think about it, it's not really cheating as such.'

'I beg to differ! I knew *cozener* wasn't a word you would have come up with, and by the way, we've only been playing for half an hour.' The irony of his word choice wasn't lost on me.

'Firstly, I could have known that word and secondly, I came

ASCEND *Billie Jade Kermack*

prepared... shoot me!'

'Men have been killed for lesser things' I grimaced accusingly with a hidden smile, picking up the letters on the board and handing them back to Beau to drop back into the green velvet pouch.

'Wait a minute, you knew I would turn down Pictionary – you played me! So, what games can you play without the help of old Mrs Booth?' I teased suggestively as I tugged at his shirt.

'Well, apparently she's never played Cluedo, but she's always wanted to' he teased, expertly side-stepping my advances.

'Beau, how do you spell *philanthropy?*'

Beau stumbled a little and I could see he was wracking his brain for the answer; I began to sing the theme tune to *Countdown* as time ticked away. The fact that Beau had no answer assured me that Mrs Booth had officially left the building. I looked over to the armchair and the cushion, which had been despressed by an invisible weight, slowly began to puff out and back into its normal shape.

With that incentive, I made a swift movement that landed me directly next to Beau on the floor. I leaned in, delicately draped my leg not-so-innocently over Beau's and tickled his neck around his T-shirt collar.

ASCEND
Billie Jade Kermack

It didn't take long for the Scrabble board and all the tiny tiled letters to end up on the rug beneath the table. Let's just say, words were no longer an issue and Mrs Booth's assistance was no longer needed. Beau had this part of our date down to a fine art!

SEVEN

With the tiles from last night's Scrabble game still strewn across the rug, a clean up was a must. The day consisted pretty much of sitting, lying and cuddling on the sofa, with the exception of toilet breaks and an occasional excursion for food and water. As the sun settled outside and the warm glow of the table lamp flooded the room, I suddenly had a usually well hidden Forties housewife urge to cook a home-made meal without the help of a paper menu or phone call.

I stood over the sink in my pink, tomato and meatball-spattered vest top and Beau's oversized ¾-length grey slouch pants that I had to roll up around my waist just to keep up. I squeezed a generous amount of Pomegranate Fairy Liquid into the washing-up bowl and as the boiling water hit the plates it began to bubble up, the heat steaming up the rear window in front of me. The evening's speckled red sky turned darker, mottled yellows and blues slowly fading behind a crow-black backdrop by the time I had finished. I could just about make out the honeysuckle bush and Gwen's wooden-slatted garden table and bench set. I pulled the sink plug and grabbed a tea-towel out of the

ASCEND   *Billie Jade Kermack*

drawer.

That's just great! Why is it that the second I drain the water I find something else to wash up?

I picked up the glass tumbler, gave the marble sideboard a quick wipe down and headed back to the sink.

The glass smashed into pieces as it hit the bottom of the ceramic basin. There was someone out there in the dark, amongst the bushes. A young woman, in her early twenties, I would guess. The darkness almost completely shrouded her face. Her battered, wounded body was partially covered by the leafy green bushes and the torn dress which hung off her. My heart rate spiked as it ballooned uncomfortably in my chest.

I glanced down at the shattered glass in the sink and back up to the lone figure outside the window. It could only have been mere seconds, but she was gone. The breeze whistled through the branches of the old willow tree, flicking leaves across the freshly-mown lawn. The wind chimes hanging above the back door clinked – their orchestral pangs were unsettling to say the least, sending an uneasy twinge surging up my back.

Calm down, there's nothing there. You're overreacting. Breathe! How is it I still don't feel settled? *Oh wait, OK, seeing a creepy woman outside your window in the middle of the night wearing barely any clothes and staring directly at you – yes, that'll be the problem.* My Inner Crazy

ASCEND

Billie Jade Kermack

Lady was definitely onto something; actually, at that moment, her mocking was oddly comforting.

I picked up the broken pieces of glass carefully and balanced them in my hands. The air around me turned bitterly cold, my breathing wispy and painful. The spotlights above me flickered on and off. Against my better judgement and a screaming gut feeling, I turned around. In a split second and a haze of slow motion my hands tensed around the glass before the shock of what stood before me loosened my grip, sending the glass shards tumbling to the floor, leaving ravaged skin in their wake.

The darkness of the night sky no longer concealed her form; her disfigured, brutally invaded form. Beneath the ornately-carved alcove three metres ahead which joined the kitchen and the living room she stood silently, assessing her new surroundings. If I had blinked I probably would have missed it, but for a millisecond she almost looked human.

Her hair fell down past her shoulders, preened ringlets of copper-tinted gold, on one side at least. The left side of her body was burnt almost beyond recognition, her skin flaked and peeling away, exposing the delicate, charred pink muscle-tissue beneath. Two large hooped earrings – one twisted metal, one bloody and bright silver – still hung from her ears, and her plastic bangles were held in place by parts of her stringy, melted flesh. Her expression was grave as she stared at me from beneath her mascara-covered eyelashes, slowly assessing every inch of me . Her head dipped towards the floor and to one side as she silently questioned my

ASCEND

Billie Jade Kermack

presence. The clock on the mantlepiece gonged, signalling that it was midnight and briefly diverting my attention.

'Who... who are...' My words were hushed and heavy. I couldn't speak, I could barely think. Purple, bloody and swollen cuts and bruises smothered her body, and the pain of her torture was reflected on her face. I went to take a step towards her, thoughtlessly planting my foot directly onto the remaining shards of glass. I recoiled in pain, instinctively dropping to my knees. As though it had been waiting to strike, the pain from the wounds on my hands began to throb. I didn't have long to worry about them though as I felt a gust of icy-cold air surrounding me from above, grazing my bare shoulders.

I glanced up slowly and apprehensively. Feet – a red patent 2-inch wedge shoe on one, the other bare but for a holey, singed stocking gathering at her broken, exposed ankle. The bone was completely detached and poked through her ragged flesh as the foot, coloured purple and blue, rested uncomfortably at an awkward angle on the floor.

Her dress was a black-and-white monochrome print, the white material now nearly completely stained blood-red. The ragged hem bordered her knicker line and was slashed at the waist, smothered with ash and soaked in what I assumed was pints of her own blood. The musty smell of old petrol lingered in the air. I didn't realise until that second that I had started crying. My vision was blurred but that didn't stop me staring into that face; that disfigured, brutalised, once-beautiful face, now filled with fear and

ASCEND — *Billie Jade Kermack*

confusion. She looked younger then I had at first assumed, innocence lingering beneath the trauma.

With no warning, she screamed. Mere inches from my face, her jaws slowly parted, wider than was normal by medical law and practices; normal for the living, that is. Her scream was agonising and shrill, her eyes alight and fraught with the memories that haunted her. I couldn't shake the feeling that maybe... she wasn't a stranger.

There was something familiar about her, a connection that made my heart plummet, a feeling of womanly solidarity that pinched at my soul and shook my very core. Her eyes were studying me, misty pools of deep greyish-blue which were slowly drowned out by her pupils until all life had been completely smothered from them. She floated backwards, her eyes still on mine, just the tips of her feet scraping against the hardwood floor with a squeak from her shoe. She stopped dead just shy of the living room sofa.

Now I lay me down to sleep,
I pray the Lord, my soul to keep.
If I die before I wake,
I pray the Lord, my soul to take.

The words were a distant, ethereal whisper. Her mouth never moved but her stare spoke clearly. The deep, booming, disembodied voice recited the prayer, dragging me back to that night, that night I had tried so desperately to forget. I gasped as the realisation hit.

ASCEND

Billie Jade Kermack

'It was you, you were there on the beach. You did that to me. Why me?' My tone was accusing but my concern was heartfelt.

How could someone do that to another human being?

I extended my trembling fingers and began to walk towards her, my hand outstretched to touch her face, to console her as best I could. For a brief and fleeting moment her body stopped dead in front of the fireplace and her face contorted, in an image of serenity and pure beauty; an image mirroring my own, as though I was staring at my own reflection.

But with another violin-chord scream that rattled around my head, she was on fire – illuminated like a fourth of July firework, ready to fully combust. The pain was etched on her face as the bright orange flames licked at her skin, consuming her. The rocking chair on the upstairs landing began to move with a creak, picking up speed. The books from the floor-to-ceiling shelves on either side of the fireplace behind her flew off, randomly sprawling open onto the large rug beneath my feet. Gwen's family photos on the walls cracked, tilting on their sides one-by-one in a domino effect around the room.

'I can help...'

My words were of no comfort – to me or her.

EIGHT

ಸಂಬ

'Grace, what the hell happened here?' Beau rushed towards me with a towel secured around his waist, his hair still dripping from the shower. 'Grace, WHAT HAPPENED?' His worry went unnoticed. I was still trying to work out exactly what had happened myself.

'I dropped it, my hands were wet. I thought... I mean, I saw... there was something in the garden. It just slipped. Sorry.' I said slowly, still in shock, staring at the now-empty living room which was clean and in order, not a book or frame out of place.

'Right, sit down and I'll get all this cleaned up. You're bleeding.' He was right; I gazed down, still shellshocked, at my glass-cut palms which were still gushing blood, staining my clothes, a haunting reminder of what had just happened.

'Wait, how did you know...?'

'Know what? I heard the glass smash in the sink when I got out of the shower. I was calling you, but you didn't reply.'

ASCEND

Billie Jade Kermack

He rushed to the drawer under the sink, grabbing some tea-towels and wrapping them round my sliced-up hands. 'Look, it's late, its been a long day.' As he dumped the broken glass into the bin the clock on the mantelpiece rang, signalling midnight – again.

Did it really happen? I'm sure it happened... how did I lose all that time? Where did she go? Who was she?

I had a flurry of questions and a baffled and concerned Beau by my side, checking my wounds.

'They've stopped bleeding for now. I don't think they need stitches but I'll wrap them up anyway, Gwen can check them over tomorrow.'

I was shook up, understandably so. My hands burned furiously, blood still seeping ever so slowly like an ink blot onto the brilliant white fabric of the bandages. I walked apprehensively into the sitting room, Beau's voice a distant background noise.

Everything was neatly in its place. The picture frames on the walls were undisturbed, as proven by the light coating of dust on top of each one. But something still hung in the air, a lingering presence, some left-over apprehension. I glanced up at the loft reading area, 20-feet up to my left beneath the high, barn-like, beamed ceiling. The spiral staircase attached to its side led up to an ornately carved dark wooden rocking chair and a side table with a bell lamp, unlit. It began to move, back and forth, to and fro, on its own. With apparent purpose it creaked, its joints whining as it rocked, picking up momentum.

As Beau approached me from behind, wrapping his glistening, warm, muscled arms around my shoulders and pulling me in to the comfort and security of his chest, the chair stopped dead, mid-rock. I didn't make my feelings known to Beau, with good reason; my wrapped wounds were a blindingly-clear reason alone to keep quiet.

I glanced out of the corner of my eye up towards the phantasmally-charged chair and onto the beechwood shelf on cast-iron brackets above it. In the ordered row of ten to twenty books, two books had haltingly edged out of place. One was a battered brown leather-bound book with what looked like gold or silver embossed italics that I couldn't make out from where I was. The other book was hefty, double the size of the first, its thick, frayed, dogeared pages sheathed by an ebony, scratched, almost skin-like cover. Seared into the book was a crudely hand-carved star. It looked old – ancient, even. It clearly had history. In fact, it looked as though it had been used as a shield in a world war.

I recognised the star embossed on the book jacket immediately; Gwen had an identical symbol on her wrist. The first time I saw it I had questioned whether it was carved, burnt or tattooed onto her skin, as it didn't look like any tattoo I had ever seen. The skin was raised and red, elevated from her arm, its texture grainy. I had only seen the mark once or twice as Gwen was very careful to keep it covered with draped tops and cardigans, the hems settling

ASCEND *Billie Jade Kermack*

just shy of her knuckles. I needed to know what was in that book.

□□

Beau's deep and restful breathing as he slept created a feeling of serenity in me. With my eyes heavy and my brain crying out for more sleep I watched him, his angelic, peaceful face buried in his pillow next to mine.

As I stroked his forehead, I caught a glimpse of my bandaged hand. An onslaught of everything that had happened set my mind racing as I tried to piece together my experience on the beach, my loss of time and the distraught woman in the living room. The woman on the beach, the woman who had subjected me to those terrible things. Were they one and the same, and if so, why had she come to me? What had I done to deserve all that pain, that torture? I knew I should tell Beau. I should have learnt my lesson – but we had only just gotten things back on track.

I would pour my heart and soul out to Gwen when the opportunity presented itself. If all this got out of control, I would deal with it appropriately. I was suddenly sure of two things: however unsettling the thought, I *had* seen the bedraggled woman that night, and when the house was empty I would be back to investigate those books. I laid my head back down so my body mirrored his, his warm, sweet breath dancing over my cheek. As my heartbeat sang in tune to his, I fell back into a peaceful sleep.

ASCEND *Billie Jade Kermack*

ℬℭ

I woke up to Beau staring at me. I yawned and smiled, rubbing my eyes; the soft, antiseptic-scented bandages were an unwelcome reminder of the night before.

'Grace, are you going to be OK when I go away?' His words caught me off-guard and it took a second for my lazy brain to get up to speed. Beau was due to join a photography group travelling around Europe in a week's time; I would have to be apart from him for fourteen days. It could have been fourteen hours, it still would have been too long.

'Damn it!' I had completely forgotten.

'You forgot all about it, didn't you?' he beamed, knowing me too well.

'No... maybe just a little. Memory like a fish, remember?' I tapped my index finger against my temple, a small smile playing on my lips.

'Well, let's hope you never forget how to do this.' Without warning, his lips met mine. Pained reassurance and a hint of worry mixed down deep as the connection vibrated between us. His silent questions bombarded me behind our loving embrace. He was more concerned than he was letting on, and I could tell. Before his lips left mine I felt a glimmer of seductive heat as he let himself fall into the kiss, leaving behind whatever worries he was harbouring for a split second.

ASCEND *Billie Jade Kermack*

'I can't leave if you're not going to be OK.'

'I will be fine, I promise. I was tired last night – I didn't mean to freak you out. Everything is absolutely, positively fine!' I stressed, not believing the words that poured out of my mouth but praying that he did.

'Are you sure? I can cancel.' I knew he didn't want to, but would if I asked him to. For now Beau was set for his trip, to enjoy life and some normality to keep him sane. I wasn't going to stand between him and any kind of normal; he deserved that at least. I just smiled in response and kissed him lightly on the cheek, getting out of bed and making my way to the door.

'Well, I have some news...' he said ominously.

Oh god, what now? I thought, feeling my legs weaken. I shuffled away from the door to sit on the edge of the bed. I realised then that his kiss had been a manoeuvre to butter me up for whatever was to come.

'I'm going to have to leave a little earlier than I had planned. Something came up while I was out yesterday.'

'Something or some*one*?' I asked, already knowing full well what the answer was. Beau picked up ghosts like the RSPCA picked up animals. It was non-stop, but I was suddenly aware that I may have picked up a couple of strays of my own, so decided not to start bickering about it. The

ASCEND
Billie Jade Kermack

likelihood that I could win an argument with Beau when it came to the deceased was doubtful.

'Ghost?' I asked. 'You're already going to be gone for two weeks...' I whined like a child, pulling at my itchy bandages.

'Three weeks, now. Its not that long – you watch, it will fly by!' He stroked my hand. 'I'm going to see you off to work this week and sort out a new set of train tickets. I leave this Friday, then I'm going to join the rest of the group in Estonia the following Tuesday, as long as I can finish up everything in France by then.'

'France? Actually, forget I asked. You have to do what you have to do!' He did, and I understood that.

'I hate leaving you. I hate not being able to protect you' he said, motioning towards my covered wounds. 'Not being able to kiss these hands' – he pulled my fingers up to meet his soft, dewy lips – 'to kiss this face.' The pads of his fingers danced along my jawline, his lips dotting feather-light kisses in their wake. 'To kiss every inch of your... neck.'

As the word left his mouth, a sly half-smile twitching at the corner of his lips, my body shuddered in response as though my ability to breathe rested on the mere pronunciation of the word. I gripped tightly round his waist at the material of his T-shirt, fearing that if I let go, I'd end up in a gooey mess on the floor. He tenderly cupped my face with one hand whilst his other skated over my now electrically-charged

ASCEND

Billie Jade Kermack

skin. His fingers fiddled with the fine, loose strands of hair at the base of my neck, gently tugging them until my head fell back, exposing my throat. Starting beneath my ear and trailing down south towards my scantily-clad clavicle, each kiss, though light, was enthralling. He returned me to normal with a guiding hand swept under my arm, supporting my back. I opened my eyes hazily, my Inner Bitch screaming on her hands and knees for the dream to continue just a few moments more. It was the first time in a long time I wanted to second her motion. He beamed at me, mere inches from my face; upset, confusion, and maybe even worry had crept into his gaze, dulling the natural light that was usually there when we were this close.

'You have to know I would be with you always if I could, right? I can't help but feel that because I attract all this death and sadness, it may rub off on you. If I go and sort this out ASAP, we can finally get on with the rest of our lives.'

He was lying. Not purposefully lying, of course I could see that; it was more like he was saying something he wished with all his heart and soul to be true, but deep down knew to be impossible.

'This ghost needs my help and unfortunately, this job doesn't offer up shift work and holiday pay. I'm all he's got. '

I decided against prying any futher. Of course I wanted to know all the details; how old was this ghost? What was their name? How did they die? I hated the idea of Beau being led around a foreign country by someone I didn't know and couldn't identify. Banishing my worry before it could play on my mind and drive me crazy, I reverted to my comfort zone and whipped some sarcastic comments from the depths of my psyche. Any knowledge I could possibly gather would only make me worry about Beau that much more.

'You're going to have a great time. You get to see what dead people look like around the world, bonus!' I teased, prompting a playful reaction, the weight of his revelation momentarily floating away. 'I'll have mum breathing down my neck at home, and I'm sure Gwen will keep an eye on me when I'm working at the hospital. All bases covered, Batman' I mocked with a sly grin. The corners of his mouth twitched up into a half-smile, but it was still laden with worry and apprehension, an expression of his that I was now only too familiar with.

I knew why Beau worried. I knew only too well why he didn't want to leave. Glen Havers, the sadistic spirit of a serial killer, was never far from our minds. After torturing me, haunting my every waking and sleeping moment and trying desperately to end my life and take over my body, it was hard to relax around the subject of the dead. Yes, Gwen and Beau had vanquished him last year, but his presence still lingered in the air around us, polluting it like a toxic fog.

'The Shadows are the only things that can truly get rid of a ghost forever, and at the moment they have a different plan for Glen.' I remembered Beau's words clearly, the

ASCEND *Billie Jade Kermack*

memory ingrained in my subconscious, ready to pounce at any moment as a cruel reminder of just how damaged my life was.

NINE

I pulled up to Gwen's house, making sure I parked out of view, shrouded by her next door neighbour's hanging apple tree. All was quiet, the only sounds the low hum of birds in the McAllister's front garden bird bath and the steady swoosh of a hose watering a large vegetable planter across the street. I crept up to the house like a Nancy Drew-style sleuth. I kept my fingers tightly crossed, closing my eyes as I crouched at the lemon-painted side door. I had already tried the rear entrance leading into the kitchen, but it was locked. This was it. *Please be open, please be open –*

Yes!

I pushed on the door and triumphantly stepped into the high ceilinged, barn-like living area . The *thump* of the door hitting against the wall echoed around the lofty, Victorian beamed room. *Right, I'm in. Nice and quick, in and out. Only target: the books,* I thought, adrenaline spiking excitedly in my veins.

I had just pulled the books from the shelf when my mission

ASCEND

Billie Jade Kermack

was interrupted. I heard the tyres of a heavy vehicle pull up onto the newly refurbished gravel driveway, a petrol-blue bonnet visible out of the front bay window. I rushed down the slim spiral staircase, almost tripping over the last step, the two books cradled in my arms. I grabbed my bag from the sofa, cramming in the books as I rushed to the open side entrance. I heard the visiting stranger kill the engine, then the tinkle of keys in the front door keyhole as I carefully and quietly pulled the side door closed behind me.

I ducked into the driver's seat of my car, throwing my bag on the passenger seat. As I pulled the sun visor down for a little extra coverage, my sunglasses fell into my lap. I pulled the round-framed, John Lennon-style sunglasses on and slipped down into my seat. I shuffled down as far as I could without crushing my legs or breaking my back, as the car began to reverse out of Gwen's driveway.

I didn't recognise the car, or the driver, but I could see Gwen strapped into the passenger seat. She was wearing a hat and a puffy jumper which was odd, over-kill clothing for such a warm, sunny day. The driver was a handsome man in his late 40s. He was wearing a blue shirt, complementing the colour of his car, and a grey pinstriped tie. His jet-black hair was shaggy, loose curls settling around the nape of his neck. He flung on some mirrored aviator sunglasses and headed off in the opposite direction, picking up speed as he approached the steep hill.

'So, what do we have here? What? Where...?' I queried out loud as I pulled open my bag.

ASCEND

Billie Jade Kermack

I counted one book, the smaller of the two, shoved up against a half-eaten breakfast bar wrapper. I searched my bag furiously, then the footwell and under the seat.

Oh my, that looked important – you haven't lost Gwen's special book, have you? my Inner Bitch questioned unhelpfully, in a giddy tone.

I retraced my steps, searching through Gwen's back garden; under wild bramble bushes that bit at my skin, in the white-picketed rose gardens either side of the cobbled pathway leading to the side entrance. The book was nowhere to be seen.

'Book! Come on, BOOOOK!' I called for it in an impatient whisper like I would a defiant puppy, not overly surprised when it didn't come with its pages flapping. I put my hands onto the small, glass-paned windows in the door to shield the sun's glare. There, high up on the shelf beyond the spiral staircase, neatly in its place as it had been before, was the book I had borrowed just minutes earlier.

'Borrowed? Don't you mean STOLE?' my inner voice barked with a smirk.

Borrowed! I repeated, vindicating what I had done but secretly agreeing with my know-it-all inner voice. I had stolen it; just not as successfully as I had thought.

I pulled at the handle to no avail; it was locked. That book

ASCEND   *Billie Jade Kermack*

would have to wait!

☐☐

After a ten-minute ordeal of trying to start up Bob, my car, outside Gwen's, I was finally on the road and homeward-bound. Sure, he clunked and protested most of the way – the exhaust taking the brunt of it – but for now at least, Bob was tucked up in the garage in one piece.

I dragged my tired feet up the stairs. Making sure my bedroom door was closed behind me, I wedged my computer chair up against it and threw my coat and bag on the already-disorganised pile of my belongings that sat in the corner by the window. I drew the curtains, their metal attachments clinking loudly on the rail and fell onto my bed, kicking my shoes onto the floor. As I opened Gwen's brown leather-bound book, its fraying binding creaked.

☐ THE SHADOWED VEIL ☐
SEEING THE TRUTH

The embossed golden writing on the yellowing, gilt-edged pages took my breath away – I couldn't explain why, but a sort of latent energy jumped from the book and felt warm in my hands. I was somehow drawn to it, my fingertips

ASCEND *Billie Jade Kermack*

stroking the pages, over the indented words.

On the first page, scribbled in almost unreadable coal-black calligrapher's ink, its age shown by the bleed of the lettering on the crisp finery of the pages, was written:

> THE JAWS OF DARKNESS DO DEVOUR IT UP:
> SO QUICK BRIGHT THINGS COME TO CONFUSION.
> YOUR LIFE IS SHADOWED, BEAUTY STANDS TALL WITHIN.
> YOURS ALWAYS –
> W, THE TELLER OF TALES

The book pre-dated my life, Gwen's life and probably the lives of many of our ancestors, yet the words appeared to speak to me, to hold great significance. 'Shadowed, confusion, darkness' – I was all too familiar with these words. The inscription matched the aged appearance of the book's exterior but as I turned over the thick, papyrus-like pages, the entries towards the middle of the book seemed to be from a much later date. Many were handwritten, often difficult to read, sometimes just a jumbled list of words and scribbled sketches.

<u>APPARITION</u>

'The supernormal manifestation of people, animals and spirits. Most apparitions are of living people or animals too distant to be perceived by normal senses.

When one experiences an apparition they bear witness to

ASCEND

Billie Jade Kermack

strange noises, unusual smells, extreme temperature changes and displacement of objects. Other phenomena include visual images, tactile sensations, voices and the apparent psychokinetic movement of objects. Apparitions may be luminous, transparent or ill-defined. They have the ability to appear and disappear abruptly, and move to and from solid matter. From my experience, some may also be able to cast shadows and may be visible in reflective surfaces. Apparitions, spirits or the souls of the dead may manifest to communicate a crisis or death, provide a warning, comfort the grieving, or to convey neccessary information.

BEWARE
Do not take apparitions lightly. Whether a gift from Heaven or Hell, a spirit may have motives for their hauntings which are not foreseeable on first meeting.'

A clumsy black-and-white sketch beneath the text was blindingly clear. A woman, floating clear off the grass, draped in a layered ankle-length dress; Elizabethan in era, I thought. I assumed this was the apparition, the shrouded peasant man kneeling on the floor beneath her feet looking up at her, the haunted. Two parallel lines above her led to an opening in the clouded sky – to the heavens. Another pair of parallel lines beneath her feet led into a crack in the ground, to the depths of Hell.

Time passed and my eyes grew heavy as I devoured each page, drinking in everything the book had to offer. As I discovered more about what was happening to me, I found

ASCEND   *Billie Jade Kermack*

an odd sense of comfort in knowing that it had happened to others before me.

'I slumber peacefully, moon high in the sky, I will now be lost in the dream-state, dancing waves of colour as they finally take rest, quiet, hushed, still. All is quiet, all is hushed, all is still.

Restore I with the name of the Intended, unless sleep be desired by the Speaker.'

I read the words aloud, squinting as I tried to rearrange them into a correct sentence. Re-reading it in my head, I mused: 'Do what with the what now?' The feeling of exhaustion didn't slowly creep up on me but instead hit me at full force; my eyes were instantly heavy, as though sandbags were attached to each lid, dragging them down, forcing rest upon me. I tried to fight it but my body was weak, and as my elbow gave way on the bed and my face hit the book below me I was defenceless, motionless. *Move, God damn you, move!* I silently screamed at my arm, now just my thoughts for worrying company as it slumped over the edge of the bed, apparently disconnected from my brain.

I gave in, unable to fight against the natural order of things any more.

TEN

୫୬ଓଃ

I woke up with the sun burning my eyes through my firmly-shut lids. I was fully dressed from the night before in blue jeans and my red hooded college sweatshirt. The book was open, face-down, on the rug next to my bed. 'Natural order of things, my arse!' I said as I jumped off my bed, my limbs still tingling as they reconnected with my body. *What the hell happened last night?* I thought, perplexed and a little on edge. Scrap that, a buck-load on edge. I felt drowsy and unsteady, like I'd had a night on the tiles that I had zero memories of.

I picked up the book slowly. It was still open on the same page it had been last night. Have you ever entered in to a contract without reading the small print, only to later regret it? Welcome to my world.

I quickly scanned through the rhyme, this time not reading it aloud, then moved onto the caption below it. In considerably darker, bolder writing it read:

Restore I with the name of the Intended, unless sleep be

ASCEND

Billie Jade Kermack

desired by the Speaker.

Beneath that line in a thin, just-about-legible scrawl were the words:

Reading this spell aloud will cause almost instant slumber. The subject's weight, height and bodily proportions may vary so allow for variations in time.

We're not cooking a bloody risotto here – surely that should have been written in big, readable letters at the very top! Where's Harry Potter when you need him? Lesson learned: don't read spells aloud! *I would make a really terrible wizard given the chance,* I thought. Then again, maybe if this thing had proper instructions, I wouldn't have gotten into that mess.

I grabbed a pen from my desk and wrote exactly that at the top of the page, regretting it instantly as I finished off by applying an exclamation point. *What the hell am I doing, this isn't even mine!* Feeling instantly as if I'd drawn in a library book, I saddled that good old prospect *hindsight* and debated ripping out the page; of course, the thought was ludicrous.

After ten seconds or so of deciding how best to mask the problem without resorting to trusty (but very visible) Tipp-Ex, my predicament was solved for me. The words, my words, began to fade and disappear. Each letter vanished, like liquid cocooning into waves and settling out of sight on the seabed. They were gone.

ASCEND

Billie Jade Kermack

I gathered the book up carefully, suddenly aware of how it had quickly gone from being an inanimate object to something wondrously magical, and tucked it safely on my shelf behind a stack of old college essays.

My phone *pinged* with a text message from inside my coat pocket, hanging on the back of my computer chair.

8.13AM
I hope you're ready, I'll be by in fifteen minutes to pick you up. Your first day at work – can't be late!

Gwen x

My toothbrush was still hanging from my mouth as I grabbed my newly-pressed uniform – thanks, mum – out of my wardrobe. The cheap, baby-blue cotton polo shirt with the *Western Hope General* logo sewn onto the chest clung to me unflatteringly, and the black cotton skirt wasn't faring much better as it bunched around my hips. I brought the necklace Beau had given me, that had once hung round the neck of his now-deceased mother, to my lips and took in a short sharp breath. I had a feeling I was going to need all the help I could get.

Nervous, are we? my Inner Bitch chastised, mocking the deep emotion of the moment.

ASCEND

Billie Jade Kermack

Yes, yes I was, but I wasn't going to give her the satisfaction of knowing that. I tucked the necklace inside my top and patted at it through the material as I often did to make sure it was still there, dangling beside my heart. The black pencil skirt and matching patent pumps made me feel like a dowdy office worker. The abrasive, knitted grey cardigan was two sizes too big for me, so I rolled the sleeves up to my elbows. With an exhale of breath and a tug at the unforgiving waistband of my skirt, I addressed my hair, checking the brochure Gwen had given me, pinned to my wardrobe door:

Hospital guidelines require that hair which reaches below the shoulders should be secured neatly in a bun. Hair which cannot be secured tidily should be pulled back from the face.

'OK, so, a bun. Shouldn't be too hard.' My voice was steady, even though my unruly tendrils normally found it difficult to comply with any style involving the word *neatly*. I brushed, teased, sprayed, pulled and secured my hair. It wasn't neat, nor did it resemble the picture on the brochure, but it would have to do.

◻◻

I sat uncomfortably in Gwen's large, split-screen VW camper van. The van was hippy chic at its best, painted bright orange and green with pink flower decals plastered all over the bonnet. *Flower power is alive and kicking in London today* I thought, as Van Morrison's grainy musical stylings rang out in waves from the updated sound system

ASCEND
Billie Jade Kermack

in the dashboard. I tapped on the battered, cream leather seats in time to 'Brown Eyed Girl' as Gwen hummed along with the tune.

Her small hands wrapped around the shabby brown leather-bound steering wheel, her fingers unable to reach around its entire circumference. Her seat was draped with an Aztec-patterned throw which was moulded to fit her perfectly, almost a second skin for the seat. Her short hair was pulled back from her face, held in place by a paisley headscarf which was secured in a knot at the nape of her neck. The hospital guidelines rang again in my head in an authoritative tone: *Hair which cannot be secured tidily should be pulled back from the face.* Glancing at her, I had noticed that Gwen's usually inviting, warm-amber coloured eyes had lost a little of their sparkle. The lightly wrinkled skin beneath them was a hollow shade of grey. She was quiet, her mood uncomfortably tranquil.

Oh God, does she know I took her book? Do I look guilty? How stupid am I – Gwen knows everything! My thoughts were manic, an onslaught of panic and residual regret. *She is psychic you idiot,* my inner voice added unhelpfully. I plastered a plausible if not overly-excited smile on my face; it pinched at my cheeks, quite possibly severing the nerve endings.

'You alright sweetheart?' she asked, concerned.

Stop smiling, you weirdo! I quickly took my own advice and relaxed.

ASCEND *Billie Jade Kermack*

'I'm fine, first day nerves probably... are you OK, Gwen? If you don't mind me saying, you look a little under the weather.'

'I haven't been sleeping much, this damn sickness bug just won't let up' she said, wiping her sweaty brow with the back of her hand.

'Are you sure you're up for work today? You don't have to show me around, I'm sure I'll survive.' Concern was oozing from me and Gwen had definitely noticed.

'It's your first day, I said I would show you around the hospital and despite any horrible illness I might be afflicted with, I will stay true to my word. I'll get enough rest when I'm dead.' I knew she was joking, but the mere mention of death made me feel uneasy. Within seconds of reading my body language Gwen's grin was now beaming, sharing a little of its brightness with her eyes. In a matter of moments, with the breeze from the open window lapping affectionately at my face, I was calm and relaxed – I was normal.

'Thanks for the lift today, Gwen. I don't think Bob would have managed the journey.' I stroked the dashboard, trying to ignite a semblance of comfort and familiarity, but it just wasn't the same. However shoddy and old he was, I missed my car; I missed Bob. For a brief moment I felt oddly guilty, as though I was betraying my car. Yes, there was rust at every corner and the interior was held together with heavy-

ASCEND

Billie Jade Kermack

duty duct tape and a bucketload of wishful thinking, but he was my heap.

'We haven't had a chance to catch up lately. Once I'm feeling a little less like death, it's you and me. Perhaps lunch today? You can tell me how your morning went.' Gwen interrupted my thoughts, which I was thankful for, as the words *inanimate object* ran through my mind. Still doing forty miles per hour on the motorway, Gwen pulled at the screw-top lid on a bottle of painkillers with one hand, the other firmly on the steering wheel. An open bottle of Evian rested between her legs.

'Sounds like a plan.' I took the bottle of oval pills, opened it and emptied two onto the palm of Gwen's hand.

□□

The heavy car door slammed shut behind me with an almighty *thud* as I stepped onto the tarmac of the hospital car park. I hadn't expected them but they crept up on me once we started our ascent up the wide brick steps, my hand gliding over the cold steel of the handrail – *nerves*. I didn't want to admit it to myself but with every step my feet felt light and uncompromising, my muscles twingeing, fraught with a stubborness they hadn't felt since Tony Blair was in office.

I tripped up the last step towards the grand white double-doored entrance of the hospital, Gwen catching me before my ankle could twist awkwardly. The automatic doors

ASCEND
Billie Jade Kermack

greeted us; once inside, the burly, expressionless six-foot-three Asian guard did not. His hand rested on the truncheon tucked into his security belt, waiting, almost hoping for a riot, praying that today would be the day that the monotony of his life would be turned on its head. His name tag was a clear contradiction to his appearance.

Hi, I'm ASIF. How can I help? it read, followed by a yellow smiley face sticker.

'Grace, will you excuse me for a moment? I really have to... use the... ladies room.' I only got Gwen's words in bits and pieces, her breathing heavy and short as she hurried away, towards the bathroom door across from the busy nurses' station.

'OK.' My words fell on deaf ears; Gwen was gone in a flash of grey and blue, but I felt compelled to answer her anyway. Drawn to their laughter, I noticed a couple of nurses exchanging patient files and chatting animatedly. Laughing about 'some dopey so-and-so who had gotten something pointy stuck somewhere uncomfortable', they quickly found where they had left their professionalism when they saw a stern, portly woman in her late fifties approaching .

I took a seat in the lobby to wait for Gwen, surrounded by the hustle and bustle of everyday A&E, still aware of the towering Asif and his accusing glare. A man with a saucepan on his head sat on one of the blue plastic chairs that were bolted to the floor, an open copy of *Heat* magazine in his hands. There were kids in school uniforms with minor

ASCEND
Billie Jade Kermack

grazes and bumps, their over-protective parents arguing with a nurse about waiting times.

A little old lady with a bandaged arm in the far corner – perched between a dirt-covered rugby player with a bag of frozen peas held to his bleeding head and a solemn young man in a wheelchair and a full leg cast – gave me cause for concern. Not so much for her wrapped wounds, but the imaginary cat she was stroking on her lap. I giggled, muffling my laughter with my cardigan sleeve. A dashing young man in hospital slacks cajoled the woman to her feet and, answering my assumptions, led her towards the hallway marked with a big sign on the wall, directing the way to the Psychiatric Ward.

'Come on Keith, keep up! Mummy's going on an adventure.' There was a childlike excitement in her voice as she addressed the imaginary animal in her clutches.

'Mrs Crane, would you like me to hold... Keith, is it?' He was polite and understanding, but I could tell by his face as they turned the corner and went out of view that he was praying she would decline his kind offer. The janitor stopped mopping the floor as they passed and dipped his head at the old lady, who returned his gesture with a smile. His prescription glasses were about three inches thick, which made his eyes appear large and his pupils dilated. His greasy hair fell lankly onto his cheeks and as he continued to clean the floors, I could see he had a slight limp.

Suddenly a booming voice came from over my shoulder,

ASCEND   *Billie Jade Kermack*

jolting me to attention. 'Tuck in that shirt!' I instantly stood up straight and rearranged the hem of my shirt, complying without question or argument. 'We have standards here – I'm guessing you are new.' It was the stern, portly woman. Her body language screamed *uptight*. Her face was taut and unfriendly, with only a seemingly glued-on, disapprovingly-raised eyebrow and pursed lips for expression.

'Did you even read the guidelines? That hair does not comply with protocol.' She laughed, but it wasn't a happy laugh; it was more critical, dip-dyed in aversion. Her hair, of course, was pulled tight and rock-solid, not a single strand out of place. The facelift effect and probable damage she was doing to her already diminishing hair line made me wince. I tugged at my messy up-do, still blissfully uncncerned about its appearance. *Head Sister Agnes Arcania,* I repeated in my head, reading her name tag.

OK – steer clear of Miss High and Mighty Agnes – got it! I agreed immediately with my inner voice; without uttering a word, I beamed and walked over towards the toilets to wait for Gwen. I didn't have a name tag, she didn't have a clue who I was or what department I worked for, so all I had to do was stay out of her way. *Seems simple enough.*

I watched Agnes make her way back to the nurses' station, followed by a young girl who was practically skipping close behind her in the wake of her footsteps. She kept her head low, very rarely making eye contact with anything other than the floor. She wore a baby-blue nurse's uniform with *Trainee Nurse* embossed above the hospital logo. Her wavy,

ASCEND
Billie Jade Kermack

bobbed chestnut hair skimmed her chin, both sides secured with daisy hair-grips. Her name tag, fastened to her uniform with a retractable *Take That* clip, read *Rosie*. She smiled constantly, her emerald-green eyes probably eternally optimistic. Although she must have been in her early twenties she had the aura of a child, a happy, beautiful child.

ELEVEN

'So Grace, welcome to your kingdom!' Gwen said with feigned amusement as she pushed open the heavy metal door which creaked at its rusting hinges. 'Ta-da!'

'Wow, it's... dark.' I gazed around the dank shell of a room, filled with thousands if not millions of papers, files, and dust-covered brown boxes; on metal shelves, in cabinets, covering the floor. The musty, twenty-year-old stale air around me clung unwelcome in my nostrils and tickled at my throat, reminding me of the onset of hay fever.

'I've found antihistamines help when working down here. Candice used to pop them like vitamins' she voiced, with a reassuring pat on my back.

'How do they find a patient's file in all this rubbish?' I asked, wiping my index finger over the computer table and realising there was dark-brown wood beneath the thick coating of grey dust.

'They don't – that's why you're here.'

ASCEND

Billie Jade Kermack

In that moment, I missed the smell of bleach and the rancid toilets at *Mr. Luigi's Pizza Parlour*. Gwen had forewarned me this job would be testing; however, with no windows or natural light and enough lint-bunnies to kill an asthmatic, I feared my minimum wage packet would soon look more like a pay off for future medical bills, rather than a way to earn some extra money. My job description was clear:

Here at Western Hope General we pride ourselves on caring for others and we are pleased to have you on board. Sort patient files with care and consideration, paying close attention to key factors: their identity, healthcare and, in most cases, their deaths. All information concerning patients and their healthcare should be transferred in full onto the computer provided. No file should be taken off premises without full written permission from a senior member of staff. Any employee not adhering to these rules will be dismissed immediately. Once you have completed a pile of exactly twenty files please pass them on to Ed Fuller, our incinerator technician. Contact him via the number provided on the desk.

You will receive a weekly list of which records to destroy, which to file and which to add to the 'indeterminate' pile for inspection. Lists can include record dates, patient names or healthcare numbers.

Gwen had spoken of Ed before – *'He has that obsessive, creepy glint in his eye every time he mentions fire; a trapped delinquent arsonist if you ask me,'* I remembered. I

ASCEND
Billie Jade Kermack

had yet to learn for myself but apparently, whether it was old papers, spoiled and stained bedsheets or the bodies of the unclaimed dead, when that first flame flickered, Ed was bewildered, almost excited. This made me more than a little uneasy and I planned to steer clear of him as much as I possibly could.

'Sounds simple enough' I said to Gwen, with an unusually positive skip in my step.

'Well then, I'll come and grab you at lunch. The hospital cafeteria food isn't the best, but it's edible. We have a low recorded rate of food poisoning, but then if the worst should happen, you're in the best place for it!' She giggled – I didn't. 'I have a group session with Rosie and the other trainees at eleven, so I'll let you know if I'm running late.'

'Rosie, from the front desk?' I mused whilst trying to clear the computer chair with my bag.

'That's her. She doesn't speak much, but she is intuitive and has a great sense of humour. Once she gets used to you, you'll see. I have very high hopes for her here.'

□□

I plodded along with my duties with only the old radio for company. Its aerial was duct-taped together, and every once in a while I had to wave it around just to pick up a clear signal. I pulled off my grey cardigan as it clung to my sweaty arms. I grabbed a dusty table fan from atop the tall cabinet

ASCEND *Billie Jade Kermack*

by balancing on a crooked chair. Falling off was a possibility, but fainting in the heat was more probable; I'd risk falling! The rotation of warm air wasn't as soothing as I had hoped, but it was better than nothing.

I pulled at one of the dented green filing cabinets in the far corner, tucked behind three rows of crooked metal shelving units. I tugged a few times with no luck, but with one final pull and an almighty screech, the drawer came loose. I fell back onto the floor with a *thud* as a colourful array of disturbed papers rained down on me.

As if there wasn't already enough work to do here – well done, Grace! I thought, fighting the urge to punch myself. The hours dragged but eventually, lunch and the possibility of my freedom was approaching. I had sorted and filed only a ¼ of the papers on the floor, but the fact that I could see grey linoleum – however small a patch it might be – made me feel overjoyed.

'Destroy files,' he ordered flatly. I hadn't even heard him approach the dungeon. He stood in the open doorway, pulling at a loose piece of wood in the frame around the lock.

'Christ, you scared me! Ever heard of knocking?' I fretted, trying to catch my breath. When I had composed myself, I noticed that the thumping of my heart against my ribcage hadn't slowed, mainly because Ed was blocking the only exit. As first impressions go, this one was unnerving to say the least. He didn't have what you would call a friendly

ASCEND *Billie Jade Kermack*

disposition and was dressed in an orange jumpsuit which made him look a little like a prison inmate, the long sleeves tied around his waist.

'Sor... sorry,' he stuttered. 'I didn't mean to startle you. I'm Ed. I collect the files to be destroyed.' The only eye contact he made with me throughout his speech was when he introduced himself, a trait that looked as though it had been ingrained in his psyche. He looked uncomfortable in my presence, his awkwardness screaming to flee the room as he pulled on the frayed edging of his grubby, once-white T-shirt.

'I'm Grace, pleased to meet you.' I held out my hand for him to shake but he just looked at me as though this was an entirely alien gesture. I could see him assessing my hand as it hung there between us a little longer than was normal. I wanted him to feel comfortable with me, especially as we would be working together. He took my hand roughly in his and shook it wildly, a trace of excitement in his eyes, my simple gesture seemingly a new experience for him.

'Very nice to... to meet you, Grace.' He swallowed hard, as though the words felt unnatural on his tongue, as though a conversation was something unheard of. He now kept eye contact (possibly a little too intensely, but we could work on that) and smiled broadly, as I did. I handed him some of the files I had sorted from my desk, and said my goodbyes. He shuffled back down the dimly-lit hallway pushing a tin bucket on wheels, so large it could have held a person and still had room.

ASCEND   *Billie Jade Kermack*

TWELVE
ℰʚɞ

13.08PM
Sorry sweetie, can't make lunch, emergency C-section on Bluebell Ward. Will catch up later. Cafeteria's on third floor, left out of the lift, follow the signs.

Gwen xxx

'Floor Three, please' I squeaked politely while checking my bag for my purse, a task of its own as I had to wade through the mountain of three months' accumulation of crap. *Why do women carry so much stuff?* I giggled to myself, the words in my head immediately taking on Beau's voice. The stereotype was most certainly true for me; if I had a space bigger than a matchbox, I would find a way to fill it.

'You're new, right?' The girl must have been about my age, twenty-one at a push. Her flawless skin was pale, her eyes a

ASCEND

misty green. Her thin, dark blonde hair was pulled tautly into a hospital-guideline-approved bun at the nape of her neck. The hem of her uniform's black pleated skirt sat below her knees and her grey cardigan with the hospital emblem on the chest was a little on the large side, as the sleeves covered part of her hands.

'Yeah, I'm Grace – head of dungeon duties, slayer of all that is unwanted paper.' She giggled whimsically, quickly muffling the sound with her hand. It put me off guard, as I knew what I had said was about as funny as a heart attack. I offered her my hand politely.

'I would, but I've got a cold' she sniffed, taking a step back, and I put my hand back down by my side. 'So, Third Floor. Are you going to grab some lunch? Can I join you?' She sounded practically giddy, seeming to levitate with joy. The cogs and pulleys managing the old service lift roared to life, lazily kicking into gear as we passed the first floor.

'You should really think about taking the stairs up to reception and then using the main lift. This rickety box-on-a-string contraption is not what you would call safe.'

'I'll keep that in mind, thanks. I've just realised, I don't even know your name!' I said. The lift pinged and then shook as we reached the third floor.

'Oh, silly me. I'm Skylar, but everyone just calls me Sky.'

"OK, Sky – lead the way!'

ASCEND

Billie Jade Kermack

□□

I picked up a suspicious looking plate of chicken curry from the food counter and grabbed a Coke from the chest fridge. If you can believe it, the brown sludge on my plate was the safest option available. A part of me wasn't even sure it was chicken; I would go as far as to question if it was actually meat. And here was me thinking the food at college was bad.

Hearing the clanking and buzz of chatter behind the closed set of double doors, I was immediately transported back to my first day of school. Why was I nervous? I laughed off the feeling and smiled back over my shoulder at Sky. With my hand on the whitewashed wood of the door, something pinned to the board on the wall next to us caught my attention. 'What's this about? They know it's May, right?'

The A3 poster entitled *Valentines Day Ball* had clearly been designed in a frenzy by a Google Image-loving employee, as there wasn't a space free of cut-out hearts and roses. 'May is when management get their yearly influx of funds from the board of trustees. June is party season here at Western Hope General, don't forget those dancing shoes!' Sky bellowed like a disc jockey introducing the latest chart-topper, as though she had heard the saying more than a few times before. I'd known her for all of two minutes, but this outburst seemed out of character to me; apparently to her too as she shook out her arms and shuddered, her expression returning to placid and neutral.

ASCEND *Billie Jade Kermack*

I grabbed a napkin-wrapped knife and fork and gazed over the crowded room in search of Sky. There she was, propped silently in the furthest corner of the cafeteria, looking slightly uneasy; she caught my eye and excitedly waved me over, almost standing on her chair in case I hadn't seen her.

'Is that all you're going to eat?' I asked, placing my tray down on the table. Sky twiddled with a shiny red apple with one bite taken out of it, the spongy inside already starting to turn brown.

'I only ate an hour ago. My mum makes me sandwiches for work.'

'Oh, right, why did you come with me then?' I asked, trying not to sound rude. Sky was a little odd; a lovely girl, don't get me wrong, but there was definitely something about her that wasn't exactly altogether there. We spent the next forty-five minutes sharing hushed whispers, getting to know each other. I had an inkling that Sky wasn't the most popular member of staff, as people on the tables around us whispered and giggled in our direction. She hid it well with a slightly plastered-on grin, but I could see how uncomfortable the added attention was making her.

She had welcomed me with open arms, so I would return the favour. I distracted her for another twenty minutes, now completely oblivious to those around us. Topics covered included parents, work and love lives – that last one a short but not surprising conversation on Sky's part. When I had mentioned the word love, she had immediately flushed a

ASCEND *Billie Jade Kermack*

deep beetroot.

'I've worked here for what feels like forever. A couple of years ago I even tried my hand at your job, in the records room – it aggravated my sinuses though' she mused, grabbing a crumpled tissue from her grey cardigan sleeve and rubbing furiously at her already pink nose.

'Have you met Ed?' I asked, trying to gauge the silence that followed. Seemingly searching for words, she moved a little closer to the table.

'Yes. He's pretty harmless, but if you can, just steer clear, he's not exactly, all there... if you know what I mean', she winked. I suddenly felt a crushing pang of guilt, deep in my stomach; I had pretty much thought of Sky in the exact same way.

'If ever you want any help in the *dungeon*, let me know.'

'You will be the first girl on my list' I smiled, which seemed to add a flush of rosiness to her face, coloured by happiness rather than embarrassment this time.

THIRTEEN

&

'Destroy pile, file pile, indeterminate pile.' I had repeated the words at least a hundred times over the past week, and was finally making a dent in the thousands records that littered the floor – *floor* being the important word. It felt wrong to trample over the files of people that might be dead; it seemed insensitive and somehow callous, especially since I had a boyfriend who could see and speak to them. I had the knowledge that they still wandered amongst us.

FOR DESTROY PILE
FILE REFERENCE : #223 - 14
AGE : Approx. 25 - 30
NAME : Unknown
DATE : 15th June 1999
CASE FILE : 221-546-544
STATUS : Deceased
C.O.D : Strangulation
CIRCUMSTANCES : Murder
LOCATION FOUND : South River, E8

ASCEND

Billie Jade Kermack

INSPECTOR ON CASE : PC Fleming

FOR INDETERMINATE FILE
FILE REFERENCE : #116 - 72
AGE : 32
NAME : Henry Forbes
DATE : 7TH March 1962
CASE FILE : 713-111-882
STATUS : Deceased
C.O.D : Heart attack
CIRCUMSTANCES Indeterminate
LOCATION FOUND : Dray's Court, N5
INSPECTOR ON CASE : DCI Canter

The records went on like that – endless facts, reports, scans, X-rays. It didn't take long for them to all blur into a black and white haze.

After two days, more than sixteen hours (four of which were overtime), and a bucket-load of coffee I was about ready to go home, have a bath and spend some time with Beau before he left for his trip.

Is there such a thing as working too hard? Because if there was, I was doing it. Although I had banished my memories of Glen, the sadistic serial killing spirit, it was at times like these that it didn't take much for him to slip uninvited to the forefront of my mind. I could have been one of those dead people, I could have had a discarded file on the floor of the dungeon. I had become an expert when it came to hiding my

ASCEND

feelings, and for once it didn't involve lying to anyone, in regard to my records work anyway. *Yes, I've lied to Beau; yes, I probably shouldn't have, but there are some things I have to work out on my own. For now, anyway.*

Fool! snarled my Inner Bitch.

I arranged for Ed to pick up the 'Destroy' pile once my shift was over, and dropped the others off at the front desk with Head Nurse Clark. I shifted my positioning so that one of the potted ferns on the desk shrouded me from Nurse Agnes, who was file-checking and giving a male intern a right telling off about some incorrect patient information.

Nurse Clark, who appeared to be saddled with the same intolerable personality disorder that Agnes had, said she was pleased with my work – her face said otherwise. Her thin lips barely broke from an even, straight line, unless she was talking. She had stress lines, frown lines, but no laughter lines to report. I had often heard her likened to the TV character Victor Meldrew, his catchphrase muttered under people's breath as she passed by their stations with a scowl. Her stunted emotional drama aside, I would take her *'Well done'* and enjoy it, with a long overdue carefree smile on my face.

I began my descent down the wide bricked path to the car park while fiddling in my bag for my keys. The sun had begun to set, painting the sky a deep, vibrant orange. Despite a light breeze, the considerably hot day still hung in the air; it felt like holiday air, the type that makes you want

ASCEND *Billie Jade Kermack*

to go to a poolside bar for cocktails. *Ohhh, that would be so nice right now!* I thought, wishing I was on a deserted, white sandy beach, somewhere far, far away.

'Watch out!'

'Sorry Sky, I was in my own world for a minute there. I'm not with it; too much work and not enough downtime, I think.' I smiled. 'Do you need a lift home?'

'No thanks, I was just taking a five minute break, thought I'd go for a wander. I'm on double shifts tonight. Thankfully we have some new girls volunteering next week, so that should lighten the load.'

'OK, well if you're free we can catch up on Friday for lunch. Same place, same time?'

'Actually, if you wanted to keep me company, I have to sort laundry... could do with a chatting buddy!' Fighting the urge to decline her offer and go home and collapse on my bed, the manners my parents had instilled in me as a young girl had answered her question before my tired brain even had a chance to articulate anything other then a grunt.

'I think I can spare five minutes' I smiled, stifling a yawn. I'd never been one to drum up new friendships and with Amelia by my side I had enough dramas to keep me completely satisfied, but there was something about Sky, something I couldn't put my finger on. I felt instantly that we would make good friends if I gave it a chance and got to know her.

ASCEND   *Billie Jade Kermack*

□□

'So, you grew up round here?' I said, emptying a wicker basket full of stiff, white cotton bed linen onto a slatted wooden table, ready to fold. The hospital name and logo was barely visible on the more yellowing sheets, their life cycle probably exceeding the last group of patients that had slept on them.

'My mother Didi and I moved here from Yugoslavia when I was two. We have never been considered *traditionally* English, you might say. My mother brought her life in Yugoslavia with her and... well, she adapted it here. I grew up in a houseboat on the river, which was excellent fodder for bullies at school.' Her usual innocent sparkle dimmed, as a faraway memory lingered with her. She shook it off and within a split second the sparkle in her eyes had returned, as though the memory had been shoved away somewhere deep and dark, away from prying eyes.

'Well at least you had an interesting upbringing, houses are overrated.' I reached out my arm to comfort her but she moved away sharply with an unsettled glare. It was a fleeting expression, but one that confused me. I abruptly changed the conversation to ease the growing tension. 'So, what made you want to be a nurse?' Magically the awkwardness dissipated, as I had hoped, quicker than it had occurred.

'My mum has always had health issues – if it wasn't her

ASCEND
Billie Jade Kermack

heart it was her lungs, if not her lungs then her kidneys. She likes to say God literally broke the mould when he made her and her insides are jumbled.' Her laugh was a soft, almost bird-like chirp. 'So the career choice blossomed from there. I was born with a need to help others, I guess. How about you?'

As I went to speak, I suddenly felt a pang of guilt stabbing at my stomach. I was there to make money, plain and simple. Yes I liked the idea of helping people, but it wasn't a life goal of mine to sort files in a basement with only my Inner Bitch for company. She cared deeply, and any response I gave her would maybe trample on what she did. Any truthful response, anyway!

'I'm still not decided on where my life is going to take me. I think I'll wait and see if I can survive college first.' She smiled in response.

'Well don't wait too long, time has a way of getting away from us when we least expect it. Look, I have to get on with my rounds, but it's been nice chatting. Thanks for your help.' I hadn't really helped; Sky's folded pile of sheets were immaculate and, I would assume, right on-par with hospital guidelines. Mine were not, and she would most definitely have to redo my pile.

I made my exit without uttering another word, just a wide smile and a limp wave.

FOURTEEN
ॐ

9.24AM
Meet for lunch – got news –
bring Beau!

Amelia's text as always, was vague.

'We're meeting Amelia for lunch' I said as I strolled into Gwens kitchen, placing my empty cereal bowl into the sink which was already piled high with dirty dishes. 'We really need to wash up before Gwen gets home' I said, eyeing Beau disapprovingly, even though I was partially to blame. I buttoned up my uniform grey cardigan and adjusted my black pencil skirt, tucking the blue polo shirt into the waistband.

'*You* do need to wash up and why am *I* meeting Amelia for lunch?' Beau replied, all the while not taking his eyes off his newspaper.

'I know you only read those for the comic strips, you're not fooling anyone.'

ASCEND *Billie Jade Kermack*

'How Snoopy spends his mornings is both informative and a key character-building tool. If you let me miss lunch today, I'll let you have a read...' However tempting his offer was, I knew I couldn't.

'Ha, ha – *we* are a couple and *we* will do things together.' I squeezed some Fairy Liquid into the sink and turned on the hot tap. 'Plus you love me and I'd really, really appreciate it' I pouted, adding an extra dash of cuteness into my voice and throwing in some 'love me' sad-face to sweeten the deal.

'OK.' He admitted defeat, putting down his paper. *Oh, how I love winning!* 'But I have some rules. You will wash, I will dry up. I am only staying for one course at lunch, any longer than that and I make my excuses. If Amelia calls me Bob, Blake, Butch, sweetheart or – my absolute favourite – 'honey', I am out of there, no questions asked. Do we have a deal?' *Beau – 1, Grace – 0.*

'You have yourself a deal. *Honey*' I taunted, blowing him a soapy, bubble-filled kiss.

ॐ

'So, what's your big news?' I asked with feigned interest.

Knowing Amelia – and boy, did I know Amelia – she had probably snagged the last pair of this season's Jimmy Choos. Coco Chanel, Prada; clothes are clothes, and I feel better when I can afford a new summer wardrobe and a cheeky lunch at Prezzo, all without breaking the bank. Thank the lord for Primark.

The arrival of Jack interrupted my train of thought. I hadn't seen much of Jack since last term; he had never been too thrilled about Beau and I, so when Beau left I hadn't much fancied the *I told you so* speech.

Dismissing the memory of being without him, I squeezed Beau's hand in mine for comfort. Jack's usual bookish, knitted vest top and corduroy combo was gone, his sleek, pompous side-parting abandoned. In their place stood a very new Jack. With his denim skinny fit jeans, tailored green shirt and Tony & Guy-inspired hairdo set in place with some wax, he looked fantastic.

'Wow Jack, looking good!' I mused, as he took the empty seat next to Amelia. Jack blushed and cleared his throat uncomfortably as everyone stared at him.

'I know, right!' Amelia squealed.

'I have Beau to thank. He gave me a little advice, took me to some new places' Jack piped up, to calm Amelia down.

'No problem mate, happy to help.' Beau raised his glass of Coke and smiled. *Beau and Jack, friends – who would've thought it?* Whilst I played catch up, I hadn't noticed that everyone had ceased to follow up with more conversation. The silence was anything but comfortable.

ASCEND

Billie Jade Kermack

'So, Amelia, news?' I pushed, filling the void.

Beau coughed to grab my attention, and out of the corner of his aviator sunglasses I could see exactly where he was directing my eyeline. My question became redundant; Amelia and Jack's hands were clasped between them. Realisation took a painfully long second to kick into gear.

'Wow, I'm so happy for you both,' I gushed.

'And that's not all.' Amelia let go of Jack and reached down into a white paper shopping bag perched near her feet. 'Ta-da!' The dress was pink and white-striped, with a lace hem that looked a few inches shy of knee-length. It had an apron panel stitched onto the front and a matching nurse's cap, also striped. *Oh, hell no, this is not happening.*

The thought was scary; no, not scary – horrifying! Sky's words rang in my head: *'Thankfully we have some new girls volunteering next week'. Oh crap!* I thought.

'I'm going to be volunteering at the hospital. We're going to be work buddies!' She grabbed me tightly in her embrace, the dress still in her hand, slung over my shoulder, the metal hanger snagging on my cardigan. I caught a glimpse of Beau sniggering, trying to compose himself. One swift kick in the shin and that was that. 'Grace, this is going to be so much fun!' My grin said 'happy', my eyes cried out with worry. I loved Amelia, her and her ditsy ways, but working with her? Everyday? Even Mother Teresa had a day off!

ASCEND
Billie Jade Kermack

'I'm going to volunteer as a candy-striper to help the sick and needy, starting tomorrow, actually! My Mr. Love Bug here thought it would be good for my university trans... what's that word again, sweetpea?' Amelia huffed, her fluttering eyes lovingly fixed on Jack's.

'Transcript' he said, kissing the back of her hand.

'That's the one. Silly me – I'd forget my head if it wasn't screwed on!' she giggled.

Amelia, Jack, sweetpea, university transcript, VOLUNTEER – all words I would never have put together in one sentence I thought, my head fuzzy with all this new information.

I was happy for Amelia and Jack; however unexpected them getting together was, they looked truly content. He was good for her, and she was good for him; who would have thought it?

'So, to celebrate everything, Jack and I wanted to invite you and Beau to dinner here tomorrow night. A sort of double date!'

'Oh, that's a shame, because... I have that thing, and Grace, you have that other thing.' I could see Beau frantically searching his brain for something, anything that could get us out of dinner.'And my dog died,' he sniffed.

'I didn't know you had a dog, Beau' Amelia added, oddly

ASCEND *Billie Jade Kermack*

concerned.

'He doesn't, and we would love to join you for dinner' I interjected, completely cutting Beau off.

'I said one course, you agreed!' he whispered through gritted teeth, so as not to draw attention to himself.

'Be thankful she never called you *honey*.' I gave him my best puppy-dog stare and fluttered my eyelashes.

'Then it's a date' he said, turning to Amelia with a fixed smile.

That's my guy! I thought, stroking the cold spot behind his ear affectionately.

FIFTEEN

I pushed open the heavy door to the dungeon with my bum. I had a half-opened strawberry Nutrigrain bar hanging from my mouth, an open can of Coke and my satchel held tight in my left hand, the set of twenty door keys on a metal ring hanging from my little finger and a stack of files teetering in my right arm. I dropped everything down on the desk and the brass keys hit the floor with a *clunk*.

□□

'Hit me baby one more time! My loneliness is killing me, and I... ' I sung along to the crackly radio, probably out of tune, but no one was around so I let loose and belted out every word with rock star enthusiasm. Without any warning, a high-pitched screeching replaced Britney Spears. I threw up my hands to cover my ears whilst struggling to pull the radio wire from the plug socket. I felt faint, the noise pulsating inside my head, my brain seemingly under attack from something sharp and heavy.

With one final tug, no effort spared, I yanked the plug from

ASCEND

Billie Jade Kermack

the socket. It came free and without thinking I stumbled back, unable to stop myself, destroying the three piles of sorted records with my backside. The radio died with a low hiss, leaving the room in booming silence.

'OK, that was new.' Filling the void with my voice was comforting; realising I had to redo all my sorting was not. 'Damn radio!' I kicked the table the radio was perched on – it wobbled, and the radio fell to the floor with a *crash*. I gathered the files as best I could without muddling them up, but gave up when I noticed I had an unsolved murder in the 'Destroy' pile. I would have to start from scratch. I sat on the floor with my legs crossed and gathered up a pile to start on. It was going to be a long day.

'*Suicide by hanging* – indeterminate. *Drowning* – file. *Murder* – file. *Jane Doe* – indeterminate. *Head trauma* – destroy.' The piles grew, as did my frustration. Two hours down, another three to go. I stretched out my arms and legs, feeling my spine creak and argue as I did. The temperature in the room suddenly seemed to plummet as my heartbeat quickened. I shook out my hands and rubbed my face as my head began to spin. My mouth was dry, and what saliva there was tasted metallic.

'I've been in this room for far too long' I noted to myself aloud, my voice a comfort amidst the silence. I continued with the sorting, shoving my feelings of dismay to the back of my mind. Suddenly I was spluttering and coughing, feeling a gripping tension, an immense swelling in my chest. I tightened my grip around the file in my hands. Blood

ASCEND
Billie Jade Kermack

gushed from my nose, and my body began to shake uncontrollably. I dropped the now blood-spattered file and grabbed my coat and bag from off the desk. What I was experiencing soon dissipated, ending just as quickly as it had started. In mere moments, I realised why the panic in me remained.

> *IT WASN'T SUPPOSED TO END LIKE THIS*
> *IT WASN'T SUPPOSED TO END LIKE THIS*
> *IT WASN'T SUPPOSED TO END LIKE THIS*
> *IT WASN'T SUPPOSED TO END LIKE THIS*

I could see the letters on the computer keyboard being struck by no one, in quick succession, the words appearing on the bright white screen as though by magic. An invisible force was intent on terrifying me.

'Who's there? What do you want from me?' My screams went unanswered, the tapping of the keyboard unsettling. As though a gust of wind was circulating in the small, dark room, the files and papers on the floor flew into the back wall, taking my bag along with them.

'No thanks, not interested today. I'm out of here!' I headed for the door, and as my hand grasped the brass doorknob, everything went eerily silent. You could hear a pin drop as the rustling papers settled. I edged into the middle of the room. On the now cleared, stained linoleum was my bag, its contents scattered around it, arranged in a near-perfect circle. I took a couple of steps, back widening my view: my lip balm, my organiser, my door keys – like the numbers on

ASCEND   *Billie Jade Kermack*

a clock face, my belongings looked as though they had been purposefully placed there.

My heart was now lodged uncomfortably in my throat, hiding out until it knew it was safe to retreat back to the comfort of my lungs for cushions. It worried me that I found these experiences way too familiar. In a strange way, I had come to expect them, even though they played havoc with my nervous system. Goosebumps started prickling up my bare arms. I shoved everything back in my bag with very little care. The temperature of the air around me suddenly dropped. I exhaled, glacial wisps of white smoke alerting me to another's presence.

They flew at me in quick bursts, the rickety, rusting metal shelves shaking. The files – old, new, thick, thin – seven in total, were now scattered around my feet. I reached for them, but before I could steady myself the rusty old water-heater kicked in with a buzzing hum, engulfing the room in humid air. I chastised myself for letting my mind wander enough for me to jump at any little sound. I fanned out the files on the floor like a deck of cards and threw my bag onto the desk chair.

The seven files had similarities; all were women, all were victims of murder, all were pronounced dead on arrival, all were Caucasian brunettes. Their details were there in black and white, their lives stored in between the dusty pages of a piece of fraying cardboard, water-stained patient numbers scrawled across the front. Some had pictures attached, some lay there anonymous.

ASCEND

Billie Jade Kermack

<u>Liza McQueen,</u> 18. She had dark brown eyes, a strong nose that tipped upwards slightly towards the nostrils, her smile baring a mouth full of metal. She could only have been a teenager, if the photo was anything to go by. *Found discarded and topless, clothes and body singed almost beyond recognition. Signs of a struggle, including restraints. Died beside Thames River North or was transported there in a vehicle from primary murder location. Ongoing investigation. Blood tests inconclusive. Perpetrator unknown. Crime scene photos missing.*

<u>Petra Halovalich,</u> 22. Studying in England, student at Trinity College, Cambridge. *Found early summer 1987, partial burns to body, accelerator identified as petrol. Signs of torture present. Face unrecognisable due to sustained blows from unidentifiable object. Dental records needed. Perpetrator unknown. No photograph available. Pages missing / incomplete file.*

<u>Alison Rose Dwight</u>, 21. There was no picture of Alison but there was a detailed X-ray of various broken bones and close-up crime scene pictures of her injuries. I couldn't piece anything together; the pictures had obviously been taken at night. *Body of Mrs Dwight discovered in Haze Trading warehouse grounds, 1991. Sustained a vicious attack with various tools including a hammer and blade, size unidentifiable.* Pages four and five were missing and page six simply stated: *Ongoing investigation. Perpetrator unknown.*

ASCEND   *Billie Jade Kermack*

<u>Hannah Holmes,</u> 24. Her face was solemn and and her poised body, pearl necklace and lace-collared chiffon shirt screamed 'well-to-do'. The next photo of Hannah was vastly different. *Law graduate, discovered February 1993, buried in Epping Forest. Burns to torso, head and face. Identified by dental records. Sustained a vicious attack from an unknown weapon, displaced force and prolonged torture prior to death by asphyxiation. Ongoing investigation. Perpetrator unknown.*

<u>Jane Doe</u>, *female, early twenties. Unidentifiable charred remains of young woman. Teeth removed. Discovered on Northern Line tracks at 6am, October 1996. Cold case. Perpetrator unknown.* Two pages were missing from her file, but like the rest of these poor young girls, the person who had murdered her was unknown.

My phone pinged from in the back pocket of my jeans. I put down the photo of Jane Doe's incinerated remains, grateful for the interruption.

7.34PM
You're late and she's calling
me 'honey' – GET HERE
ASAP!
Beau xxx

I gathered up the files and stuffed them into my bag for scrutiny at a later date. Even though I still had two files left to inspect, I somehow already knew that they weren't going to have happy endings. There's only so much brutality

ASCEND
Billie Jade Kermack

someone can look at before it starts seeping into the forefront of their mind and sticking there. I switched off the table lamp, almost burning my fingers on the hot bulb as I did.

□□

I glanced over at Amelia, beautifully poised and exquisitely draped in a mauve satin halterneck summer dress, her painted fingernails tracing suggestively over the Specials menu. I took a look at myself, suddenly wishing I had bothered to go home and change, rather than rummaging through my work locker. My black vest top, cut-off denim shorts, holey Converse and loose bun hairstyle combo clearly wasn't the attire Amelia had had in mind when she arranged the double date.

'Oh really Grace, couldn't you have made a little effort?' she tutted disapprovingly, signalling for the waiter's attention. It wasn't a fancy place; the waiter was wearing jeans with a browning washcloth hanging from the pocket and a white polo shirt with a royal-blue anchor insignia sewn onto the chest. The bar down the stairs directly in front of our table adjacent to the beechwood dance floor was nautically-themed, ropes and buoys hanging from the walls. A toy fish hanging high on the wall which sung once its red button was pushed interrupted the music on the jukebox every so often, sending the slightly inebriated rugby team propping up the bar to roar in fits of laughter, in a lager-fuelled mist of testosterone. The barman wore a sailor's hat, a sea-scene printed apron and a displeased expression as he wiped away

ASCEND

Billie Jade Kermack

the remnants of a spilt beer.

'Four Cokes, please.' She didn't even look at the waiter as she ordered which he picked up on, rolling his eyes in response and probably questioning his choice of quitting school to take this job. I remembered only too well the joys of working in the service industry. The familiar scent of bleach coming from the back of the resturant accompanied my memory of scrubbing floors at *Mr. Luigi's Pizza Parlour*.

'I think you look lovely.' Beau kissed my cheek and rested his arm on the back of my chair, stroking my bare shoulder with his thumb. I immediately wanted to grab him and kiss him, but decided it would be best saved for some alone time. I settled for a kiss on his cheek and a rub of his other hand, resting on his knee.

'I found something interesting at work earlier. Remind me to tell you about it later,' I whispered into Beau's ear. If anyone had an insight into why someone wanted me to see those files, Beau would.

'Grace, you look a little peaky – are you feeling OK?' Jack asked, concerned. I wiped my sweaty brow with my palm, still unable to shake the feeling of dread that lurked in the pit of my stomach. It was an all too familiar feeling that never really went away, even in the happiest of moments. The files, like the blinding weight of a frightful memory, were tucked in the bag that hung on my chair.

ASCEND *Billie Jade Kermack*

'She's fine. Honey Bunny, lets check out the jukebox! I think they've finally updated it with a little Barbra Streisand.' She hopped off excitedly, dragging Jack along behind her like a plaything.

'He's right you know, you do look pale. Is everything OK Grace?' Beau's words blended in with the bustling chatter from the table of college students beside us, as he felt my forehead with the back of his hand.

'I'm fine. Little dizzy, but I'm fine. Probably just need to eat something' I said, batting his hand away as his proximity suddenly felt suffocating. I took a bite out of the dry, complimentary bread roll. I couldn't swallow properly, my throat constricting as I coughed and spluttered, trying to catch my breath, any breath. The doughy, white filling of the bread now oozed a murky, black, oily substance, mixed with clotted, crimson arterial blood. It curdled together, dripping from the table and onto the floor. Beau turned to the waiter to order our food, menu in hand. I spat the piece of bread out of my mouth and tried to steady myself as I jumped to my feet.

'... feel... dizzy. Beau...' I whispered, unable to muster anything more.

My chest tightened; like a balloon expelling air, it withered into a rubbery mess. I felt increasingly weak, my eyes heavy. As my organs screamed at each other to do their job, my heart was working overtime at great speed, causing a banging, disorientating thump in my head. Everything

ASCEND

Billie Jade Kermack

around me began to fade. It all happened so quickly a blur of shapes, a buzz of disjointed gasps and noise. Then I heard it, amongst the sullen, oxygen-deprived silence of my deepest consciousness: *'It wasn't meant to end like this.'*

'Grace, Grace! Breathe, Grace. Someone call 999!'

I could hear Beau's panicked voice, laden with desperation, but it was distant. I hit the floor with a *thud*, my head catching the corner of the table as I went. Something gripped my heart, squeezing the life from it. I could feel the blood rushing aimlessly beneath my skin in a frenzy and my face felt excruciatingly hot. I knew people were rushing around me, I knew they were hysterical, but everything seemed to be moving in slow motion, bright, white snapshots. I was detached somehow, my body compelled to bow to the ramblings in my head as I hung there in an unknown limbo.

'Gracie, you need to stay awake, help's coming. PLEASE STAY AWAKE.'

A weird calm enveloped me as Beau's voice drifted into the background of rush and panic. I lay there against the cold wooden floor, struggling to keep myself awake, strands of my sweat-sodden hair falling over my face. Suddenly, some clarity, a parting in the fog that was masking my pain and detaching me from what was really happening; in my eyeline were her feet, hanging in mid air. One red patent-heeled foot and the other shoeless, snapped awkwardly at the ankle, exposing the bloody, ash-coated bone.

SIXTEEN
ଛେଔ

> We fear death, the unknown.
> Death fears us, the unknowable.
> We fear death's necessity.
> Death fears our Divinity.
>
> *- Sri Chinmoy*

Beep, beep. Beep, beep.

The tubes and needles in my hands were hooked up to a bag of clear fluid hanging high beside me. A plastic fingertip heart-rate monitor glowed red, plugged in to a machine which looked like a TV, my lifeline pitching in hazy pinnacles on the black screen. It peaked with a low beep, slowly and steadily at first. My breathing was restricted, a heavy shadow crushing my lungs from inside my chest.

'What am I doing here? I can't be here!' I was panicking, and the quickening *beep* of the machine was only fuelling my worry.

'Grace, you have to calm down. They can't know I'm here –

ASCEND *Billie Jade Kermack*

I'm meant to be working.' Sky's voice was shaky, her words missing 'soothing' with a giant sidestep into 'distressed'.

'What the hell is going on, and what do you know about it?' My tone was brutal and accusing. I ripped off my blood pressure and pulse monitors, sending the bleeping into a flurry of activity. Sky was hurt, tears threatening to fall from her eyes.

'Sky, I'm sorry, I didn't mean...' but she was gone before I could finish, her almost childlike whimpering fading into the distance as she ran down the corridor, her black boat shoes squeaking on the freshly-buffed floors.

'Grace, what are you doing?' Beau grabbed at the wires, trying to figure out what was meant to go where whilst attempting to cajole me back into bed.

'I have to find Sky, I upset her' I said, using the IV-drip stand to steady myself as my legs buckled.

'You don't have to find anyone, you need to lie down and do as you are told.' Beau was sharp and demanding, much like a mother would be – like my mother would surely be. I didn't argue, it was pointless to. He dropped the wires back onto the floor, realising he realised he had no medical training and absolutely no idea what went where. 'You are not well. We need to see what the doctors say before you can even think about leaving.'

'It felt like someone was gripping my heart, squeezing the

ASCEND   *Billie Jade Kermack*

life out of me from inside my chest. And the bread. The feet. What's happening to me?' I blubbered, completely losing my already erratic composure. Beau's tone had lightened as he stroked the hair out of my face and planted a warm, almost urgent kiss on my cracked, fluid-deprived lips. Reading my mind, he grabbed a plastic cup of ice water from the table next to us, directing the straw into my mouth. I weakly lifted my hand to my chest, in search of the necklace Beau had given me.

'Where's my necklace, what happened to it? Beau, you have to... you have to... ' I couldn't breathe. The tail end of the hurricane that had stirred inside me when I collapsed in the restaurant – effectively ruining the first sane and possibly romantic date I had had with Beau in a long time – rumbled in my chest and made me feel lightheaded. Beau grabbed at the breathing mask hooked up to a tank of oxygen hanging on the wall behind my hospital bed and pulled the tight elastic over my head.

'Calm down, have you not learnt a thing so far today? You scared the life right out of me in the restaurant. I thought I'd... I mean, what if I had lost you? I couldn't live with that, Grace. I need you to start actually caring about yourself, about what happens to you. I can't be with you every second of every day, however much I'd want to.'

For once, the silence between us was welcomed. I had taken a knock, and the special part of my brain that processed sarcastic comebacks was a little on the slow side. This was the time when normal people would kiss, cry, hug out their

ASCEND   *Billie Jade Kermack*

emotions. That wasn't us.

'Every day? I'd give it a week, max! I have been told it's quite possible that I purposely annoy people for my own amusement, and from where I'm sitting, you're people. If I was you I wouldn't risk it!' I wheezed with a grin.

'Well I was actually thinking more like five days – but the sentiment was there!' he chuckled. The jovial punch I would usually give him in response to his cheekiness would at least knock him off balance; it was now about as powerful as a two-day-old pawing puppy. I had been stripped of energy and could no longer fight it. I was exhausted.

'But, the necklace...'

Beau reached into the back pocket of his dark blue jeans and let the heavy charm and its sister jewels dangle from the gold chain that was wrapped securely around his fingers. I extended my arm to grab it.

'Not so fast – you promise to look after yourself?' Beau teased, waving the necklace in front of me, just out of my reach. I winced and doubled over. Beau quickly closed the space between us, practically jumping on the bed beside me and checking me for wounds. He pushed the hair away from my face, his eyes alight with panic.

'Is it your head, your stomach, do you want me to get a nurse?' I sat up, and for the first time since the ordeal I felt an unfiltered, warm flush of playfulness that alienated all

ASCEND *Billie Jade Kermack*

the pain still coursing through my body.

'No, what I want is what's mine!' I grabbed the necklace from his hand and quickly fastened it around my neck, where it belonged. He smiled lovingly and kissed me, long and hard. It didn't take long for the stirred optimism between us to wane and crumble as someone entered the curtained cubicle.

'Grace O'Callaghan?' The doctor, dressed in creased, light-blue theatre scrubs looked weathered, no doubt many hours of overtime making him sluggish as he pulled out my chart. He didn't make eye contact with us as he eyed the tubes on the floor which should have been hooked up to my body. It didn't take long for a duty nurse to strap me back up to the machine and tuck me a little too tightly into the scratchy hospital bed linen, all the while mumbling disapprovingly about me under her breath.

'Everything looks fine, surprisingly. It seems you had a panic attack. Induced by what isn't clear, as your review shows no problems.' He hooked an X-ray of my chest up to a light machine on the wall and flicked on the switch, which made a buzzing sound as it jumped to life. 'This area is a little cloudy, but as you can see by this second X-ray, it's now clear. You must have moved during the first one, causing a slight shadow. You will need to pass these on to your local doctors for them to file.'

'Moved? You mean while she was unconscious?' I gripped Beau's hand in mine as I felt his anger creep into full view.

ASCEND   *Billie Jade Kermack*

Maybe he should be hooked up to the blood pressure gauge. My inner voice was caustic, oblivious to the situation but very much on Beau's side; I imagined her flipping the doctor off with her neatly-manicured middle finger in protest at his idiocy.

□□

'Maybe I shouldn't leave. My trip can wait, I should be with you. It seems like every time I'm set to go, something wild happens – this isn't the first time I've had to see you bed-bound and injured, but I can promise you, I wish it would be the last' Beau said, fussing with my pillow and glaring at the industrial, oversized plaster on my forehead that masked a golfball-sized bump and seven stitches.

'It's not my fault I'm accident prone.' This was actually true, it wasn't my fault. The ghost on my case didn't get her inspiration from a Patrick Swayze film; she wanted to slaughter me, not save me. 'I'm home now and you haven't let me leave this bed for two days, I haven't slept so much in ages! The hospital gave me the all-clear, Gwen's checked me over and said I'll live to fight another day. I'M FINE! Boredom has officially kicked in – I just need out of this room! You need to go on your trip. I'm sure I'll have my mum watching me like a hawk after everything you told her about my... accident.'

'Accident' didn't feel like the right word, but I knew playing down the whole situation was the only way to make Beau go on his trip. He needed to get away, and I needed the time to sort out exactly what was happening to me. Beau sat down on the massive goosedown-filled, rose printed duvet and slid my breakfast tray, still full of cold toast and eggs, onto the other side of the double bed. He took my hand in his.

'I love you. You know that, right?' His sincerity made my heart skip a beat and my Inner Bitch swoon. For once she was lost for words, for which I was grateful, as I could bask in the glory of the moment.

'I know, and I'm not going to be forgetting it any time soon!' I smiled, but it didn't reach my eyes. I was grateful that he didn't seem to notice, his tension visibly dissipating as his shoulders relaxed.

'I forgot to ask – what was it you wanted to talk to me about the other day? Something about work?' I didn't want to hurt Beau. I could wave him off on a long trip where I would miss him desperately, but I couldn't pour out everything that I had been witnessing, the torture that had become an everyday occurrence. I didn't want him to worry. It was an onslaught of thoughts, feelings, visions and dreams that just weren't plausible, messed-up storage probably left over from my run in with Glen.

I glanced over to my bag, hanging on my desk chair; it was still partially open, exposing the seven files I had stolen from the dungeon for closer inspection. They were a reminder of what was happening to me, and quite possibly a major part of everything I had been experiencing since that night on the beach. He had left me once because his gift for

ASCEND
Billie Jade Kermack

seeing and communing with the dead led me into a cat-and-mouse game with the psychotic spirit of a dead serial killer. I couldn't go through that again. The heart-wrenching memories of being without Beau sparked a reaction in me. I needed him; I feared, much more then he needed me. He reached out and stroked my cheek with his thumb, my broad smile finally meeting my eyes.

'It was nothing, a joke someone told me – can't even remember the punchline now. By the way, I packed you a little present for your trip, but you can't look at it until you leave. Promise me!' I said, changing the subject. I grinned, recognising that excited glint in his eyes.

'I promise' Beau agreed, beaming back at me with a calming breath. I pulled him in close and whispered lovingly, 'Never forget: I love you too. Right to the moon and back again.'

Each and every day with him was brighter somehow, coloured with a honey hue that enveloped me like a soft fur blanket on a frosty winter's morning. My body tingled, each cell and vein vibrating. My heart swelled as it made room for all the love that I had for him. My stomach fluttered aimlessly, always fearing for a split-second it could be the last. He was my world; watching him leave would probably break my heart in two, but watching him come back – that could make me feel an eternal wave of happiness that would go on in this life, and the next, and the next. I couldn't fight it. I refused to fight it. He was my all!

SEVENTEEN
ಬಿಂಞ

BEAU

If I was completely honest, I didn't want to leave her. Grace was going through something; I would have had to be deaf, dumb and blind not to see it. There was something... something I couldn't put my finger on. A part of me still felt guilty for leaving her that day, for waiting all those months to come back to her. Even if she wouldn't admit it, I knew a little apprehension still lingered between us. A scrap of uncertainty, lost trust. I had left Grace, and regretted it almost instantly. I felt the pain she did. The immense and uncontrollable urge to be with her had made me crazy, but I had done what I thought was best at the time. Now, I wasn't not so sure.

I saw how she looked at me sometimes – like something was missing. I watched her folding my clothes, neatly and motheringly sorting my jeans, tops and underwear into organised piles; we both knew I would have thrown them in

ASCEND   *Billie Jade Kermack*

without a second thought. Grace packed them into my duffel bag and turned to me, with a beautiful smile. Knowing she was OK, I relaxed. I never wanted to lose her again, but maybe for now she needed some space. She wanted me to go... maybe distance really would make the heart grow fonder?

She pulled me towards her, my fingers reciting the loops of her long hair. How did I get so lucky? The empty space between us heated to near-boiling point. I couldn't take my eyes off of her. Mesmerising, hypnotising, stunning: no words could explain how I saw her, or what she meant to me.

If I did anything with my life, ghosts or no ghosts, it would be to show her just how much I love her. A few weeks apart would be nothing we couldn't handle. Her sweet, balmy, rosebud lips lightly caressed mine for a few long and delightful seconds before reality snapped back in and she pulled away from me.

'WOW,' and I meant it.

'Wow yourself, handsome!' Grace said, slapping me playfully on the arm. By the way, I packed you a little present for your trip, but you can't look at it until you leave. Promise me!' She patted the side zip-pocket of my duffel bag, with an excited smile on her face.

'You know I love you too, right Grace? So much more than I could ever explain.' For a brief and fleeting moment she looked sad, but it was quickly washed away with a flutter of her eyelashes. Something inside me popped. She was mine, I was hers. Everything else was kind of... meaningless.

֎

FLOOR 5: MORGUE

I made my way up the stairs, the rubber soles of my boots squeaking on the freshly-waxed landings as I took them two at a time. Whenever I could bypass a lift trip, I would. Memories of my parents' deaths and that macabre accident were never far from my mind and I still found it difficult going into lifts, especially ones in hospitals.

'Mace, long time no see mate!' I shook his hand, and he pulled me in for a manly pat on the back. Mace and I had known each other for a few years, a few *long* years. With what I could do, getting to know people and making lifelong friends wasn't common in my life.

'How's it hanging, Beau? Still seeing the dead?' He lowered his voice, glancing uneasily around at one of his colleagues who passed by us holding some pretty intense looking cutting tools on a metal tray. I may deal with ghosts, but the part just before they visit me – the part with the cutting and examining by a trained professional – that part made me gag.

ASCEND

Billie Jade Kermack

'You know me, a sane and simple life is what I live for,' I replied sarcastically. I could always sense Mace's underlying uneasiness with my gift, the things that I saw.

'Your life is anything but sane and simple! So, is this a personal visit. Has someone got a message for me? Because you know how much all that stuff freaks me out.' He wiped his clammy forehead with his latex-gloved hand.

I had found that over the years, since my gift had first presented itself, talking about what I could do was easier with strangers than with the people closest to me. I would often help whoever I had to and then cut all ties, never seeing them again, just to spare me the heartache of how differently they behaved around me. Mace had been an exception. Considering his choice of career I had hoped that with time he would have relaxed, knowing what I could do; he never did relax, and I found it hard to cut him out. So, friends it was.

'No, no one with a message this time. Saying that Mace, your... patients, is that the right word for them? I don't think they're all very happy.' I felt cruel, but the opportunity to mess with his head was just too inviting.

'You're kidding, right? Is it Mr. Wagner? It wasn't my fault, I didn't lose it. We found his foot eventually!' I could no longer keep a straight face as Mace panicked and threatened to fall head-first into oblivion.

ASCEND
Billie Jade Kermack

'I'm pulling your leg, Mace – excuse the pun!' I laughed. Mace reached out and slapped me without a second thought.

'Very funny Mystic Meg, lost your optimistic snowglobe already?' I could see he couldn't fully commit to his mocking, which made me realise how on-edge I had made him feel.

'I am here on a ghost matter, but I promise, the ghost isn't attached to you. I'm looking for some remains; someone's ashes, to be exact.'

'I told you after the last time mate, this makes me feel very uncomfortable. If I got caught, that would be it: my job, my life, most probably my freedom, if my boss pressed charges' he said, tugging at my jacket sleeve and ushering me through a set of double-doors. We headed into a bright white, overly sterile room that made me feel immediately uneasy. I glanced around at the six perfectly positioned metal slabs, four of them covered with people-sized sheets with the contours of what (or who) lay beneath protruding at familiar angles. I shuddered, catching Mace's attention.

'Oh I'm sorry, is this place making you feel uncomfortable?' His caustic tone did not go unnoticed. 'Now you know how I feel about you bringing your Steven Spielberg, 'I see ghosts', 'We live on an Indian burial ground' bullshit my way. If I wanted this drama I'd rent a film' Mace babbled, enjoying that for once, when it came to the dead, he was ahead.

ASCEND

Billie Jade Kermack

'Touché, dude. I see you got tickets to Fright Fest this year,' I beamed. I had to give it to him, it was a point well made.

'I can't see why it is relevant but yes, I did go, and considering I hate horror films, it was bearable at the most. Now, let's get on with this so I can get back to work. Name, date he died, how he died? Do you have any details, or is this another shot in the dark like Darcey Lewistein?'

He pulled open the top drawer of a stainless steel filing cabinet, which scraped and screeched as he worked it over the rusting slide fixtures. Darcey Lewistein was one of my more... traumatic encounters. Mace and I had spent almost three months, day after day, trying to find out who Darcey was and what – or in her case, who – had caused her death. Darcey was a stuck up, butter-wouldn't-melt, 'I've already raided your wallet' sort of girl. I had felt her presence often, but it was Mace she decided to concentrate on. She had latched onto him, playing with his psyche. He was on the brink of completely giving up when we chanced upon her file; thankfully Mace recovered, and bypassed the nuthouse with one giant leap into the safety of his work. 'I can't work another one of those cases with you. All this Cagney & Lacey, looking for the truth, *Murder She Wrote* bollocks gives me the heebie-jeebies.'

'Heebie-jeebies, really? You need to lay off on the 80s TV on your lunch breaks, mate' I chuckled, picking up a two-pronged tool that flew wide open, taking me by surprise.

'Don't touch!' I held up my hands as he grabbed it from me,

a sneaky, amused smile still settled on my face.

'This one is straightforward Mace, I promise – you know I'm good on my word.'

He replied with a silent nod. He didn't like what I did or how it sometimes affected him, but Mace being the good guy that he was, he would always agree to help.

'You'll have him down as John Doe.' Joking aside. Time to get serious.

'Beau, you best be kidding. That filing cabinet alone holds all the John and Jane Doe cases from just the past ten years.' He motioned towards a green filing cabinet that reached high above our heads, a rickety stepladder pressed up against it. 'You know I don't work as a magician, right?'

'You don't? And there's me telling everyone I'm friends with Mr. Magoo! Look I haven't got much time on this one Mace, I'd really appreciate your help – and the side order of sarcasm you're offering keeps me jolly and on my toes, so that's also welcomed.'

'OK, so no name; do you have a place, a date maybe?' He thumbed through the files in the drawers.

'I have a name, it's just of no use to you in this case, they never identified him!' I said, realising that I may have underestimated how much work may be involved in this crossing over.

ASCEND *Billie Jade Kermack*

'It was four years ago. January 23rd I think... actually, it may have been February 23rd. Thinking about it, it may have been three years ago.' Jacques spoke intensely as he paced the floor behind me, his translucent form passing through the computer table.

'Gonna need a decision here. Just relax and think hard, we will find it' I said through gritted teeth as to not alarm Mace, which stopped Jacques in his tracks. Apparently, I wasn't being as discreet as I had intended.

'Who are you talking to? Please tell me you didn't bring a ghost along again. Was I not clear last time? I swear you bring them along just to freak me out.' Mace shook animatedly as he stepped away from me. 'This wasn't part of the deal!' He almost sung the words, which made me smile. He was completely right – messing with him was a little on the fun side.

'Look, he says it was roughly four years ago, around the end of January or February... a hit and run outside Mason's on Bixberry Lane. I know this makes you uncomfortable but the sooner we find his file, the sooner you give me his bag of human dust-bunnies and the sooner we'll be out of your hair. We can laugh about it over a beer next month, mate. I'll pay and everything. Please.' It wasn't often that I had to use the hurt-puppy look to get my own way, but I had learnt with Grace that it could be very effective. I couldn't tell

ASCEND   *Billie Jade Kermack*

whether this one fell under the category of successful.

'Mate, I will find your file if you stop eyeing me up! Rearrange your knickers, you woman' he chuckled uneasily. *Not successful at all, it seems.*

'I guess my powers only work on Grace – I'll be sure to mention that to her.'

□□

'So, I have found your mystery man!' His words were positive, his tone was not. It had been a five hour search that had the other staff members asking questions, awkward questions that could have led to a very sticky situation if it hadn't been't for Mace and I thinking on our feet.

'OK.' Mace handed me a tin urn, wrapped with black and grey marble. The embossed silver plaque had a date on it and a reference number. I weighed it in my hands.

'Wow Jacques, I thought you would have been a little on the heavier side' I said flippantly, glancing at him as he wandered around the metal slabs.

'Very funny' he replied caustically, a small smile on his face as he rubbed his stomach, which had seen fitter days. By girl standards, Jacques wasn't ugly; he was dressed smartly in blue suit pants and a white button-down shirt with the sleeves rolled up to his elbows. His short brown hair was tidily cropped and secured with a handful of styling product.

ASCEND   *Billie Jade Kermack*

He had minor cuts to his forehead, and the left side of his shirt was stained red from a more substantial wound to his stomach.

'Do they mind you being so... disrespectful?' Mace whispered, shielding his mouth with the sleeve of his white lab coat.

'It's not disrespectful. It's my job to make their transition as relaxed as possible. It's not my fault I am naturally hilarious.' My remark cut the tension in the room. Mace exhaled a sigh of contentment, as he rested against one of the morgue tables.

'Uh, Mace, you might want to move – you're sitting on him!' Like a cartoon character about to be eaten by a sea monster Mace jumped into the air and away from the table, his dainty, girlish scream the pretty pink icing on the cake that was this moment.

'That was brilliant!' Jacques beamed from behind me, laughing so hard he began to tear up as he watched Mace jumping about and freaking out like a court jester. As Mace caught a glimpse of my face, my wide grin bursting out from behind my fake neutral expression, he stopped and dropped his hands to his sides.

'Why are you smiling? He wasn't there, was he?'

'No, but that was amazing. Jacques also enjoyed it.' I couldn't mask my laughter now as Mace scowled at me.

ASCEND *Billie Jade Kermack*

'Take your little friend –' he pointed at the urn in my hands '– and your poltergeist buddy, and get out. I don't know why you find it so funny, you know the dead freak me out!'

'Mate, you work in a morgue. How many people have you chopped up today?' I asked knowing full well he would have a smart-alec answer to follow up with.

'I don't chop, I *dissect*, and its all in the name of science. The idea of them hanging around to check out my handiwork... that's just not right.'

'You have your job, and I have mine. If you think about it, we kind of work in the same field!' I used, tinkering with a selection of sparkling stainless steel tools that rested neatly on the cloth-covered workbench next to me.

'What did I tell you? If we were in the same field, you would know not to touch those!' He grabbed them from me and placed them neatly back where they belonged, covering them with a blue towel. I could already see the makings of a smile on his face as he ran our encounter over in his head.

You probably wouldn't believe it but this was the twelfth time I had visited Mace requiring his services, and every time I had I brought a ghost with me. Actually, that's a lie; on the occasions I hadn't been accompanied by one of my – let's call them *clients* – I had lied to Mace and said I was. The first few times I came it had taken nearly a full hour to calm him down and steady his nerves. This time, we were

ASCEND
Billie Jade Kermack

hitting five minutes cooling down time; any way you look at it, that's progress! I knew I drove him crazy and I knew it wasn't what you would call a traditional friendship, but I could be myself with him. I didn't have to hide, and I liked that.

'Shall we freak him out again?' Jacques asked, the sadistic prankster within him blooming as his eyes lit up with a childlike need to cause havoc. My face obviously spoke volumes as Mace turned to face me, pointing his blue biro that was nibbled at the end directly at my chest.

'If you don't want to give me a heart attack and see me on one of these slabs, you will stop playing with me now.' He couldn't help but smile, knowing he had trumped me and my plan to mess with him further. 'Checkmate!'

'You love it really, don't you Mace?' I teased, pursing my lips, grabbing his cheek in my fingers like his grandma would.

'I wouldn't use the word love. I *love* football, I *love* half-naked women, I *love* beer. I'm only mildly amused by you and your parlour tricks. It's a sick fascination I have, and I'm currently seeking a healthcare professional to sort it out. That's it: I'm crazy!' His tone had again become playful and relaxed. I knew I had to make what I do as normal as was possible for Mace. He made my life a lot easier, and our monthly beer meetings helped ease the tension my job brought me.

ASCEND *Billie Jade Kermack*

'It's always good to be a little insane, so keep quiet, and if they offer you the blue pills – run!' I laughed, almost uncomfortably, as my soul was laid bare and exposed. It wasn't uncommon for me to mix the truth of my past experiences in with light-hearted conversation to dampen my memories. Being held against my will in a padded cell, with only the company of deranged inmates who had shuffled off this mortal coil, I had seen another side to my gift.

Criminally insane spirits didn't joke about; they didn't let up with their taunting because I was a kid. I had told the doctors the truth about my gift and was force-fed those blue pills for months. No ten year old should feel that alone, that separated from the real world. I hadn't expected it, but suddenly Grace's beaming face, her understanding, warm, cobalt eyes shone brightly in my head, pushing away the darkness of thoughts I usually refused to give light to. She was my star in the blackest night that was my past; she was my saviour.

'Wait, this can't be right' Mace said, interrupting my train of thought, his attention piqued by an open document on his computer screen.

'What? Mace, what's going on?' I pressed.

'He isn't a John Doe – he never was.' Mace looked confused, his brow furrowing as he clicked the *Print* button on his keyboard.

ASCEND   *Billie Jade Kermack*

'I don't understand, what were his remains doing in the Doe drawers then?'

'It says here that he was identified by dental records. His family were informed, it says so right here.' He pulled a sheet of paper from the printer, circling some information with his pen. He handed it to me, his eyes wide and telling. He didn't want me to show Jacques. I dipped my head to let him know I understood.

'Can you believe this? I can stick my head right through this! No material made by man can stop me now!' Jacques bellowed, his inquisitiveness a great distraction for me.

Patient #45221445559 identified by family but remains refused for reclamation. Permission given by immediate family for cremation. All rights of family relinquished upon request. Body is now property of the state.

I re-read the statement three times, the callousness of it making me question whether Jacques was really who he thought he was. He must have known why he was left here.

'How could they do that to him?' I whispered to Mace, who was still digging for information in the online folders.

'My family knew I was here, and they did not want me?' Jacques was distraught. I had no idea he had been reading the piece of paper over my shoulder. Before I could respond be was gone with a stifled sob, a cooling breeze the only thing left in his wake.

EIGHTEEN
ഓരു

GRACE

The day had come. I waved Beau off onto the waiting coach which would take him onto the Eurostar to Paris. With a shuddering pang of loss already vibrating through my body, I did consider making him stay. The fact that I *could* make him stay meant that I didn't. The engine grumbled, and I watched through the dusty windows as he took his seat at the back. I did the only thing I could, something a supportive girlfriend should do in situations like these – I blew him a kiss and smiled, as broadly as I could. It made my jaw ache a little, but as he beamed back at me, I immediately knew I had done the right thing.

I love you, I love you, I love you! My Inner Bitch was on bended knee professing to Beau loudly, annoyingly, still snubbing me for allowing him to leave us. *Us,* I laughed, realising my alter personality that popped up pretty much every time she wasn't welcome or needed was screaming out my feelings the only way she could.

ASCEND
Billie Jade Kermack

I willed my legs to move as the coach made its way up the hill and into the distance. I wanted to run after him, but I couldn't. I stood there, silently watching as once again London transport swept my boyfriend away. At least this time, he was sure to come back. *Oh no – what if he doesn't come back?* my little inner voice whimpered. Though I tried to ignore her, I knew it was a shared worry.

What if he gets hurt? What if he decides he wants to stay out there, what if he meets a girl and suddenly feels the need to elope? What if she can give him a normal life? What if she gets my happily ever after? A bombardment of panicked thoughts kept me still and solemn for almost ten minutes. His coach had left but I couldn't seem to move; I didn't want to increase the distance between us.

☐☐

'So, Beau's gone?'

'Yes Amelia, he left yesterday morning' I sulked, clearly still not over Beau's departure.

'Let me guess: you're missing him already. It's written all over your face. *Grace and Beau, sitting in a tree, K-I-S-S-I-N-G! First comes love, then comes marriage, then comes a baby...*' she sung.

'Righty-ho, I'm going to cut you off there.' I had completely lost my sane train of thought thanks to Amelia and as usual, she loved to watch me squirm.

ASCEND
Billie Jade Kermack

'Talking of kissing, love and marriage, how's it going with you and Jack? Is true love blossoming?' I mocked. Amelia lived in a Mills & Boon, rose-tinted glasses sort of world – perfection was always close at hand, failure was not an option. Her long blonde hair fell down her back, each curl the same as the one next to it, the sides pinned up just above her ears showing off her long, delicate neck.

'He treats me like a princess, which I like. Now it's time to crank it up a notch – this princess wants to be a queen. Jewellery should cost more than £29. No problem, though; as usual, Amelia's got it covered.' Her words were so *decisive*. Unromantic almost, like she was discussing what cheese was best to put on her pizza.

'You know it's creepy when you refer to yourself in the third person, right?' Amelia shrugged off my remark and continued to separate coloured pills into numbered cartons on her hospital trolley.

'Grace, do you think I'm a joke?'

Her question knocked me for six. Her usually *I-couldn't-care-less* front melted away, exposing her inner fears.

'No, why would I? You have strong opinions. It's kind of the reason I love you, keeps me on my toes. What would make you think that?'

'I know I'm not popular here. At college I'm top dog, but

ASCEND
Billie Jade Kermack

here... everyone whispers behind my back.' I wasn't used to seeing Amelia's fragile, emotional side. She never really let her guard down, but now that she had, it warmed me through – she was just like anyone else. Maybe it was her newfound love with Jack, or maybe the light of the big bad world had finally presented itself. Either way, she obviously hadn't been prepared for it.

'Is it the dress? Be honest!' She tugged at the hem of her skimpy pink and white candy-striped uniform which rode high on her thighs and had quickly shot her to the patients' number one helper on duty. The staff, however, didn't approve; their old-fashioned ideals of proper conduct and hospital guidelines had cast Amelia out.

'Maybe you could tone down the dress a little, it may be too...' *Damn it, what's the word?* '... extrovert.' She looked miffed, first at me then down at her dress.

'So you're saying that if I wore a different dress, people would like me?'

'That's the gist of it, yeah.'

'OK, so when we go shopping, will you help me pick something else out? Don't tell anyone, but I actually like working here – helping people.'

Who are you and what have you done with my friend?

'Sounds like a plan.' I said, leaning in for a hug.

ASCEND
Billie Jade Kermack

I walked away from my bemusing encounter with Amelia to attend to the hundreds of other people that needed my help. The papers of their lives, their deaths; these were my work, and they weren't going to sort themselves into piles.

Amelia was tending to a sick old man with a greying beard and bald head, putting a cooling compress on his forehead. She bent down to his side and before I even reached the door I stopped dead, brimming unexpectedly with fear. 'Now I lay me down to sleep, I pray the Lord my soul to keep. If I die before I wake, I pray the Lord my soul to take' Amelia whispered softly, almost angelically, from behind me.

'What did you say?' I turned on my heels, confused, not entirely sure I had heard anything at all. Reality had comprised mainly of blurred lines recently, and weeding out the crazy stuff was becoming a chore.

'It's OK Grace, he'll be dead shortly, just making sure he's sorted before he goes.' Her voice was eerily calm and even, lacking any empathy. The overhead light began to flicker. *Off, on, off, on.* The machine the old man was strapped up to began to beep a little faster and his hands shook, as did the bed frame. It was only for a moment or two, and the second it ceased I questioned whether I had really seen and heard what I thought I had. Did that just happen? Am I crazy?

'Amelia. Amelia, what did you just say?' I shook her almost

ASCEND *Billie Jade Kermack*

violently, my fingernails digging into her shoulders.

'Grace, you got a screw loose in there or something? Why the hell are you shaking me?'

'You said... I heard you say...'

'Take your hands off the Gucci!' she squealed, brushing off any particles I may have left on the sleeve of her dress before she could return her gaze to me. 'I'm pretty damn sure I didn't say anything – and Mr. Morris has been in a coma for twelve months, so I'm pretty sure he didn't say anything either. Are you getting enough sleep? You look really shook up.'

I *was* shook up, there was no doubt about that. Although I appreciated her concern, I knew I had heard her speak those words, plain as day. I wasn't dreaming. I wiped my forehead with my cardigan sleeve, catching the now-purpling bump and stitches on my forehead, making me wince.

'Amelia, I'm going to go. I've got work up to my eyeballs. I reckon you're right, I'm probably just tired.' Excuses made, I left, without a backwards glance.

□□

It didn't take long for the days to merge into an onslaught of tiresome repetition. With the exception of reading Ibsen at bedtime (it was incredibly boring and I was determined to find an audiobook version to catch up on), my days played out the same. Like clockwork I slept, worked, studied and ate – probably not always in that order – but without Beau, everything was quiet and mundane. *Wake, work, sleep. Wake, work, sleep.* And washing, of course; I was depressed, not disgusting, and showering was still on my to-do list.

<u>29th June</u>

1) Hair *against* hospital guidelines: check. If I can annoy Agnes, it may at least add a new chapter to my day.

2) Daily catch-up with Sky over lunch, today a tuna melt sandwich and a Diet Coke. The tuna felt furry and against my better judgement I finished it, which led to a pretty severe case of heartburn.

3) Tea with Gwen. She still looks a little under the weather, should maybe check in on her tomorrow. Checked on Amelia for any new personality glitches. Hung on herevery word during her rounds. Nothing strange to report, or nothing new anyway. We had a very interesting conversation about whether or not Sherlock Holmes was an actual, once-living person. She said yes, I screamed no. The argument was left undecided.

4) Packed files from the hospital to show Gwen. (I hadn't intended on stealing becoming a second career, though it seems I'm great at it.)

ASCEND *Billie Jade Kermack*

5) Bedtime. A few chapters of Ibsen for Mrs Crayman's English class and a hot chocolate, then back to the grind tomorrow.

ASCEND *Billie Jade Kermack*

NINETEEN
ೞCR

The ailments came on thick and fast. To begin with I didn't notice the small stuff: a ticklish cough scratching at my throat, a gripping bellyache momentarily swelling in my stomach, dull pain swamping my frontal lobe, quickly spreading to behind my eyes. Beau had been gone for thirteen days and as each day passed, my ability to holster my feelings became harder. I snapped at staff, patients, Amelia, Sky, I even had a good crack at Agnes; I was on my last nerve, and she was sadistically playing it like a banjo string.

I decided that putting in some overtime hours in the dungeon was the best way to go unseen. Funny how nobody wants to visit a place drenched in depression.

I picked up a file, and as my palm connected with rough yellow card a shot of searing heat enveloped my heart – like an empty box holding a clump of ice, it fought off the fire. I dropped the file, grabbing at my chest. It was gone; the pain, the heat had vanished in a flash. The file I was holding

ASCEND   Billie Jade Kermack

had landed open, its pages spread across the floor: *Andrew Lake, Heart attack, May 1991*. A desire to pull another random file from the shelf was overshadowed by a yearning to touch a file from my bag – the files I had stolen – the ones that had jumped out at me, screaming for my attention.

'OK, lets see now. File one: *Bobby (Roberta) Jones, died March 1994, cause of death – Murder.*' Flipping the page over with my fingertip to make as little contact with it as possible, I took a deep breath and went for it. I pushed the palm of my hand down onto the coroner's report of Miss Bobby Jones and it happened. The veins in my arms vibrated beneath the now-translucent skin of my arm. A pressure built up in my shoulder, the socket holding on with dear life to its counterpart. I was stuck, and with every second I made contact with the paper, removing my hand became even more impossible. The vicelike grip reaching across my collarbone felt as though it could tease my bones to snap and shatter.

In a sudden surge of adrenaline, I used my free hand to tear the paper from my palm with an almighty scream. I collapsed onto the computer chair, distancing myself from the files, even though something in me still felt compelled to investigate them. As though stuck with glue and dotted with the blood from my torn skin, pieces of the paper had adhered to my hand. Any that I had removed had taken some of my skin along with them as a souvenir. Not knowing what the hell was happening but getting a *refer-to-Gwen's-special-book* kind of feeling, I made a note to

ASCEND

quickly sort the files listed with more violent causes of death. Heart attacks, ruptured organs and broken bone cases threatened a trip to A & E, but with my reflexes on top form and my bloodstream hyped up on caffeine I worked quickly, thankfully without any lasting damage.

The beams of bright white fluorescent light from the hallway that flooded into the room from behind me were suddenly interrupted, casting a black grainy shadow on the floor beside me. I ran my fingers over the floor, distorting the grainy projection, questioning whether I wanted to turn around and find out to whom it belonged.

'Rosie. Are you OK?' I asked, concerned the moment I saw her. She stood there twiddling her fingers and fiddling with the hem of her cardigan, her stare fixed to the floor, her usual smile beaming.

With a click of her fingers and a splutter of buzzing activity from the radio on my desk, Rosie straightened her posture, stopped fiddling and dropped her hands to her sides. Her smile curdled into a grimace. She raised her head. Her eyes, firmly fixed on mine, were no longer sparkling emerald green but sickly yellow curdled with emotionless grey. 'Find me Grace, find me. Find me Grace, find me.' Her tone was deep and self-assured; she repeated the phrase precisely, as though someone had hit the *Rewind* button on a remote control.

Whatever or whoever had taken control of Rosie's body suddenly moved out of her in a quick, sharp shock, returning her to her innocent, carefree self. She skipped off down the deserted hallway, trailing her fingertips along the wall and giggling. I didn't know whether this was more haunting than the misty-eyed stranger that had inhabited her. I was now truly out of my depth; there's only a certain amount of crazy that one person can deal with.

1.33PM

Gwen,
We need to talk –
something really
strange is going on!
Grace xxx

I re-read the text and hit the *Send* button.

BOOK OF AURORA
ଖଓ

☐ The Shadowed Veil ☐
Seeing the Truth

A Channelling Empath

Whether by mystical force, preordained fate, death-induced intervention or a gift delivered at birth, the power an empath receives is only correspondent to the belief and understanding they put into their gift. Naturally-occurring empathy tips the scales in varying degrees according to the individual harnessing their gift. Empaths resonate a silent echo both internally and externally, an echo which intensifies the more power the person acquires.

Without proper use, history has shown that this gift may be dangerous; sometimes propelling the channeller or user into destruction, sometimes even leading to their demise. A channelling empath, if not instructed wisely, will slowly slip into madness. Their thoughts, feelings and actions will no longer be their own, as a higher power tears them apart from the inside.

ASCEND

Billie Jade Kermack

Emphatic resonating is a dangerous, beguiling gift, a tool that can be used by the wicked to challenge the good and tip the scales in the balance of evil.

An empath is open and available to the highest bidder, whether they be of Heaven or Hell.

TWENTY

We walked into the pub garden surrounded by hanging baskets full of multicoloured posies and took a seat at a round wooden table, away from the other patrons. I took off my cardigan and dumped it on the back of the wooden chair, the rays of the exposed sun beginning to colour my bare arms a healthy brown.

'So Grace, what's going on?' Gwen seemed to have missed the sweltering heat, sitting across from me under the shade of an oversized blue parasol in a large brimmed hat, her uniform cardigan still on and buttoned-up.

'I've been seeing some things.'

'Some things? Before we start, have you told Beau? You do remember how upset he got last time you decided to keep a secret, right?' She was completely right. Last year I had decided against letting Beau know everything that was happening with Glen, the psychotic spirit. I was afraid he would leave me, and in my defence, I was right – he had left me. Being right in that instance funnily enough didn't fill me with joy, and kept me squarely thinking that I should run my problems past Gwen first.

'I haven't, but it only started happening once he left,' I lied. 'I can't make him come back from his trip early.' She agreed with a worried but understanding nod.

'OK, fill me in.'

'Right, I think I've been seeing a...' Words failed me.

'A...?' she urged.

'A spirit. But it's not like Glen. I can feel the torture and the pain, but I think she's trying to show me something. I don't think she actually wants to hurt me.' As the words left my mouth I remembered that excruciating experience on the beach, the indescribable pain which had torn at my body that night, each unrelenting and brutal blow she had rained down on me.

Did she want to hurt me?

'Well, that's a bonus. You are most probably seeing a spirit... she must have something to do with Glen. Although we banished him, echoes of his past will still resonate on this plane. After everything you went through with him last year, I'm not surprised that this is happening. You said *she*; do you recognise her?'

'No, I don't think so. But if what happened to me happened

to her, I have ways of finding out who she is.' I sipped my refreshing orange juice, the ice-cubes tinkling in the glass, the almost freezing liquid drenching my dry throat. I thought I would have found it more difficult explaining everything to Gwen, but after half an hour of deep and revealing conversation in which I brought her up to date with everything about my mystery visitor, we had decided on a plan that would make the *Scooby* gang proud.

'Chances are she is one of Glen's victims. She clearly has a connection with you, so we can hopefully use that to help her cross over. You would tell me if you had seen Glen though, wouldn't you Grace? We can't afford for that to be a secret you keep from me right now. If my spell has worn off, I need to know!' She cradled her clammy hands around mine. 'When something like this happens and a tortured soul attaches itself to you, it isn't uncommon that you will experience other things, strange things.'

I remembered immediately the reason I had first wanted to talk to Gwen.

'Rosie came by the dungeon to see me. To tell me something. But it was strange, she wasn't... herself.'

'What do you mean, wasn't herself?'

'She was different – assertive, uncaring, solemn. Her whole body language changed right there in front of me, it was major eerie. She said I had to *find her*.'

ASCEND   *Billie Jade Kermack*

'Well, it's most probable that you were in fact talking to a spirit. Sounds like the spirit of your young woman friend, if I had to guess.'

That felt strange; the ghost wasn't my friend, not even an acquaintance. She had tortured me, ripped savagely at my body, left me in excruciating pain. I was only helping her so that I could get rid of her. This realisation suddenly filled me with a sense of guilt that I kept to myself, forcing it and my confusion down into the pit of my already unsettled stomach.

'People with mental issues, Down's syndrome, learning difficulties – these people, among others given the gift to see, are affected on another level. Like children, they can see spirits, and spirits find it easier to use their bodies as portals. They are uniquely wired and find the mythical and usually unexplainable reasonable. They don't understand that these spirits can be bad for us, or that it's unusual to see them. Rosie is an open, untainted vessel, easily channelled by the dead. People open to these sorts of... visits, people like Rosie, appear momentarily unaffected by their disability or their usual characteristics, oddly centred and calm. They are trusting, allowing otherworldly presences in with little question as to their motives. A lot of people are branded 'crazy' merely because their brain works differently. Usually spirits can't keep it up for too long, as the soul of the person cottons on to the unfamiliar intrusion and fights back, pushing the spirit out without understanding what they are even doing.'

ASCEND *Billie Jade Kermack*

'So the spirit used Rosie as a walking, talking meat-suit and I shouldn't be concerned?'

'For now, no. Possessions are not uncommon, they're widely reported all round the world. You are only noticing it now because you know about our world. It happens, but more often than not, ordinary people simply can't see it. This ghost in particular is trying to tell you something, something you haven't yet understood. Until you do grasp it, she will use any means necessary to talk to you, get you to listen.'

Gwen's words hit home as I realised I hadn't actually pieced anything together. I wasn't helping her yet, I wasn't even really listening! Even under her bundled layers and wicker sun hat Gwen seemed to shiver, her face a little pale, her fingers momentarily shaking. Reading my concerned gaze, she filled the silence with an answer to a question I had only asked in my mind.

'I'm going down to Cornwall to visit some friends tomorrow – will you be OK while I'm gone? It will only be for a few days and when I get back we will sort this out, once and for all.' She stroked my face and edged slowly up to her feet, steadying herself on the table. For a fleeting moment she looked her age; no, more than her age. She looked old and frail.

You know she's not going to see friends, right? That handsome man at her house was probably her new toy boy – you watch, after a weekend away with her fancy man

ASCEND   *Billie Jade Kermack*

and some necessary hours of totty action, she'll be good as new! My Inner Bitch dismissed my worries excitedly.

I had to agree with her as I thought back to all Gwen's little 'trips away.' She could definitely do with a break, and she certainly deserved the companionship of a handsome young travel buddy.

□□

The weekend passed by – uneventful as it was, I think that concerned me more. When something creepy wasn't happening, all I could think about was if and when it would strike. Would I be eating breakfast and have it change into that thick oily sludge? Would I wake up with my body set alight, the flames eating through my skin, boring pitilessly through to the bone?

Having free time that didn't involve the dead spirit of some poor tortured girl but actually involved me, a pot of Ben & Jerry's and a Leonardo DiCaprio movie box-set felt strange and unfamiliar these days. Strange, but definitely welcome.

TWENTY-ONE

૪૭૦૪

'Eyebrows, armpits, legs... ½ leg or full leg?' The tiny Asian woman behind the high-top black desk had an air of arrogance about her that didn't comfort me any. She fiddled and picked at her French-tipped manicured nails, her attention fixed on the latest copy of *Heat* magazine open in front of her.

'Go full. I honestly don't know the last time they even saw a razor' Amelia answered, looking me up and down.

'Oh no! You have got to be kidding me.' I was awkwardly laughing on the outside, but inside my Inner Bitch was donning her running shoes and searching around for possible exits.

'Grace, we need to work the overall look, we can't just throw an outfit on you and send you packing. In the spirit of full disclosure – and so you can't moan and complain later – I have a list of what we will be doing today. A Beautification Itinerary, if you will' she said, her eyes alight with excitement.

ASCEND

Billie Jade Kermack

'Really? I think I'm feeling a little under the weather. It could be mumps, strep throat, pneumonia... it could be deadly.' I forced out a wheezing cough to no avail.

'Lying is a sin, you know. Today is happening, Grace. You can fight me on it, but you will lose.' Her shrewd glare alone spoke a thousand words. I valued my life; I could bypass my dignity for a little while. After all, I had learnt only too well that what Amelia wanted, Amelia got. The woman behind the desk flicked her waist length, table-straight black hair over her shoulder and huffed. Our one woman audience was growing impatient, tiring of our pointless squabbling.

The baby pink walls around us were decorated with large framed pictures of models with lustrous hair and French-manicured nails holding flowers, long thin legs perfectly waxed, bronzed and airbrushed.

'OK, I give in. I'll have what she's having.'

ೞಣ

One, two, three... ouch! I gritted my teeth, almost grinding them into dust as another young Asian woman coated my legs in hot sticky wax and patted down the strips of material. Well, they definitely didn't look like the picture hanging above me but at least they no longer resembled wild cacti.

'Bikini line?' Her strong, sickly sweet and oddly bubbly

ASCEND
Billie Jade Kermack

Chinese accent filled me with dread as she ripped off yet another strip that was now coated with my hair and quite possibly a couple of layers of my skin.

'Pain is beauty Grace, pain is beauty.' Amelia, experiencing the same torture I was on the papered fold-out bed next to me, didn't even flinch as she read the problem pages of her copy of *Heat* with a deep-seated fascination.

□□

We sat out on the pine-decked veranda with an oversized cream parasol shielding us from the warm rays of the sun. I edged uncomfortably in my wicker chair as a light breeze stroked the now completely hairless skin of my calf. My underwear rubbed against me, the subtle yet very present sting reminding me of my torture. *You must have to be a little bit of a sadist to enjoy applying boiling hot wax and a hair removal strip to some poor innocent person,* I thought. Then again, I had willingly paid for the discomfort. I looked at Amelia as she sat there assessing the menu, cool as a cucumber.

A young man who even I could admit was cute, with shoulder-length curly brown hair secured back into a ponytail, strolled over to our table. He wore a burgundy polo top and black apron over his dark denim jeans. Although he was good looking, he was nowhere near Beau's level of hotness. It was strange, every other man just didn't have that... sparkle. He pulled out a pad and a pen and without a word looked at Amelia, anticipating her order.

ASCEND
Billie Jade Kermack

'The niçoise salad with breadsticks, not croutons, please' she said curtly, the *please* sounding more like an insult than politeness.

'And what would you like to drink, sweetheart? I may not be on the menu, but for you, I am definitely willing to bend the rules!' he said in a Cockney, jack-the-lad tone, ending his question with a creepy wink.

'Uh, I will have a Long Island Iced Tea, and if you call me *sweetheart* again in that sleazy way you just did, I will have you fired.' She smirked, knowing full well she had just obliterated any sense of self-worth the poor boy had built up in his life. I watched on, mesmerised, unable to blink as his face fell.

'What do you fancy, Grace? Don Juan over here needs to get back to washing dishes, so you better make it snappy!' she added, empowered by his silence.

'OK... I'll have the cheeseburger and chips with extra gherkins please, and a Coke.' I rushed the words and kept my eyes on the table, trying desperately not to laugh as my Inner Bitch rolled around on the floor howling. He picked up the menus from in front of us and made a speedy getaway, his eyeline now firmly fixed on the sandstone paving beneath his feet.

'Alright, he was a bit much, but did you have to lay into him like that?' I laughed, still not believing what I had just

ASCEND *Billie Jade Kermack*

witnessed. Amelia usually buckled under the mere weight of a cute boy's glance.

'I have a boyfriend, my uncle now owns this restaurant and he was dating my friend Ashley not so long ago before he cheated on her with Charmaine. He deserved it!' she retorted, a princess's air of smugness about her.

Without a word he placed our orders onto the table, careful not to make eye contact, and scurried away back towards the restaurant dining hall with his tail still firmly secured between his legs.

'So, what do you think?' Amelia asked, unwrapping her knife and fork from the burgundy napkin.

'What do I think about what?' I said from behind my hand as I chewed and swallowed my first chunk of cheeseburger.

Amelia was fiddling with her fancy niçoise salad, almost wary of its colourful contents, stabbing at the whole anchovies which lay on top of the crisp green salad leaves. 'Do these eggs look a little suspicious to you, Grace?'

'Forget about the eggs, what do I think about what?' I pressed on, silently agreeing with one glance that the eggs didn't look completely kosher. The plate was smothered in a thick and grainy vinaigrette, suffocating any goodness the vegetables once had.

'About me and Jack? I don't want things to be weird

ASCEND *Billie Jade Kermack*

between us. I know you two had that...'

'That what?' My attention was piqued.

'That thing. Jack tells me everything' she cooed. It was becoming clear that Jack's idea of *everything* was a normal person's idea of a full-blown pack of lies. She discarded the pink umbrella and single cherry that sat on the edge of her glass and took a large swig of her cocktail through her tasselled straw, the smell of the varied mix of undiluted alcohol tickling my throat even from across the table. I had seen Amelia drunk, and if I could avoid a instant play-by-play, I would.

'Firstly, that straw isn't going to disappear so stop abusing it, and secondly, Jack told you wrong' I exclaimed with a disbelieving chuckle. 'The only *thing* that Jack and I ever had was an awareness of each other's existence which then moved painfully slowly into an uncomfortable friendship. He disapproved of Beau almost instantly, any feelings' – I shuddered at the thought – 'that *he* may have had for *me* were not, and never would be, reciprocated.' I blurted it all out quickly so Amelia wouldn't have the chance to interrupt me.

Catching my breath and awaiting her response, I grabbed her glass and took a big sip of her drink – plain old Coke just wasn't going to cut it. Boy, was it refreshing; the sweet nectar sat in my mouth, caressing my taste buds long after I had swallowed it. For a brief and unclouded second I forgot what we were talking about. Sadly, that blissful moment

ASCEND   *Billie Jade Kermack*

didn't last long.

'It's OK Grace, I can see the appeal now, obviously, I'm dating him!' she purred. I chose not to argue my point, knowing full well Amelia was like a dog with a bone. In this case the bone was a complete fabrication but nevertheless she believed it, so in her quirky mind, it must therefore be true.

'I'm happy for you and Jack, it's nice to see you in a content, stable, grown-up relationship. You were made for each other.' I smiled, and I can assure you it was genuine, because what I had said was exactly on point. They both lived in their own little worlds sometimes, they both made snap judgements of people on a whim and they both idolised Amelia. It really was a match made in heaven.

It was at times like this that I questioned the validity of our friendship; after all, we were so different. Still, I knew it all rounded down to one thing – whenever it was called for, she had my back and I had hers. What can I say? I love the girl.

'Well, how about you and Mr. Elusive then? Are you still madly in *loooove*? she asked, dragging out the word and pursing her lips. 'There's still something strange about him, something I can't quite put my finger on.' Little did she know there was something out-of-this-world strange about Beau. 'You're different since you met him, you know. Don't get me wrong, you look better for it, but you are definitely different.'

ASCEND
Billie Jade Kermack

Without realising it, after spending twenty minutes pushing her smelly fish and egg salad around the plate, she had speared one of the anchovies and placed it in her mouth, her eyes still firmly fixed on mine. Her face screwed up, her lips tightly clenched as she bit down. I could tell by the tear in her eye that she instantly regretted it. I held out a napkin but being the girl she was, with the well-to-do upbringing she had, she shook her head and declined. Amelia would never be so uncouth as to spit in public, so she swallowed uneasily. She bypassed her flimsy straw, downing two-thirds of her drink to wash away the unpleasant aftertaste of the fish and pushing the plate to one side with her free hand.

'I'm happy, he's happy – we're getting along great!' I announced, a pang of loneliness swamping my belly at the mere mention of our relationship.

'Is he coming to the hospital's Valentines dance?' she asked, stealing a few chips from my plate.

'I don't know. His work means planning for things isn't always that easy, but I really hope he does make it. It won't be the same without him!'

'His work?' Amelia asked, her lacquered lips pursed, one of her preened eyebrows high and questioning.

Crap. I had to think fast but all I could think about was my Inner Bitch giggling at my predicament and standing with her arms outstretched, holding back any bright ideas that just might have been able to help me. *La, la, la, la, la, la,*

ASCEND
Billie Jade Kermack

she hummed tunefully, taunting me.

'Fish!' I almost yelled it – it was the first word to jump clear past my Inner Bitch and into the forefront of my mind. *Fish? What the hell?!* I immediately had the sneaking suspicion it wasn't an accident that this had been the only word to break free. It was at times like these I realised that naming my consciousness my 'Inner Bitch' was an apt and fair description.

'Fish?' Amelia mimicked my internal questioning and disbelief, her jaw slightly off-centre at an unflattering angle, her plucked eyebrows raised high.

'Erm, yeah, fish.' I couldn't possibly abandon the lie now, that would have been more suspicious. 'He packs it up for local fishmongers.' *What are you rambling on about – do fishmongers even still exist? It scares me how badly you have run this conversation into the ground.* That ever-helpful voice rang in my head.

'You know what Grace, I did smell something a little... fishy, last time we went for lunch.'

No you didn't! It was oddly comforting to hear my Inner Bitch on my side for once, as she petulantly screamed the words in Beau's defence.

'So, Jack's coming with you to the dance then?' I knew changing the subject to a more Amelia-centred conversation was my best and only bet to get out unscathed.

ASCEND

Billie Jade Kermack

'Of course, I wouldn't let him wriggle out of that one. We've been deciding on what romantic couple to go as.' *Oh damn, I forgot about the 'couple' theme idea.* Beau's handsome face, his inviting, warm blue eyes, his soft lips that parted slightly as he listened to me talk floodeded my thoughts, pulling me softly into a brief memory of us lying blissfully content in each others arms. I missed him terribly, and every time I thought of him it ruptured a pang of pent-up longing and desire that I had pushed down deep into the quiet crevices of my still butterfly-filled stomach.

'So what did you come up with?' I asked, quashing my feelings before they broke free.

'He suggested Romeo and Juliet – talk about predictable! Obviously my idea was much better. So we're going as Barbie and Ken. I have the perfect pink shimmery dress and matching heel combo, and let's be honest, my hair is perfect for it' she giggled, stroking her hair flat and playing with the ends. 'Do you think your mum might have time to trim my hair, Grace? Split ends are *defo* not Barbie,' she frowned animatedly. I edged closer and still couldn't see anything wrong with her hair; mine, however, could do with a complete overhaul. I mirrored her movements, holding a strand of my own hair and gazing at the dry, broken ends. I hated having my hair cut, but there was a bonus to having a mother who was a hairdresser.

ASCEND *Billie Jade Kermack*

TWENTY-TWO
ಸಂಚ

The unusually warm summer's day meant that Soho was heaving with people, carefree in their sunglasses, shorts and dresses, clothes that hadn't been aired since winter. The farmer's market that ran down the cobbled road and beneath the redbrick arches of the train tracks above was crowded to near bursting. All around us were smells of fresh, doughy, rosemary-baked bread, zingy goat's cheese that had never seen a supermarket shelf and home-made raspberry jam in a mixture of glass containers of all shapes and sizes, covered with red gingham fabric and secured with elastic bands.

The heat lingered, stifling the slight breeze that travelled North which didn't cool me in any way; I tugged at my T-shirt, wishing I had chosen to come out in a bikini top. The walls and doors of garages, businesses and homes in every direction, whether they be metal, brick or wood were covered in bright and beautiful graffiti, artist's renderings of their inner thoughts and feelings plastered high and low for all to appreciate.

ASCEND

Billie Jade Kermack

After taking a picture of a rainbow coloured, Banksy-style mural of a gorilla smoking a pipe, I realised Amelia had wandered off ahead of me. Catching up with her wasn't a problem. The row of three warehouses that would usually be empty and devoid of any character were now packed out with self-assembly metal clothes rails. Everywhere there were stunning outfits; dresses, skirts, tops, jackets and stacked blocks of recycled wood dotted artfully around displaying numerous pairs of shoes. Women were frantically searching the rails, pulling at the garments and their hangers, the scrape of metal on metal setting my teeth on edge. Every piece of clothing was unique, you couldn't find something you liked and ask the assistant for it in a bigger size; there was one and only one of each item.

'Grace, why are you not looking? I want something pink, sequins, size 10.' I stared blankly at her, as though she had spoken in German. 'So help me God, Grace, if you do not start searching then I won't be held responsible for my actions!' The pulsing vein in her temple was on show, highlighting just how much water her warning held. 'I have a Freshers Week mixer coming up and it clearly states we must dress to impress. I took the *Marie Claire* quiz this week, it demands I find this top, and this apparently is the place to be to get it hanging in my wardrobe before the day is out.'

□□

'So you're happy now?' I asked, placing my Lennon-style

ASCEND
Billie Jade Kermack

tinted sunglasses over my eyes as we exited back into the sunshine. Amelia was clearly sated as we made our way further down the street, leaving the hoards of bickering women to fight over the last crystal-encrusted satchel or draped hippy skirt with original beading. She beamed as she patted down her newly acquired cerise sequinned top.

'Where is your other top, Amelia?'

'Some tall bloke liked it – wanted it for his daughter, I guess' she replied nonchalantly, her questioning stare not fully understanding why I was asking.

'You gave a stranger your top? Am I missing something?'

'It wouldn't surprise me Grace, you have been a little away with the fairies lately,' she snorted. 'Look, it's a stop-and-swap shop – you can't buy anything, but you can swap clothes. Each rail has a brand and is categorised in types of clothing. I swapped my vest top for another vest top. It's pretty simple when you think about it.'

◻◻

'This one looks OK right?' *Mrs Masterson's Costume Emporium* was a fancy dress shop tucked away down a deserted alley in Soho. We passed the heavy-duty trailer bins that lined either side of the alley and I kept the stink at bay with the sleeve of the jumper tied around my waist, my feet uneven as I trampled over the cobblestones. The familiar clink of trays, pans and kitchenware and the hustle-

ASCEND *Billie Jade Kermack*

and-bustle chatter of staff flowed from the open doors that led into the back kitchens of the swanky restaurants, their storefronts bright and appealing on Carnaby Street, patrons aplenty grabbing the sun-soaked outside seating.

'I don't know Grace, have you decided who you want to go as?'

'I don't have a partner, so this whole trip is a moo point.'

'Moo point?'

'Yeah, a cow's view on the subject: pointless.'

'Just saying, but it would have been a lot quicker just to say pointless!' she baited me, trying to prompt a response. Of course she was right, but there was no way I was going to tell her that.

For the twelfth time that afternoon Amelia glanced down at her beeping phone, tapping at the keys to answer whatever text she had just received.

'Who do you keep messaging?'

'No one! I can't help being popular Grace, now back to you. Are you serious about your choice, because you look a little on the frumpy side. I know your dream man isn't going to be there but you can still dress up and look pretty.' Who was I kidding, she was right. The below-the-knee yellow flowered summer dress was more like something my nan would have worn – definitely not a party dress.

Beep beep. I glanced at Amelia as she once again shifted her attention to her phone.

'Think of your favourite film or something. You and Beau love a good movie, so maybe we should start there.' I had it, and surprisingly, it was all thanks to Amelia.

'Natalie Wood' I mused, almost internally.

'Natalie who now? Was she one of the Spice Girls?'

'She was the female lead in *Rebel Without a Cause*; Beau loves James Dean, it's perfect.'

'So we're looking for what era?' she asked excitedly as she helped like a parent to unbutton the unflattering dress I was wearing. I wiggled it over my hips and on to the floor as I worked out the dates in my head.

'Fifties' I said after a moment or two, ashamed that I had to even think about it. There was a glow in Amelia's eyes as she went tottering over to the rail with a placard marked *50s* in fancy red ink, searching for appropriate candidates.

☐☐

After two hours of trying on everything Amelia waved in front of me, we finally had a winner. Amelia picked up a few bits for herself, but before I could get a good look she had

ASCEND   *Billie Jade Kermack*

already paid and Mrs Masterson was bagging them up into a bright orange paper bag with a white hanging dress logo on the front.

As I approached the front desk next to the till and dumped my armful of clothes and accessories down with a *thump*, Mrs Masterson stared at the last remaining blotchy brown and yellow bruising on my forehead.

'I had a fall' I answered meekly at her unasked question.

'A fall? Ha, more like a nosedive into a table,' Amelia added unhelpfully. I turned to glare at her but luckily her phone started to ring; she raised her hands apologetically and turned to answer the call.

'It isn't as bad as it looks.' I smiled, which seemed to satisfy Mrs Masterson as she continued to ring up my purchases, folding them neatly and placing them in another of her orange paper bags.

ಸಂಘ

So three hours later, with lunch eaten, a costume for the dance acquired and enough sunny vitamin D to keep me glowing for a month, I was pretty beat. However, even trawling through the aisles at the fancy dress shop or the confusing trip into the stop-and-swap shop where strangers greet each other with *'I like your top, I want it, can I have it now?'* hadn't satisfied Amelia's thirst; with a Shopaholics Anonymous meeting nowhere in sight, I knew our day

ASCEND   *Billie Jade Kermack*

wasn't over yet.

We visited *La Senza,* the third underwear shop in the town square (under Amelia's orders of course) where she badgered me into buying a purple and black lace 4-piece underwear set. Now, I was used to a simple bra and knickers set – this matching belt thingy and the stockings looked confusing and totally not me, but I knew better than to argue. As we approached my tired Beetle Bob, lonely under the shady area of the car park with not another vehicle in sight, my arms laden with bags full of goods that I wasn't overly sure I wanted or needed, Amelia's words rang clearly in my head.

'He may not be there to hold your hand at the dance but at least if he calls you, you'll feel all that inner beauty flushing out. Guys can sense that in your voice apparently – or that's what Jack tells me. At least when he does finally come home, you have something fabulous to wear!' Her words made one side of my mouth curl into a small, brief smile. I dropped my bags onto Bob's bonnet with an exasperated huff.

'Careful Grace, it might just fall apart under the weight.' Amelia chuckled, not even a little fazed by her trolley load of bags, at least double the amount of mine, that hung off her arms. 'Oh no, I forgot!' She dropped her bags, and as they hit the concrete, she pulled her hands up to her mouth. I rushed to her side.

'Forgot what?'

ASCEND

Billie Jade Kermack

'I was meant to get a new uniform for work! My shift is tonight and I was determined to go in with my head held high. All the shops will be closed now...' she rambled. I unlocked the Bob's passenger side door and pulled out a large black and white striped box with a white ribbon tied round it in an ornate bow.

'This is for you. I wanted to say thank you... for everything, really. I knew you would make today special for me.' I blushed as I handed the box to her. 'We didn't forget, I've just been trying to distract you. I got this for you the other day.' She tugged unceremoniously at the ribbon like a kid on Christmas morning, pulling open the box without an upward glance. As she pushed aside the white tissue paper inside, her eyes were giddily alight with surprise. I waited for her approval, which came quickly as she beamed up at me, racing across the oil-stained gravel car park, box still in hand, pulling me tightly into a one-armed embrace.

'Amelia, I – can't – breathe!' I spluttered, still smiling.

'Sorry, this is just so... wonderful! Thank you, Grace!'

'Lets just say it's an updated Amelia fashion-conscious hospital uniform.'

In the box was a tight black pencil skirt with a white crystal beaded hem, and a light blue pearl button-down shirt with short ruffled sleeves that allowed for a little cleavage on show. More 'welcoming receptionist' than 'lady of the night';

ASCEND *Billie Jade Kermack*

the balance was perfect! Never one to wear flat pumps – EVER – I had also bought her a pair of patent black peep-toe cork wedges. Gushing and for once speechless, she hugged me again, only this time in a little less of a bear hug, for which my ribs were grateful.

TWENTY-THREE
ೲ

BEAU

'How much further?' I asked, holding myself back from whining *Are we nearly there yet?* like a small child stuck in the back of a packed Metro with no air conditioning on a tour of the Australian outback. Any air that was in the car smelt stale and dusty as the sun's rays cooked the tired seats.

'About twenty minutes, then you will take a left at *Francio's Meat Market*, carry on up the dirt path past the orange grove and it is the house on the hill' Jacques recalled from memory, without taking his eyes off of the road in front of us. The revelations that Jacques had overheard in the morgue about his family had never again been mentioned again on our trip. Looking at him now I could sense the foreboding haunting every second which edged us closer to the house on top of the hill. With no knowledge of what or who he would find at the end of our journey but a sense deep down that it was where he belonged, Jacques was slightly (at times, almost dangerously) on edge.

'You know, we could have been here yesterday if someone

ASCEND *Billie Jade Kermack*

had agreed to travelling on the Eurostar' I pointed out, as he continued to complain about my driving.

'So I am afraid of tunnels. We cannot all be as brave as you, big-shot' he snapped. I was tired and dehydrated, which didn't seem to bother Jacques and his determination. My bagged lunch of a ham hock and mustard bagel was decidedly rushed; as Jacques grew tired of waiting, he sped up the process with his rendition of 'Ninety-nine Bottles of Beer on the Wall'. By the time he got to fifty-six, I was just about ready to take one of those beer bottles and smash myself over the head with it.

The few minutes that I did manage to get alone were sadly only possible because Jacques had little need or interest in watching me go to the toilet in a stand alone cubicle that smelt of blue cheese and week-old crab meat; you might not think it, but there were definite up points to being dead. I reached into the side pocket of my satchel, pulled out the brown rectangular box that Grace had hidden in there and opened the small silver card attached to it:

> *I now have your mother's necklace to
> keep me safe, so this is for you.
> Keep this close, it's for good luck.
> Today, tomorrow, always and forever.*
>
> *Love & kisses,*
>
> *Your Miss Gracie xxx*

ASCEND
Billie Jade Kermack

Sitting in white tissue paper inside the box was the St. Christopher medallion I had given to Grace before I left her. It now no longer hung from a chain, but instead was set in a bracelet of brown, wound-leather straps. I turned it over, running my fingers over the words inscribed on the back, remembering fondly how excited I had been for her to read them. *Love will conquer all.*

The thought of her smile was warming. However brief it was I was suddenly a million miles away, lying beside her, my fingers running through her hair, her kisses mine for the taking. The shallow dip of her chest when she laughed at one of my awful jokes, the creases around her eyes when I made her smile. What I wouldn't give to be with her now.

ೋ

The crappy tan-coloured rental car we had picked up near the docks huffed and spluttered as we veered round the next corner, my pressure on the gear stick forcing clouds of thick black smoke out of the exhaust. Suddenly – with the state of our car, Jacques' newly-discovered car sickness (which I contested was impossible for a ghost) and my throat as dry as the desert – I surprised myself, glancing out of the dusty windscreen with an impromptu smile on my face.

'It's beautiful,' I mused. Hundreds upon hundreds of rows of vine-ripened oranges hung from the branches of neatly spaced trees on either side of the dirt track we were on. The sun, high in the sky, rained down a bright shine that turned the leaves an emerald green.

ASCEND

Billie Jade Kermack

'It is just as I remember. I think,' Jacques added, his eyes now alight with a mixture of excitement and trepidation at greeting his past with open arms.

'That is not a hill! More like a mountain' I exclaimed as I stepped out of the car and slammed the rusting car door, making the hinges whine. Jacques simply wafted from the car onto the pavement in one easy, fluid motion, the metal construction of the door of no concern to him. We climbed the hill and approached the eight-foot-high, slatted timber front door, climbing ivy from the large terracotta plant pots either side of the entrance now shielding us from the sun.

'So, do you have a plan?' Jacques mumbled, rubbing his hands together nervously.

'No... you?' was my response, as I quickly realised that we had forgotten a key element of our journey.

'What? We have come all the way here, and you do not have a plan? What are we going to do, Beau?'

With the lack of water in my system and a niggling headache from Jacques' bout of hypochondria, I decided to act first and ask questions later. Without another thought, I knocked twice on the door and stood back.

Jacques, though invisible, cowered behind me as squeaky footsteps on what I assumed was the freshly-waxed marble flooring behind the door grew louder.

ASCEND

Billie Jade Kermack

'*Bonjour*,' he smiled. Now that word I knew, thankfully. The man was about thirty or so, with only a few strands of grey around his temples in his short, neatly arranged jet-black hair to show his years. He spoke in a thick American accent, the twang maybe originating from New York. His big green eyes were friendly and complemented his olive skin, while a wide smile sat welcoming on his face as he waited for my response.

The next collection of words that he spoke were lost on me. I did make out the rise in his voice and an inquisitively-raised eyebrow which led me to conclude that he was asking a question of some kind. *Year Eight French, Year Eight French;* I pleaded with my brain to remember anything that could help me, but I was greeted with only silence and a searing visual snapshot of the French word for *ham*.

Jacques expertly read the rushing beads of stressed sweat down my face as a sign of panic. Although he went unseen, being in the presence of this man had clearly knocked him for six and left him speechless. He took a deep breath and stood tall beside me.

'Repeat exactly what I say,' he whispered in my ear. I mumbled the words, my voice stumbling over the rolling *R*s. I didn't know what I had said but it seemed to do the trick, as the man chuckled in response.

'Sorry, I've lived here so long that English has kind of become my second language. Where are your tools?' *Tools?*

ASCEND *Billie Jade Kermack*

Why would I need tools? As though reading my mind and sensing my panic, Jacques leant in behind me.

'You're the plumber, idiot' Jacques smiled, knowing full well that I couldn't come back at him with anything smart as we were in mixed company. If I was to speak, to argue with thin air, this guy would probably slam the door in my face.

'I left them in the van! I thought I would check out the problem first. That trek up here was no picnic.' I gestured in the direction of my imaginary van and smiled, pumping up my chest and secretly praying I could pass as a plumber.

'Come on in. It's up the stairs, third door on your left. It's the en-suite that I'm finding is the root of all evil.' He chuckled, stepping aside and gesturing to a grand, creamily marbled staircase which took up most of the foyer and led up to a balcony with hallways in both directions. I wiped my dripping forehead with the back of my arm, enjoying the air-conditioning unit above the door which fanned a cool breeze down my collar.

'I'm Roscoe, by the way. Head on upstairs and I'll go get you some water; seems like that walk has taken its toll.' He closed the door behind us and strode off into a room to his left.

'So, now what?' I asked Jacques quietly as we climbed the stairs.

'I don't know – I got us through the door, didn't I? I think I

ASCEND
Billie Jade Kermack

pretty much saved your ass back there. Who comes to France and does not learn at least basic French? I bet suggesting you buy that translation book in the boat gift shop doesn't seem like such a stupid idea now' he tutted, revealing just a smidge of a superiority complex.

'Who's doing who a favour? I didn't have to come here, so rather than bitching at me, tell me who he is and how I can get you to finally cross over. I very much doubt your final wish was for me to learn French, so let's get on with it.' I walked along the corridor, counting the doors as I went, remembering the directions Roscoe had given me. I quickly realised there was no need, as Jacques was already ahead of me and had entered the room. *Silly me, of course he knows where he's going.*

He walked around the room, the familiarity of the surroundings bringing a tear to his eye. I left him with his moment and kept my mouth shut. For the first time since we had met, however crazy it seemed, it looked as though Jacques was accepting that he really was dead; being in this place made it real for him. He ran his hands along the striped-silk lime bedspread, tracing his index finger over but not disturbing the layer of dust from the top of the black metal fireplace.

'I was always on at him about dusting up here. Magda, our cleaner, is about four foot nothing and could never reach it.' Jacques laughed at the memory, acting as though it had been only yesterday. 'And those bloody throw cushions – I always hated those.' As Jacques attempted to pick one up

ASCEND   *Billie Jade Kermack*

his hand sank straight through it, his misty palm translucent, a hint of lime-green shading his knuckles from the fabric beneath.

'You're getting tired, aren't you? It's perfectly normal, Jacques – or however normal this whole situation can be. It's the emotional pressure of being here...'

Knock, knock.

'*Merde,* someone is here, what do we do?' Jacques panicked, manically rushing between the dressing table and the bedroom door, clearly wishing he could pull aside the cream curtains and hide behind them. 'Damn it, damn being a ghost!'

'Calm down.' Trying to placate a spirit on the verge of a panic attack was new to me, and as his already greyish appearance began to flicker with the oncoming implosion of stress, I realised I wasn't as prepared as I had hoped. I rushed out into the hallway and stood peering over the balcony, hidden by a brick beam. Roscoe opened the front door and smiled at the guy standing on his doorstep: '*Bonjour.*'

'*Merde* is right, Jacques. I'm quite happy to throw a few curses around about being a human right now – you have it easy, no-one can see you!' We were in trouble. A short, portly man with a full strawberry-blonde beard and matching toupee beamed at Roscoe, removing his worn baseball cap and almost taking his hairpiece along with it.

ASCEND

Billie Jade Kermack

He was holding a toolbox and wearing a blue boiler suit with a leaking tap insignia on the chest. This meant that we had to think – and FAST!

They continued to exchange pleasantries on the doorstep. The French I had learnt at school may not have stuck, but even I could tell the conversation between Roscoe and the man at the door was getting heated.

'What made you think of the plumber? When you gave me that excuse earlier, why would you think of telling Roscoe I was a plumber?' I pressed, realising the window of opportunity was closing fast as our cover folded like a cheap suit around our feet.

'I don't know, for a moment before he answered the door I kind of heard a phone conversation, I think. It was the only thing I could think of.'

'Damn it, you blinked.'

'I did what now?'

'You moved, switched, blinked through space, allowed your astral aura to travel through subconsciously and make a connection. Chances are you did it without even knowing. You probably overheard him complaining to the company that the plumber he rang for was running late. Hence why there is now a plumber – who, by the way, is way more convincing than us – standing at the front door. You obviously have a very strong bond with this guy, I've only seen a handful of spirits blink without trying.

'Loving the chat and this new found rapport we seem to be sharing, but we have a problem far greater than the fact that you cannot act your way out of a paper bag.' Jacques pointed towards the front door and the approaching occupant, whose house we were in with no good reason.

TWENTY-FOUR

ꜱoꜱ

'Who the hell are you? What are you doing here?' Roscoe yelled, chasing us back into the bedroom. He had asked me in perfect English, yet the anger furrowing his brow and his tightly-clenched fists made my mind go blank. Then I saw it. On the bedside table was a framed photo of Jacques, with his arms around the ball of rage that stood before me.

'Jacques, Jacques!' I yelled in response, the only answer I could muster, my arm raised above my head in case I had to protect it from an unwanted blow. I watched all bravado and tension wash out of the man as he collapsed onto the edge of the bed. I lowered my arm, almost immediately feeling sheepish at my panic.

'How do you know about Jacques? Where is he, have you spoken to him? Did he send you here for his stuff finally?'

'You don't know?'

'Know what?' he pressed, concerned and wide-eyed.

'Jacques is dead – he died about four years ago. He

ASCEND *Billie Jade Kermack*

obviously needed you to know before he could cross over. You were his unfinished business. I can see you guys were close' I said, gesturing towards the photograph. 'How did you not know?' I fought to answer my own question without the help of the now-silent Jacques, as Roscoe fought with his own inner demons and cradled his bowed head in his hands.

'We had an argument before his business trip to London. We'd had arguments before, but this one was explosive. His last words to me as he shut the door behind him that day were *I'm done*. We had decided since day one that if either of us ever wanted to call it quits we wouldn't make it messy, we wouldn't drag it out. We didn't have any kids and the house is in my name. *I'm done* were our get-out words; it killed me that day, and every other day since, but I just couldn't break that promise. I couldn't track someone down when they wanted to be alone – no matter how much I loved him.' Jacques had listened silently as Roscoe laid his heart bare to a stranger. The words had been trapped within him for God knows how long, and even though Jacques could no longer be with him, he now had the chance to hear the truth and say his goodbyes.

'I'm so sorry for your loss.' My concerned autopilot switched on as I figured out my next move. It was now time for an honest display of the truth. I took a deep breath, but before I could speak, Roscoe beat me to it.

'There's one thing I don't get.' The man practically jumped up from the bed, his index finger extended. 'You say Jacques

ASCEND   *Billie Jade Kermack*

died, but I have been receiving messages from him; phone calls, e-mails. Maybe you have the wrong person.'

Nervousness bubbled in my stomach, as it did every time I was about to out a ghost. My palms were sweaty, my consciousness screaming for me to get it over with.

Like a band-aid, quick, like pulling off a band-aid.

'The reason I know that Jacques is dead is because I can see him, as clearly as I can see you now. He is here with us and he led me here to speak with you. He has been able to commune with you even after his death because the bond, the pull between the two of you, is so strong; it's why he has managed to keep his human sensibility and emotions for as long as he has. It's why he can connect with you and why you haven't moved on with your life. Although you have received messages from him, he has no knowledge of them. It's a sort of loop – he's been projecting his feelings without even knowing it.'

'You have to leave' he said abruptly, running his shaking hands through his hair and tugging at the neck of his polo shirt.

'Tell him he has to hear this. I can't leave until he listens to what I have to say' Jacques finally piped up as he stood tall beside me, his eyes unmoving from Roscoe's face, the torment flowing from him in waves.

'Jacques wants you to hear him. Please, for your sake and

ASCEND *Billie Jade Kermack*

his, just listen. I think I have a story to tell you.'

෴

'Jacques? Jacques! Where are you?' I yelled. After half an hour of trying to convince Roscoe that I had in fact brought the dead love of his life with me for the kind of reunion only seen in books and movies, I had taken my eye off the ball and lost the one thing that could prove I was telling the truth.

'What is this? So now he's gone. What sort of con artist are you, playing on the sadness of others?'

'It's the emotional connection, he's worn out, I've seen it happen many times before. He will be back, I promise, and then we can carry on. There is something I can try in the meantime – if you're willing to help. I'm going to need that photograph.' I pointed to the dresser and the framed photo of Roscoe and Jacques that sat alone upon it.

෴

Roscoe had done as I had asked and the blackout curtains in the bedroom were now drawn, simulating night. Every surface held lit candles that flickered and spluttered whenever one of us spoke. The air in the room grew heavy as I took my position on the bed. Roscoe pushed the scatter cushions onto the floor, chuckling to himself: 'He always hated these bloody cushions.' He took a seat in the corner of the room and watched as I made my final preparations.

ASCEND *Billie Jade Kermack*

'This may get strange, so don't freak out. I haven't done this for a while...'

'Wait, haven't done what for a while?' Roscoe interrupted.

'Channelled a spirit's past. I will most probably speak aloud, so don't be alarmed by anything. I can answer your questions once I come out of the trance. It's probable that at some point I will look like I'm in pain – I'm not gonna sugar-coat it, I will be, this isn't exactly a walk in the park – but you *must not* touch me or try to intervene. Do you understand?'

'Sounds simple enough, just a regular Friday afternoon for me!' Roscoe was clearly nervous as he bit his fingernails, laughing a little off-beat at his own joke.

I held onto the photo frame, my knuckles turning white as my grasp tightened and the searing pain in my temples began to build. Like a crazy game of Jenga, I mentally waded through Jacques' life experiences, stacking them one-by-one in chronological order.

My brain was a Filofax, filled to the brim with random Post-it notes and scribbles. Photos, names, dates all jumped out at me, none of which were mine, all things I was experiencing for the very first time. With certain questions in mind – his life with Roscoe, his absent family, his death – the pile of memories had been halved.

ASCEND *Billie Jade Kermack*

I was so close to seeing the answers for myself but faced a hurdle of stabbing pain; the brick wall that stood in the way, the intense pressure that built up as I snooped deeper and deeper into Jacques' life pounded incessantly in my head, making me feel queasy. I marched on, bounding through the pain as best I could.

With the wall now defeated and the pain no longer holding me back, I was locked into my first vision of Jacques' life.

They were married – Roscoe and Jacques – in a secret wedding, beneath a white rose-studded arch with only a handful of guests. They were dressed in matching blue suits; Roscoe relaxed in an open collar, tie-less white shirt and Jacques the polar opposite, immaculately put together with his crisp white shirt done up all the way and a coral-blue silk tie tucked into his buttoned up suit jacket. The wide smiles on their faces, the light of possibility and hope that lingered in their eyes; it was a memory that looked so real. They were truly happy. They were in love.

'You will forever be my family' Roscoe whispered in Jacques' ear, as they embraced and turned to their guests. Warmed by the moment but apprehensive as to where I was going to end up next, I knew I had to move onto the next memory in the pile.

Happiness was not rife in this next one – it wasn't even present. The room was dark, lit only by a dusty table lamp in the far corner. An older man sat silently beside it in a beaten-up black leather armchair, his coal-black stare fixed

ASCEND *Billie Jade Kermack*

on what was playing out in front of him. There was a small portable TV on a wicker stand and above that, fixed to the wall, a large carved wooden cross with a depiction of Christ nailed to it.

I watched on as a dark-haired woman chastised Jacques, screaming at him; he could only have been about eighteen. It was his mother. The disgust in her eyes was oddly compelling. I had never known my mother, and the substitutes I had been forced to live with after her death had looked at me this way – as though I had personally tried to ruin their lives, bringing shame upon them and their families. It was becoming clear why Jacques' body was left unclaimed after his death, and why he hadn't wanted to see them before he crossed over.

The woman spat at the young boy and ripped a gold cross from his neck. My heartbeat quickened as it threatened to break in two. Her words were strong, her eyes lacking any compassion or love; the pain in my chest made me buckle to my knees, mirroring the boy's movement.

'You are no longer my son. I will never speak your name again, as long as I shall live.'

I felt deflated, as Jacques' life played out in front of me; such wonderful instances of love and life, and then the bottom of the barrel, pain and suffering. I witnessed him lose everything he knew as his family heartlessly disowned him.

ASCEND *Billie Jade Kermack*

I had one final memory to explore. I had to see how it happened – how Jacques had lost his life. I knew this would be the most painful flashback of them all, which was why I was accustomed to saving it till last.

Sucked away from the childhood dwelling of Jacques' past and the memory of his parents I was suddenly standing in a busy street, the sun shining high above me, its heat colouring my skin with a healthy glow. I was outside *Larry's Locksmiths,* across the busy road from Mason's Deli. I breathed in heavily, knowing the painful truth of Jacques' demise would soon be an experience I would never forget. My body would soon feel what he had felt, his wounds mine whilst I remained in this vision.

From the church steeple at the end of the road where overgrown reeds and grass almost drowned out the lot full of graves, a bell rang loudly, signalling midday. I had entered this memory a little earlier than was expected. Everything looked different, the street, the people. I couldn't quite put my finger on it, but I was sure this memory was older then four years. As I gazed at the people passing by, my suspicions were confirmed. Something caught my eye; I immediately recognised those big blue eyes and waves of chocolate brown curls, pushed away from her face by an Alice band.

'Grace' I breathed, the vision of her welcomed. She must have been about eight or nine. She skipped along the pavement across the road from where I sat with a honeycomb-dusted ice cream cone in one hand, the other

ASCEND
Billie Jade Kermack

holding onto her father's. Surprised and now completely oblivious as to what I was doing there, I suddenly saw the blond-haired manifestation of my ten year old self, with his troubled gaze and arms laden with paper bags filled with groceries. He stood beside a beat up turquoise Honda which I remembered had belonged to my old social worker.

Grace's eyes met his; even as children held captive in a passing moment, we had shared something.

'We had met before,' I smiled. My smile was short-lived however, as the watercolour of the picture perfect memory which had momentarily bypassed Jacques' – the reason I was there – was doused. I screamed, as a torrent of stabbing pain tugged at my side. On all fours and in the middle of the road, I staggered to my feet. Still gripping my side as the sensation dwindled, I caught sight of the blood spot that was seeping through the material of my T-shirt.

'He's been stabbed, call an ambulance!' I looked across the road towards the woman yelling as she propped a wounded Jacques up against the wall of an alleyway. Not ready to give up, Jacques struggled into a jog in pursuit of his attacker. The young Asian man was shrouded in a dirty green trench coat, his face covered in dirt, his scruffy five o'clock shadow more of a ten to twelve.

He held Jacques' brown leather briefcase tightly in one grotty gloved hand, a crumpled wad of banknotes and a bloody switchblade in the other. He scrambled through the crowd, knocking people over, finally breaking out onto to the street and dodging a moving vehicle; its occupant hit the horn in argument and the thief's feet beat against the tarmac at speed as he turned the corner, out of view.

Jacques wasn't as fortunate as his attacker. He was swept up off the street at full force into the windscreen of a rusting yellow pick-up truck.

For a moment, everything around us was silent. Nobody dared move, hoping to see Jacques jump to his feet, unscathed. Once realisation had set in passers-by ran to his aid, but it was too late.

A shock-induced calm held the ghost of Jacques in place on the kerb outside the post office. The only thing he could do was watch on at the horrific scene in which his body was the feature.

The traumatising confusion was clear on his face; ghost or not, the reason why he had blocked this memory out was now blindingly clear. The fatal injury which had caused him to bleed out whilst in pursuit of his attacker was now very much my problem. It may have been a vision, but I was forced to experience it as though I had lived it. I applied pressure to my torso, the open wound pumping blood uncontrollably as it panicked to find its course. The thick red liquid ran down my side, onto the leg of my jeans, pooling on the ground around me. I felt light-headed, sick and desperate as I fought for control. I knew it was a vision, but that didn't stop the pain. Nothing ever seemed to stop the pain.

TWENTY-FIVE
ಸಿಂಧ

GRACE

On the short ten-minute walk to Gwen's house, I found myself blissfully unaware of everything around me. Actually *everything* is a little extreme, but for the time being, all was well and good. Beau would be home soon, and that day couldn't come soon enough. When I had waved him off, I hadn't realised just how much I would miss him. I wandered leisurely over the grassy hillocks in the nearby kiddie park, kicking the stones and twigs beneath my feet, every so often exploring what I had unearthed. The bright-green leafy trees with their draped, almost alive branches swaying cautiously in the light summer breeze sent an array of dancing lights and shadows onto the grey stone path in front of me.

I gazed up, my eyeline following a flock of birds as they ducked and dived amongst the trees. The mottled white clouds floated heavenly amongst a perfect, sea-blue sky. *'What do you see in those clouds, sweetheart?'* Elephant

ASCEND
Billie Jade Kermack

wearing a bonnet, baby holding a monster truck, snake wearing a bow-tie.'

I remembered lovingly our walks through this park when I was young, my arms stretched to the limit to reach up and hold my dad's large hands. He'd whip me up onto his shoulders in one swift movement; perched there, exploring the world from my new height, my fingers ruffling through his black curly hair, we would cloud-spot. My imagination alight, the feeling of unfiltered happiness bellowing from my little face, excitement flushing rose in my cheeks. The memory drifted into the passing cool breeze but my broad smile stuck around, accompanying me like a giddy tinker-bell fairy to Gwen's.

□□

'Sky, this is a surprise. What are you doing here?' I stepped up the kerb, looking up at Gwen's house.

'You told me to meet you here, to go get some lunch,' she replied timidly. It seemed strange, but for a fleeting moment she seemed as surprised to see me as I was to see her.

'Did I? I'm so sorry Sky, I must have completely blanked, I've had a lot on my mind at the minute. I see you have your uniform on, off to work? How's your mum doing?'

'She's better thanks, my shift starts at four. How are you doing?' she asked, looking at the now near-invisible crusty scab on my forehead from my head banging accident in the

ASCEND *Billie Jade Kermack*

restaurant that night.

'All good thanks, but you might want to hurry, it's already a quarter to' I said, glancing down at my faux-Gucci silver wristwatch, a Christmas present from Amelia. 'Maybe we can meet up for lunch next week?' I added.

'Sounds like a plan. I best get a move on then,' she smiled.

I watched her stroll away, still a little mystified by our encounter. I hadn't seen Sky since that night in the hospital when I had shouted at her and reduced her to tears. When had we arranged lunch? She had texted me every other day with little more than *'My mum's ill, so I wont be in today.'* I didn't know why, but looking at her, I still felt bad.

'Hey Sky,' I called after her, running to catch up with her. 'I think I can probably make a hour or so for lunch tomorrow, if you want to meet up. I feel like I haven't seen you in ages.' At this point I would usually reassuringly tap a friend on the shoulder or give them a hug, but I refrained from doing so. Sky was anything but tactile and I knew it.

'Brilliant.' She strolled off into the distance again, but this time seemed a little more light-hearted, with a happy-go-lucky skip to each step.

I glanced down at my watch. I hadn't planned it, but I was over an hour early. I strolled up towards Gwen's front door along the paved brick path, lined with flower solar lights. Her usually perfectly-kept front garden looked a little

ASCEND *Billie Jade Kermack*

shabby, the grass littered with falling pink flowers from the trees, grass overgrown, weeds popping up in the cracks of the pathway. Before I could extend my hand to knock and announce my arrival, Gwen appeared in the doorway. Her choice of hat today was a grey wool flat-cap, strands of her copper hair poking out around her neck.

'How do you do that?' I asked. Her gifts still managed to amaze me.

'Just intuitive, I guess.' She welcomed me in and closed the door behind me. 'Grace, this is Dietra, a good friend of mine and a highly regarded member of our coven.'

Dietra had long, dark-brown hair speckled with grey that reached past the small of her back and was secured in a loose plait. She was much broader than Gwen and had a round face with full, pink cheeks and light grey eyes. She wore a red and green checked long-sleeved dress which flowed around her ankles. Her brown strappy sandals were worn in, her cardigan of the same colour fraying at the sleeves.

Dietra extended her hand, pulling me towards her with a little more force than I was anticipating, which caused me to stumble forward and momentarily lose my balance.

'Hello, Grace. I have heard A LOT about you.' She emphasised, wide-eyed. Her voice was deep and had a hint of a foreign accent that I couldn't place which made her roll her Rs.

ASCEND
Billie Jade Kermack

'All good, I hope!' I said nervously. If Gwen had told her even half the trouble I had gotten myself into, this conversation could be interesting. I glanced down, immediately recognising what I had interrupted. Gwen was known around town as a psychic and she was giving Dietra a reading. Those lavender candles perched high on the dining table in the twisted metal holder, the glass of water to cleanse the area, the pack of oversized Tarot cards. Gwen had given me a reading last year before I had let slip about Glen and the problems I was having. She had read me like an open book, never straying far from on-the-point direct truth.

'I must have ran over schedule – that's you, Dietra, and all your chatting.' Dietra let out a girly, high-pitched giggle which didn't seem to suit her. 'Go and make yourself comfortable in the kitchen Grace, I'll be with you in a minute.'

I did as I was told, waving goodbye to Dietra as I went. After another five minutes or so I heard Gwen's front door close with a *thud* and the scent of freshly-extinguished lavender candles wafted into the kitchen around me. I hadn't seen Gwen since before she took her trip, and my Inner Bitch was right; she looked healthier, with a glow to her skin and not as much tiredness swamping her eyes.

'So, are we ready to rock and roll?' she asked. I jumped down from the stool and grabbed my holdall from the maple work surface, not realising that the zip wasn't fastened all

ASCEND
Billie Jade Kermack

the way.

'Let me help you with those.' Gwen was crouched on the floor by my side before I could blink, a handful of pens in one hand and my hefty photography textbook in the other.

'How on earth do you carry all this stuff?' she mused, handing them to me and using the alcove frame to steady herself and get to her feet. Once upright she continued to run her fingers along the swirling grain of the wood, over the indentations and permanent marker which charted the dates, names and heights of her foster children as they had grown. All the while a sweet smile settled on her face, as their memories warmed her.

'Can I ask you something Gwen?' I asked, my stare still fixed on the beam.

'Always sweetheart, you know that' she beamed, the sincerity clear in her eyes.

'Why is Beau's name charted on the wood? You have his height marked every year since he was four.'

'Three, actually. If you look down there it's a little worn now, but it was actually the first name I ever carved. I dreamt of him long before I met him; a cute sandy-haired boy with chocolate on his face and yoghurt in his hair who sat by himself, a little smile curling on his lips. He would visit me in my dreams every year on the same date, and with each year that passed he changed – he grew. I felt compelled to

ASCEND *Billie Jade Kermack*

acknowledge him, even though I had no proof whether he existed or not.'

'So when he walked into the hospital that night, you recognised him?' I asked, enthralled by her story.

'That I did, and I think a little part of him recognised me too. He felt like my son; I felt like his mother. Fate has a way of bringing things about when you least expect them... even if she does take her sweet old time sometimes,' she chuckled.

'So you believe in all that? Fate, I mean.' I hadn't realised until that moment just how pessimistic I had become. Being grounded in one world but with a part of me floating in another, I had lost an innocence of sorts. I had awoken into a reality that threatened everything that I knew on a weekly basis.

'Of course I do. You are living, breathing proof that fate exists. The fact that you don't already know that is a little worrying, though. You and Beau were destined to be together, and I wouldn't be surprised if at one point or another you had already crossed paths. I see...'

'But I...' I tried to interrupt, before Gwen raised her hand to silence me.

'No buts. We have to take the happiness in life where we can find it. He is yours, you are his. I have every belief that you two are a real life, twenty-first century Romeo and Juliet.

ASCEND *Billie Jade Kermack*

You are stronger together.'

She stroked my cheek, pulling me into a hug. I sighed and settled into her embrace, enjoying the comfort of her wise words as the thought of Beau washed over me. She stifled a spluttering cough with a lace-edged white handkerchief that she pulled from her cardigan sleeve, and the moment was over.

'Now, enough of memory lane. You should know better than to argue with a psychic. Let's get to it.'

◻◻

She welcomed me into the living room. A tray with her signature home-made sweet lemonade, the melting ice cubes inside frosting up the walls of the jug, and two tall glasses were already laid out on the coffee table.

'You were expecting me this early? I didn't even know until I cancelled my morning shift!'

'I may be old, but my intuition is still bright-eyed and bushy-tailed,' she chuckled. 'Right, sweetheart. I'm ready, so if you're ready, lets get started.'

In front of the Georgian, carved fireplace was a six-foot-high A6 whiteboard on a metal easel, dotted with a colourful array of blank Post-it notes.

'Where did that come from?'

ASCEND

Billie Jade Kermack

'I told you I was ready,' she laughed.

'Is there anything you don't know in advance?' I mused, knowing full well that the answer was *no*. If Gwen didn't know something, it probably wasn't worth knowing.

'Yes, I didn't know you was going to ask me that!' she beamed. I wouldn't have put it past her, though. Gwen's gifts appeared to be growing stronger every day. Or maybe, the deeper I delved into her world, the more comfortable she had become with sharing. Either way, there was still a lot to learn.

'I've looked through a couple of these briefly, but I thought I would wait for your opinion. I think this is the best place to start.' I handed Gwen the stack of stolen hospital files from my bag, trying not to make too much contact with the papers, diverting my eyes to anywhere but into hers.

'You know you're not supposed to take these home? You could get in a lot of trouble for this.'

'I didn't want to take them home, believe me; it's not like they make for light bedtime reading. They practically threw themselves at me. There's a reason I got a job in the dungeon, a reason why I'm surrounded by the files of dead people.'

'Fate's a bitch, huh?' I could tell by her consoling grin that in one way or another she had probably experienced far worse,

ASCEND

and could relate to the inner doings of the dead.

'I wouldn't want to completely smack karma in the face by admitting that, but on this occasion *fate* certainly has a messed-up view of where my life is heading. I can't put the files back. I've tried to – every time I get them back on the shelves, they turn up in my bag hours later. There is something I am meant to see and I need your help to find out exactly what it is.' I may have sounded confident, assertive and under control, but inside my stomach was somersaulting to the point where I wanted to throw up.

□□

After two hours, four pages of scribbled notes and theories on the whiteboard, a whole plate of chocolate digestives, the entire pitcher of lemonade and three toilet breaks, we had trawled through all the information in the seven files from the dungeon and some of the boxed newspaper clippings from Gwen's stash.

'So we have seven victims – that we know about' Gwen said, pacing in front of the now-lit fire. The room was sweltering, and if I was forced to take off another layer I would be sitting in Gwen's living room in just my underwear. Gwen, however, apparently hadn't felt the depths-of-Hell heat, sitting opposite me snuggled in her chunky knit cardigan.

I nodded as I looked at the stacks of paper messily spread across the coffee table. 'All the files have pages missing, all the victims were young females with similar attributes. All were murdered in a similar fashion and all are unsolved. Some were murdered whilst Glen was alive, some after his *unfortunate* demise. The word 'unfortunate' was heavily burdened with a sarcastic tone, as Gwen shrugged off the memory of his existence.

'Are we sure they were all Glen's victims?' I asked, my nose buried in the box of newspaper clippings. It was a silly question; Glen was a monster, capable of far worse things than these horrific murders. Having met him, it surely wouldn't be too long before more of his victims floated to the surface. If he could hurt me the way he had whilst being a ghost he could have easily done these things to those poor women. Knowing him, he'd have taken way too much pleasure in doing so.

'The question I need to ask you now is: do any of these women look familiar? Are any of them the woman you have been seeing?'

I glanced at the pictures to make sure of my answer. 'Well, no. But there are some photos missing. There are two on the list that don't even have a name. I'll search the records room top to bottom if it means I can finally put all this to rest. Somebody had to be filing all of these; somebody had to have noticed the inconsistencies.'

'I wouldn't be so sure – you work in the dungeon, how easy is it to misplace a file or some loose papers in that place?' She was right of course, but the thought didn't settle me. 'There is a connection, and we will find it. It's all a matter of time and patience' Gwen soothed, rubbing my shoulder affectionately.

With my patience rolled up tightly into an impending ball of constant fear, I knew I would have to delve deeper if I wanted to solve this. I looked at the whiteboard with its list of victim's names scrawled in black marker.

> Cassandra (Casey) Michaels, 27, murdered 1991
> Elizabeth (Liza) McQueen, 18, murdered 1996
> Hannah Holmes, 24, murdered 1993
> Jane Doe, approx. 25, murdered 1991-1993
> Alison Rose Dwight, 21, murdered 1991
> Petra Halovalich, 22, murdered 1987
> Jane Doe, approx. 21, murdered 1989

I tapped away at my laptop keys, exhausting twenty or so keywords in the search engine. As my finger tired of hitting the *Enter* button, I was finally rewarded with an old news report covering one of the murders. The footage was grainy, the focus-pull at first a little unsteady, the sound out of sync like an old Bruce Lee movie. The reporter was short and slim, her dark skin blemish-free and taut around her chiselled cheekbones. She pushed her harshly-bobbed black hair behind her left ear, pulling the microphone up to her mouth. The twang that resonated through the camera as it got a little too close to her earpiece showed her inexperience. The time stamp simply read *1991: 4.42pm.*

'Viewers, as you join us today I can report that another

ASCEND

Billie Jade Kermack

body has been found, a mere ten metres from where I stand. With the police still unable to shed light on who is responsible for these heinous crimes, I have to ask – is this the final body to be found, or is this just another in a long line to come? The body of this young Caucasian woman is yet to be identified, but as you can see behind me, interest in this murder and the sheer volume of police attention means that this is a high-profile case, of which every young woman in London should be aware.' Officials in jackets with the word MORGUE branded in yellow letters on the back zipped up a black bag on a gurney, sealing the charred remains of the body inside.

'Sources tell me that as in all the previous cases documented in the search for this serial killer, this young woman sustained blows from an unidentified blunt object and there are signs of prolonged torture and repeated strangulation. We can also confirm that the victim was set alight prior to death.'

'I can't watch any more.' I felt physically sick as I watched as them load the body-bag onto the back of a large black van. The crowd that had formed stood behind the yellow tape cordoning off the dump site. Anger, sadness, concern, the mixed emotions were clear on their faces as they slowly realised the horror of what had gone on there. There were a few tears spilt for the victim, questions from some reporters not able to get a good enough view with their cameras, and a few cries of police incompetence from some picketing protesters. *'More on this breaking story at six tonight. Keep safe out there, viewers. '* I slumped down onto the sofa feeling deflated, my hands cradling my head as I struggled to process all the new information.

'It was never going to be pretty, sweetheart. Murder has a way of making you see cruelty and destruction around every corner. We have to do this, we have to find out what is going on here.' She stroked my hair to calm me. 'Grab the hospital files over there, and we'll see if we can match a girl to this news report.'

'OK, so we have two files that match that date. No wait, three – Jane Doe wasn't discovered immediately, her time line is between 1991 and 1993, so it could be her.'

'We can eliminate Jane Doe. I caught a glimpse of that girl's body on the video, and no signs of decomposition means she was found relatively quickly' Gwen added, realising quickly that referring to the video was making me feel uneasy.

□□

'I think we've made a good start. I have to go and pick up a few last-minute things for tomorrow.' I fussed with the papers as Gwen sank into the padded armchair next to the fire. She winced as she found a comfortable position with her legs crossed. 'You look exhausted, Gwen. Is everything OK? You really haven't seemed yourself recently' I asked, concerned.

'You don't look so chipper yourself, sweetheart – it's been a *looooong* afternoon. I will be right as rain after a little

ASCEND *Billie Jade Kermack*

afternoon nap' she said, fanning herself with one of the empty file covers. 'When is Beau due home?' she added, trying to change the subject.

'We were hoping he would make it home for the Valentines dance at work tomorrow, but unfortunately his flight has been delayed. I know it's June so it's not technically Valentines Day, but it was going to be our first one together. I'm really going to miss not having him around for that.'

'The dance – I completely forgot! Is it really that time of year already?' Gwen said, closing her eyes and rubbing her forehead.

'No need to worry Gwen, I bet we can rustle up something for you. I have a three-hour shift tonight but I don't have to be in work until two tomorrow. We could hit the shops! I know where *not* to go if you're against self mutilation with a wax strip' I giggled, feeling the air run up the leg of my jeans over my bare and hairless calf.

'I can't help but think maybe I should give this year's dance a miss. I still haven't shaken my cold, and to be honest I'd much rather be sitting here with a cup of tea and a good book' she said, her skin clammy and her eyes translucent and glassy. 'While I have you here Grace, I was wondering if you could help me solve a little mystery; I've lost something.'

'Oooh, sounds intriguing.' A cheeky smile briefly fluttered across my face. It was rare that Gwen asked me for a favour, and after everything she had done for me I relished the chance to pay her back.

'Did you take a book from my reading area?' Her russet eyes bore into me, searching for the hidden truth, wading through my desire to fib. I was clearly nervous; Gwen had caught me off guard. My Inner Bitch bitingly sang the *Countdown* theme tune with a grin, signalling the continuing uncomfortable silence between us. I didn't want to lie, and Gwen's question only had two possible answers: Yes or No.

'Yes, I did. I'm sorry I didn't ask first. I was only borrowing it, I hope that's OK, I was kind of confused by everything going on and for some reason I just felt compelled to read it.' I diverted my stare to the ground, dreading Gwen's response. As usual, she shocked me.

'It's no problem lovely, it's just I have a few spells in there that I need. You are welcome to borrow any of my books, just let me know first.'

I felt awful – no, more than awful. I felt abominable. Strange though, before I could filter the next string of words to tumble out of my mouth, I found I had asked a question I shouldn't have.

'Why couldn't I get the big black book out of the house?'

Gwen's stunned silence and surprised stare spoke volumes.

ASCEND

Billie Jade Kermack

Well done smarty-pants, you've really screwed the pooch on this one. Get rid of the spade, I think that hole's more than big enough. Sadly, this time I couldn't argue with my inner voice; she was absolutely right.

'I've had it for as long as I can remember' she mused, staring wide-eyed off into the distance at a painting of a farm scene hanging above the alcove to the kitchen. She cupped her hand around her branded wrist, scratching at an invisible sensation.

TWENTY-SIX
ಇಂಡ

The painting was no longer just an amalgamation of watercolours on a canvas, but instead a skewed reality. The picturesque scene in front of me was calming, an array of multicoloured pastels tinted burnt orange from the low-hanging afternoon sun. Every tall, leafy tree of the surrounding forest, the crystal blue water of the babbling brook, the stand-alone, cosy, thatched cottage in the distance; everything had a warm hue of high definition, a world coloured with serenity and purity, the view of a painting by Monet.

It didn't take me long to realise that though I wasn't there, I somehow was. My feet were grounded, yet floating. I couldn't pinpoint anything but a bursting emotion of relaxation that travelled in waves of pins and needles through my fingers and up my hands.

Without acknowledging me, a girl of no more than eight or nine with bundles of long, curly red hair swamping her beautiful pale elfin face ran giddily past me. Her smile reached from ear to ear, her big brown eyes full of hope and excitement as she waved me forward, her actions laboured,

ASCEND   *Billie Jade Kermack*

as though she moved in slow motion.

For a brief moment I thought she could see me, but as I lifted my foot to take a step toward her, another girl ran out from beside me. This girl was the first girl's mirror image.

Their hair, those eyes, even their shabby patchwork dresses and handmade aprons meant that I couldn't tell them apart. I watched the twins clasp hands and run through the overgrown green field, their fingers flitting between the high stalks of barley, their bare feet leaving imprints in the dirt. The sun shone brightly down as they washed their feet in the water, and after a short game of hide-and-seek they collapsed amongst the fallen leaves of a withered oak tree, its one good branch supporting a rope swing.

They were now a good twenty metres from me, broad smiles etched on their faces. The warm breeze frolicked through the tall reeds as their laughter and chatter were drowned out by the light but very loud chiming of the metal ornament which hung from the wooden porch roof of the cottage.

'The book.' I spoke the words at a whisper but as I did both girls glanced up in my direction and I could tell, they saw me. The first girl – or maybe it was the second – pulled the big black book into her chest.

It couldn't be the same book, there's just no way! I thought. But it was, though it was not ruffled, frayed or dog-eared. Although the book the girl held looked used and a little

ASCEND *Billie Jade Kermack*

battered, it was years away from the tortured appearance of the one that sat on Gwen's shelf.

The girl ran her hand protectively over the carved star design on the book's jacket, trying but failing to shield it from me. They were now certainly aware of my presence.

As a droplet of rain grazed my cheek, I realised I hadn't even noticed the dramatic change in the sky. The now ashen spotted clouds had collected together, completely masking the sun and coating the picturesque scene in a depressing grey. The hanging chimes on the cottage porch collided frantically against each other as the wind rose angrily, taking me off my feet. The reeds hummed manically, swaying around me as though in warning of what was to come. The rain, at first light, was now pelting at full force like an attacking army. My white shirt was now see-through, my skin damp and cold to the bone.

The girls stared at me for another second, assessing the growing feeling of apprehension that hung on the wind. A shot of bright-white lightening and then bellowing thunder interrupted the chiming, and sent the girls running along the waterlogged dirt path towards the cottage, out of the rain.

I didn't move, I couldn't move; held in the moment, not knowing exactly where I was or in fact *what* this was, I decided against following the girls into the comfort of their home. Beneath the tree where there had been an idyllic scene of two little girls frolicking and having fun was now a

ASCEND *Billie Jade Kermack*

manifestation, a shadowed human whose face I could not see.

He had no features, his coal-black mask shielded him from recognition. His presence was unnerving, his energy debilitating as it washed over me, tugging at the valves around my heart. He watched through the cottage window at the girls, at their mother who served a warm stew for dinner, at where they hid that special book.

I had a feeling that the book, Gwen's book, was a big deal; that it held secrets that could be very, very dangerous in the wrong hands.

TWENTY-SEVEN

℘‍◈

6.31pm

Grace,

I'm sorry I can't be there with you. I hope you have an amazing night, and please, look after yourself. You and crowds never end well – I'm happy at least that this time you'll be surrounded by doctors and nurses. EasyJet have cancelled yet another flight out of Hamburg, so as soon as I know anything, I'll message you. I miss you like crazy beautiful girl, and can't wait to get my hands on you. I have a feeling there are a few things we need to talk about but for now at least, love you always, with you always, miss you always,
Beau xx

ASCEND

Billie Jade Kermack

Talk about? What does he want to talk to me about? He knows! On some level, he knows I've been keeping something from him. Damn that man and his mindbogglingly special gifts!
I pulled on my 50s bell-shaped skirt, ensuring the ruffles and the layers of extra material beneath it were loose and not tucked into my knickers – I had been burned by this before at my Year Ten prom. Being called *Gracie-Lacey-Panty* had haunted me for a whole year. Kids could be cruel.

I brushed at my skirt, finally satisfied that it was fine, and pulled at the buttons on my white, tight-fitted, short-sleeved shirt. I toyed with the idea of unhooking another button, venturing to show a little more flesh whilst glancing at my reflection in the door-length mirror on the inside of my wardrobe. *Screw it, have a little fun!* my Inner Bitch squealed, throwing her hands up in the air without a care and then returning to her pout as she applied another thick layer of bright, fire-red lipstick. So that was decided.

I left the button loose, able to see the slight curvature of my bust. Thankfully, the underwear set that Amelia had practically forced me to buy was barely visible underneath my top. The lacy tops of my sheer stockings hugged my thighs, the straps of the garter belt tickling the tops of my legs as I moved. I secured the sheer black neck-tie around my throat and took one last look at my costume. *James Dean-worthy?* I thought, still feeling like I had forgotten something.

ASCEND   *Billie Jade Kermack*

Black pumps – check.

Baby-pink frosted poodle skirt – check.

Sexy and most probably inappropriate underwear that I would never usually buy but thanks to Amelia I have, but if I'm honest feel fantastic in – check.

Black neck-tie and matching bow headband – check.

I was ready. Well, almost ready; I was yet to rummage around in my mum's make-up bag and attempt to slap on some cream/powder/foundation – whatever it is that makes your skin radiant and blotch-free, I needed some of that.

Looking at the new picture of mum and Cary at the Sanderson's BBQ last weekend sitting proudly on my mum's dresser made me pause. I hadn't realised how distant I had become since Beau had left. I managed to hold up day-to-day conversations with others and plaster on an acceptable smile, but the second I was alone, something deep inside me felt broken. A yearning to find the missing puzzle piece had left me worn out and exhausted from over-thinking the situation.

Though I hadn't let Amelia or my mother see my crushing disappointment, I really had hoped Beau would make it back for the dance. Yes, I knew it would probably be a complete drag, the night ending with the radiology team storming half-cut (and probably half-dressed) into the fountain as the surgeons looked on disapprovingly, but it

ASCEND *Billie Jade Kermack*

would have been nice to have my man, my *backup,* by my side.

I felt a tear teeter on my eyelid, threatening to ruin the slapdash but acceptable make-up cover job on my face. I sucked it up, blinking like a crazy woman, diverting the salty water away from my cheek and back where it had come from, along with the tension building in my chest. I reached into my shirt and pulled out the necklace Beau had given me, the one that had once belonged to his mother, now secured safely around my neck. An errant ray of light from my bedroom window caught the gold at an angle in the mirror, almost blinding me.

I furiously rubbed my eyes, careful not to smudge the steady markings of black eyeliner and mascara. I pulled the trinket up to my lips; as I made contact with it, I closed my eyes as tight as I possibly could and for one unfiltered, unassuming moment, allowed a memory of Beau to jump into the forefront of my mind. For a brief moment, I just allowed the emotion to swell and multiply inside me.

Hey, princess! We kind of have an event to be at, how about you stop thinking of your dream guy and get a bloody move on! My tormentor yelled at me from within, dispelling any goodness my thoughts of Beau had stirred in me. *Patience is a virtue, you know* I thought in response, goading her.

My big eyes were usually a wide, bright powder-blue, but today, as I added yet more concealer to the grey bags under

ASCEND   *Billie Jade Kermack*

them they looked misty, darker pools of an indescribable shade of indigo. I flushed my cheeks a rosy pink with a large brush and some blush, nodding my head in silent approval at my reflection.

The phrase *you can't polish a turd* jumped to mind but I quickly disregarded it, even though my comfortable onesie and the TV remote on the end of my unmade bed momentarily offered me the option of a very different evening. With a deep, steadying breath I pushed my hair behind my ears and tightened the bow around my head. I grabbed the black and pink-chequered clutch purse that Amelia had lent me and made my way out of my room.

'If I'm not ready now, I never will be. Deep, steadying breaths!'

TWENTY-EIGHT
☙❧

I strolled up the hospital stone steps amongst an eclectically-dressed bunch of my work colleagues, their laughter and chattering a soothing noise in comparison to Amelia and Jack's somewhat... *confrontational* conversation. It wasn't news that I was uncomfortable in unfamiliar surroundings, and I was a little annoyed at the fact that I had to dress up for the pleasure.

The car drive over had been interesting, to say the least. With Jack driving and Amelia riding shotgun I was left squashed up in the tiny back seat, sandwiched between stacks of coursework and Jack's gym bag, forced to hear their rowing like a small child would their insufferable parents – parents who should have got a divorce a long time ago. They bowled through the double doors ahead of me into the now very different hospital cafeteria, Amelia waving an aggressive finger in response to Jack's questioning glare.

'I'll see you later then guys?' I started my question off loudly and assertively but as they mingled into the crowd and out of sight I trailed off, my voice almost a silent thought once I

ASCEND
Billie Jade Kermack

was finished.

Elongated swirls of draped red, white and blue silk streamers filled the ceiling, almost completely masking the bright and unflattering glare of the buzzing overhead strobe lighting. The whole thing had an American Patriot feel to it. June Lowery – events co-ordinator for hospital functions by night, medicine dispenser by day – had only arrived in England three years ago, and her Southern Belle accent lent a hint of musicality when she spoke. She was tall and thin, her brown skin flawless; it was hard to believe she was forty-five. Her braided hair was secured in a blue bow high atop her head, her make up harsh, neon contouring lines highlighting her cheekbones and eyebrows. Very 80s!

'Hey Grace, let me have a look at you. Grace Kelly?' she mused. *Damn, that would have been a good one*, but I guess I haven't strayed too far past the era. My outfit oozed elegance, even if my inner confidence was ten steps behind.

'Natalie Wood actually,' I smiled. I hadn't realised I was doing it but I had been swaying, innocently enjoying the bell movement of my skirt, for once feeling like a proper lady rather than a trainee-in-waiting.

'Oh, that's nice sweetie' June lulled, refraining from the urge to tap me on the head as she passed. *OK, she has no idea who I am*, I thought. *When did people stop appreciating the classics?*

'Henry, put – the – bottle – down!' She said the words

ASCEND

Billie Jade Kermack

slowly, authoritatively, attempting but failing to coax Henry into listening to her. It didn't work, and before he ran off into the crowd, his head of bleached blonde hair bobbing up and down like a whack-attack arcade game, he had emptied a litre of pure Russian Red Label vodka into the large crystal punch bowl. Henry was only nineteen, with the youthful tenacity that usually incited playful disobedience. Even with his love of prankster antics, everybody was very fond of him.

'Henry knows that June is an ex-Olympian hurdler, right?' said a doctor dressed as Sweeney Todd to my left, his own Mrs Lovett giggling heartily in response, nursing a cold beer in one hand and a dirty – and very fake – meat cleaver in the other. She smiled warmly at me though I was rudely staring at her without even realising it, running my tongue over my teeth in response to the black special effects make-up caked on hers which made them appear dirty and missing in some places. This was one of the times I was grateful for Amelia's interruption.

'I might as well become a lesbian!' Amelia yelled, a little too loudly. The dramatics had officially begun, and I don't mean the band. I sighed, already able to see how the night was going to unfold.

'Or *hello* also works. But you know, tomato/tamato.' Her glare silenced me, and being the good friend that I am I dutifully listened to Amelia as she babbled on about her woes. If I'm completely honest, I didn't hear much past 'He said he would buy me the purple shoes, the idiot is colour blind, who mixes up purple and maroon?'

ASCEND

Billie Jade Kermack

Red helium balloons were dotted round every corner and entrance of the room. It looked like a fantasy land, worlds away from how it usually did; the stained brown curtains had been replaced with lengths of glitzy gold material which shot off rainbow stars in every direction as the lights below them flickered. Where rows of cheap, mass-produced metal table and bench combos would usually be were now round, French style, ornately crafted cast-iron tables with red cotton tablecloth runners along their centres which had been pressed to within an inch of their lives. There were twenty or so tables, all surrounding a newly fitted black and white-chequered dancefloor that bordered the stage. Centred on each table was a clear glass vase, a red ribbon snaking around its neck, stacked high with an array of roses and chrysanthemums.

A stunning Asian woman in a backless silk chartreuse gown, her eyes illuminated, mesmerising the crowd, stood proudly on the wide teak stage overlooking the dancefloor, her band of merry men also enraptured by her beauty and seductive voice.

As the beat softened from an intense power ballad to a romantic symphony the crowd around me changed pace; almost instantly couples banded together, singletons quickly searching for their exits. She sung of love and loss, happiness and anguish. I had to get out quickly as Beau jumped to my mind, causing my lip to tremble. *Don't cry, don't cry*! I chastised myself, politely making my way through the swaying couples who were the picture of

ASCEND　　　　　　　　　　　　　*Billie Jade Kermack*

happiness. I needed to get out, and fast.

ॐ

'Getting some fresh air?' Her voice was low and mousy, her shyness, as always, in full bloom. She took a big bite out of a shiny red apple, wrapped it in a napkin and placed it in her hanging cardigan pocket.

'Sky. How are you?' I piped up excitedly. I wanted to hug her but decided against it, remembering immediately her aversion to touch. 'Are you coming into the party?' I quickly realised my question was redundant, as she was wearing her hospital uniform of guideline pencil skirt and fraying grey cardigan that hung a little too long on the arms, which thanks to the warm night air was now tied in a knot around her waist.

'I can't. I had to take time off to look after my mum, so now I have to make my shifts up.' She looked pale, her face ashen and almost bemused for some unknown reason. 'It feels weird, like I've lost a whole week of my life, but I'm determined to jump back in the saddle and get on with it.' She smiled, but it did not meet her mottled grey eyes.

'So you're OK missing the party?'

'More than OK – I'm not great in big crowds, more of a lone wolf. Except when I'm with you of course.' She chuckled girlishly, which was uplifting. 'I've never been a people person. Popularity tends to roll right off my back in waves, I see how everyone looks at me!' Or sadly in Sky's case how they *didn't* look at her, her shyness smothering her like an invisibility cloak. *Am I her only friend?* I felt immediately guilty for thinking it, but quickly realised that it was a fair point to make.

'Oh, OK. I'm sorry I missed lunch today, but we will definitely have to catch up soon. If you need help on folding duties, I'm all yours' I beamed. She diverted her eyes, now uncomfortable, clearly not wanting to hurt my feelings. Who was I kidding, I was useless at folding. I knew it, and now I was assured that Sky knew it too.

'I can manage thanks, but a rain-check for lunch would be great.' *She was right to decline,* my Inner Bitch giggled with a snort. I expelled a sigh of relief and a smile that made her visibly relax again. 'What are friends for?' I added lightly, briefly lifting the sparkle back into her eyes. Way too briefly.

'I have to... to go. I'll see you... soon, maybe.' If she could have run without tripping over her own feet I think she would have. Her words came out in spluttered dips as she spoke and jogged awkwardly up the stairs away from me, her little legs taking them two at a time, eventually heading into the West Wing side-entrance towards A&E. Her expression was uncomfortable, almost haunted as she flitted out of view. *What did you do?* my inner voice snarled. Before I could run through a list of my possible misdemeanours I heard him, and my question was answered.

ASCEND

Billie Jade Kermack

'Hi Sky. Bye, Sky.' He sounded disappointed, his brown puppy-dog eyes full of sadness. I turned to face him, walking down the steps to meet his gaze. I don't think he even saw me until I waved my hand in front of his face, breaking his stare at the now empty path that Sky had chosen as her escape route. I knew Sky had said she didn't mix well with people, but as soon as Ed tried to instigate a conversation – and he had done on several occasions with her – she checked out as quickly as she could.

'Ed?'

'Hi Grace!' Ed's voice was weirdly a few octaves higher than usual as I pulled him out of his trance.

'How you doing?' I had grown more comfortable in Ed's company since starting work at the hospital, but being alone with him in a deserted parking lot with no witnesses within screaming distance made me uneasy, and I was chomping at the bit to rejoin the celebrations.

'Good, good. Maybe only OK actually, but can't complain.' It had been clear from the moment I met him that Ed was a little... slower than everyone else, and his poorly-nurtured social skills were evident from the start. But on the whole, he was polite and pleasant.

He wasn't wearing his uniform of grubby T-shirt, holey jeans and an orange all-in-one jumpsuit, the sleeves usually secured around his waist. His calloused, soot-covered hands were now gleaming, not an inch of dirt in sight. 'Do you like my costume?' he beamed with an excited, boyish grin, lovingly running his slender hands over the breast panels of his expensive blue suit. His sleek, gelled hair was neatly scraped back into a side parting, his usual over-eye-hanging fringe firmly in place behind his ear.

The suit was clearly made for a man at least two sizes bigger than him, but although out of place and ill-fitting, made him look smarter. At roughly six-foot, with his arched posture and slender frame, his facial expression whimsically giddy as he glanced once more at the dancing rainbow lights of the party edging out of the cafeteria double doors, Ed looked almost sweet and innocent. He looked like a son wearing his father's best work suit, the pant legs swamping his black, scuffed tennis shoes and the sleeves just about allowing his hands to see the light of day, hanging down at his sides and already folded back once.

'Grace, do I look OK?' he asked, making me jump. He seemed tense and upset, which scared my vocal chords into compliance.

'Very dapper Ed, I almost didn't recognise you' I smiled, watching his shoulders relax. 'Do you have your eye on someone tonight, a special lady maybe?'

'Maybe,' and his eyes flitted over towards where Sky had been just a hop, skip and a jump away from us. *Ahhhhh*, my inner voice cooed. *He likes Sky!* I didn't know Ed's precise age, but I would have assumed he was quite a bit older than her. This would need looking into, and I would have to get

ASCEND

Billie Jade Kermack

Sky's version of events before I interfered.

'Well, these feet weren't made for walking – I've got my dancing shoes on!' he chirped, with a celebratory nudge to my shoulder. In a very faraway, Oz-land, flying monkeys sort of a way, Ed was quite cute, his excitement radiating from him. Before I could reply he was off up the stairs, letting out a great howl of peer-pressured excitement as he entered the double doors and mingled with the crowd.

The night steadily drifted into my past; happy memories, sure, but memories without Beau never seemed as bright, their clarity dampened by the constant niggling feeling of sadness that crippled me from within. My face fell as I fiddled with the single white rose that Henry had rushed by and given me on bended knee, June still hot on his tail, determination furrowing her now sweaty brow.

'Hey Mrs – fancy a dance?' Amelia was considerably happier than she had been, and by the smudged remnants of pink lipstick on Jack's mouth as he propped up the drinks table across the dancefloor, I could tell they had kissed and made up. I was immediately grateful that they hadn't included me in their display of affection; sometimes sharing really wasn't caring.

'I don't want to' I replied petulantly, my gaze still fixed on the table.

'What do you mean you *don't want to*?' She mimicked my whining, which caught my attention. I huffed and sat back

ASCEND *Billie Jade Kermack*

in my chair. 'This is about your Mr Right? You miss him?'

'Hey Amelia, meet the obvious' I said caustically, holding my hands out palm-up in front of her for a visual reference, slapping them together when she finally got my point. She held out her hand to me without a word and gave me a cheeky pout, wide-eyes and head tilt combo. I shrugged a response and gave in – fighting her was futile. I dropped my guard and although slightly hesitantly, as I fought the idea of running home to the comfort of my room, put one foot in front of the other and followed her back into the cafeteria.

Slightly intoxicated and feeling the effect of the masses of people and their body heat around me, I wasn't sure I was still in the territory of *good decision-maker*. In a haze of inebriation, bright strobe lights that would have been an epileptic's Hell and the soft lulling of the beautiful singer, the talented green goddess gliding round the stage professing her love to someone unknown, I relaxed; for the first time that night, I felt at ease. I pulled my necklace from Beau out of my shirt and fiddled with it, rubbing it between my fingers, smiling at the memory of when he gave it to me. God, I missed him!

Amelia chatted animatedly to Mavis Monroe, a receptionist on B-Ward who had abused the spiked punch more than most and had candy pink lipstick spread across her lips and front teeth. She was dressed, as if you couldn't guess, as Marilyn Monroe. Unfortunately for Mavis, she was the complete polar opposite of the legend that was Marilyn, but you had to respect her determination as what was meant to

ASCEND *Billie Jade Kermack*

be a white flowing sun-dress hugged her body like cling-film.

TWENTY-NINE

ೞಣ

'Grace, shake it!' Amelia demanded as she sung along animatedly to the Lady Gaga/Rihanna mash-up that was now blaring out of two speakers that towered above us, each thumping bass note shaking the dancefloor beneath our feet. It was a spliced tune of R&B and pop with a side-order splash of Bajan buzz, and instantly cajoled the crowd to swamp the dancefloor. The song signalled the live performers' break as they made their way off of the stage and down to the bar, a lone PA with a clear thirst to succeed but not enough hands to complete the task dabbing their foreheads tentively with a towel..

'Shake what?' I laughed, as Amelia followed through with a selection of complex dance moves that were music-video-perfect. I should probably just have opted out and sat down, because the mere idea of following in Amelia's footsteps made me immediately question the inane ability – which I didn't possess – to balance whilst shaking any of my body parts, even the aforementioned *it*.

'Your junk!' she replied with a confused *duh* expression on

ASCEND *Billie Jade Kermack*

her face, as though what she had said was a given. She gyrated her hips, pointedly shaking her bottom in my direction.

'When did you get all Jenny from the Block?' I shouted, trying and almost failing to throw my voice above the music.

'About the same time you became a boring housewife' she replied, panting, not letting her feet stay planted on the same patch of floor for very long. I sniggered in response, more at the idea of how wrong Amelia was, rather than what she had said. Thankfully, as I bopped apprehensively from side to side along to the beat, she had a beaming smile on her face; I knew she had no idea what I was thinking, which sated me slightly.

Little did Amelia know I was being stalked by the battered spirit of a murder victim – *screw it, I can do this!* I mused triumphantly, in protest at my unwilling body, with a cheeky smile on my face. Mimicking (to the best of my ability of course, I wasn't delusional) Amelia's moves, I jumped head-first into a *Stars In Their Eyes*-worthy performance, complete with believable lip syncing. For the first time in a long time, I actually had... what's it called again? Oh yeah – fun!

It was clear almost immediately that I looked more like Kenny from the block, my moves hindered by the fact that dancing wasn't one of my naturally God-given talents. After what had to have been at least thirty-five minutes of dancing and animatedly chatting (or quite possibly shouting) with

ASCEND

Billie Jade Kermack

Amelia, I was exhausted. As the chorus to Bon Jovi's *Living on a Prayer* kicked into play so did everyone else, responding to some unanswered question with joyous screams, almost matching in unison the melodic chorus bursting from the loudspeaker. Whoops and *whoas* erupted from a table beside the stage as people circled it, clapping and cheering.

'Mrs Benson has some moves – who'd have thought it?' Amelia chuckled, still two-stepping, her stiletto heels tattooing against the now-scuffed wooden floor surrounding the dancing area. We watched on as Mrs Benson – or Dr Benson, as she was more commonly referred to – wound her hips like Shakira. Well, almost like Shakira; she was fifty-four, after all. Her shoulder-length auburn wig was static and in disarray, the fringe sticking to her sweaty forehead. She tugged at her black, backless mini-dress, revealing a little more of her already exposed thighs – yes, I said *mini-dress!*

'Wow, Dr Benson has changed a tad since I knew her' Jack piped up from behind us, his close proximity making me jump almost clear of my skin.

'Is it legal for paediatricians to dance like that? ... WHOA!' he yelled, covering his eyes with his forearm, a shudder raging through him as an inadvertent panty-flash from Dr Benson threatened to mentally scar him for the rest of his life. Amelia was almost on the floor in stitches of unrelenting laughter, as Jack turned away from the floor show.

ASCEND

Billie Jade Kermack

Amelia took a sip of her fluted glass filled with pink champagne, then said 'I overheard her in the toilets earlier. She's meant to be Julia Roberts, and I don't mean sweet and innocent *Notting Hill* Julia Roberts.'

'So who's that guy she's dancing with?'

'Well he's definitely not Richard Gere, and I'm pretty sure he isn't Mr Benson.'

'How could you possibly know that? She could just be into younger men.'

'I can tell because that balding man in the black Gucci suit with a face like thunder, wading through the crowd with a plastered-on scowl, would be my best bet at good old Mr Benson. I could be wrong, though.' He said the last part ever-so-nonchalantly, with a cheeky smile. I glanced over in the direction Jack had hinted at and immediately agreed with his observation, however untactful a response that it was.

The raging Mr Benson screamed *average*; his height, his build, the wispy grey monk-like hairline and matching trimmed beard. The scene that followed wasn't pretty, but the commotion was forgotten as quickly as it had begun, and as the performers took their places on stage everyone continued on with their nights – although now more intoxicated and with a little less composure and dignity than they had started with. As another girly giggle touched at the edges of my mouth, I realised I wasn't exempt from my observations.

'I think I'm going to go.' It was only 9.30, but I had already had enough; displays of affection were beginning to grate on me, and my white-wine-fuelled urges were reminding me of what I didn't have and who was missing in my life.

'There's only a couple of hours left and then they'll start kicking us out. Do you really want to be the sadpuss that left early?'

'One more dance, and then either I sit down or fall down. Your choice, as I officially impart the job of taking care of me onto you!' I smirked, cutely touching my index finger onto the tip of her crafted button-nose.

'Where's Beau when you need him?' she mused, grabbing Jack around his waist and leading away from the conversation he was having with a junior nurse who had once attended school with us.

Her comment was sobering: *Where was Beau? Was he thinking about me, who was he with now?* No! I couldn't think like that. If he could be with me, he would be. As sadness crippled me from the inside out, I realised the emotions of the evening were overpowering and mentally exhausting.

'That's it – I'm done. But thank you for tonight Amelia, it was needed.' I went in for a little hug, but she held me at

ASCEND
Billie Jade Kermack

arm's length.

'You can't! Please... just...' she shared her attention equally between me and the stage. 'Yes, OK, one more song and then you can go' she pleaded, her beautiful doe eyes fluttering. '*Pleeeeease,*' she begged, clasping my hands.

'Okaaay...' I dragged the word out, mimicking her, still unsure of her motives and eyeing her suspiciously. I fumbled around with the buckle-lock clutch bag in search of my phone, not realising that my feet had been drumming along familiarly to the tune drifting towards us from the stage.

Where do I know this song from? I thought, glancing up at Amelia who was now beaming and giddily jumping on the spot like a kid hopped-up on sugar on Christmas morning. Without realising it I was tapping my feet along to the beat, mirroring the drummer's steady beat on the bass drum as the melody quickened.

Two beautiful young women wrapped in matching figure-hugging silver cocktail dresses swayed in time, rattling tambourines against their palms and humming silkily into their mics. Suddenly that voice chimed into action, the memories it evoked, the lust, the familiarity. An explosion of desire erupted in my stomach and I nearly toppled over in suprise.

'Beau!' I choked.

THIRTY

'Listen, baby. Ain't no mountain high, aint no valley low, ain't no river wide enough, baby...'

His tuneful rendition caused tears to prick at the corners of my eyes, sending my vision into a blurry mess. As the words enveloped me in a smouldering warmth, wrapped suddenly in a blanket – for the first time in what felt like forever – of unquestionable certainty, I felt like a whole person. I was glued to the spot.

He sang our song at first to the crowd who joined in without hesitation, women of all ages flooding towards the stage to get a better look. He moved round the stage with the microphone at his lips like a performer at the Albert Hall who had been doing this all his life, interacting with the beautiful songstress who sang along with him on the chorus.

His was the only face I saw, as everything around me shadowed into nothingness. A pang of jealousy niggled at the pit of my stomach; my hands urged to be on him, watching the stunning singer sharing not only the lyrics and the stage but also her emotions with my boyfriend. My gorgeous, rock-god, never-stops-surprising-me boyfriend.

ASCEND *Billie Jade Kermack*

In battered dark blue denim jeans that were rolled up at the ankles, a fitted white T-shirt and with the collar of his black biker jacket turned up, it was becoming clear just how planned this really was. His hair was slicked back into a 50s duck-tailed style, and then it hit me: the truth of Amelia's part in it all.

'You!' I accused with a smile, turning on my heels to face Amelia.

'Yes, me! Who do you think has been messaging me all weekend? He wanted to know who you were coming dressed as, he was practically giddy when I told him. He wanted to surprise you and he asked for my help!' It was becoming clear why Amelia and Jack had been arguing; I can't imagine he was very happy with her and Beau's cosy event planning, even if it was for me.

'I can't believe... I mean, how...?' I muttered, unable to drop my silly grin.

'I think someone's looking for you' she beamed, only briefly taking her eyes off of the stage.

And so he was. With his hand up over his eyes cutting off the overhead bright white spotlight, his eyes met mine, immediately stunning me into submission and making my entire body flush fuchsia. My yearning to be close to him threatened to smother my other senses. He pointed at me, making the partygoers around me stand to attention and swoon. I felt the boning of my new bra tighten as my chest swelled and pushed defiantly against it.

~~~

AMELIA

I was happy for Grace, but I'm not going to completely lie; an instant tightening around my midriff alerted me to the unwelcome arrival of the green-eyed monster. I glanced over at Jack, who was now locked in conversation with Paolo from Reception about a poker game they were planning for next weekend.

I watched as Beau winked at her, inviting her in with his drop-dead gorgeous smile that managed to make even my knees weak. He jumped off the stage and into the crowd, the overhead light following his every move. He only ever took his eyes off Grace for mere seconds; as he danced around everyone who by the looks of it had also fallen under his charming spell, they made a pathway on the dancefloor for him to travel down. He shimmied, light on his feet, over the waxed dance floor, closing the space between them.

A handsome Romeo for thine indescribably beautiful Juliet I thought, sighing. For an instant – a brief, but boldly there instant – I wished that he was mine, that I was special, that I was *the one* instead of being Grand Supreme at always coming in second.

ASCEND

Billie Jade Kermack

A fleeting expression of sadness and shock passed over his face as he edged closer to Grace. His performance acted as his mask as people cheered around him, but I knew why he worried; I had seen it since he had left. Even with the layers of make-up she had used to help disguise her thinning and worry-weighted skin, her sleep deprived, tired eyes, you could see the weight she had lost. Sure, she tried to hide it, but I knew it was there, lurking – she was lost without him, and now he knew it. She wasn't a complete person without him.

Her cobalt eyes were alight with wonderment as he edged closer to her, the space between them a heated trail of anticipation, of longing. She fiddled with her chocolate brown locks and straightened out her skirt, unable to keep her hands still. It was clear to not only me that they were meant for each other.

In that instant, I panicked. My worries for Grace had been bubbling up for a while but it wasn't until I saw her now, with her body tightened and rigid, instantaneously a slave to him, that I realised the hold he had over her. I shrugged it off quickly, knowing that I couldn't keep my mouth shut about most things so it was a dangerous train of thought that would undoubtedly lead to trouble. *What would happen if he left her again? What would be left of my friend?* I thought.

'I'm sorry I shouted at you. This was a good thing you did.' Jack grabbed me around my waist from behind, ripping me back to reality. I quickly dispelled my thoughts of a different life and the perfectly-trimmed greener grass that sat on the other side of the fence, just out of my reach. I took in a deep breath and plastered a smile on my face.

Who was I kidding? That smile was my backbone, the thing that ensured my feelings stayed hidden. With the remnants of a chocolate éclair from the snack table still messily present on his lips, Jack's smile slipped slightly. 'Why don't you look happy, Amelia? Grace is made up!'

ಸಂ

BEAU

I had been planning it tirelessly. She deserved the best, and with the surprisingly undramatic inclusion of Amelia, it all went to plan without a hitch. I hugged Vanessa for agreeing to include me in her set and singing along with me and shook the hands of the house band, before descending the stage stairs onto the dancefloor. A sea of people bounded towards me, blocking my view of her. I graciously and politely acknowledged them, thanking them for their compliments, but all I wanted was to see her, to be with my Gracie.

'There's my girl. What happened to you, Gracie? I go away for a couple of weeks and you decide to stop eating?' I

ASCEND
Billie Jade Kermack

grazed my fingers over her taut jawline, her rosebud lips now fuller on her face, her collarbone hard beneath my palm. The energy between us felt electrically-charged, as in a dream. I had counted down the days until I would see her again but now that I had, I felt like if I hugged her as much as I wanted to there was a chance she would break.

'A couple of weeks is an understatement, it's felt like forever without you here.' She grasped my hand, moving her lips softly to my palm, taking a deep and steadying breath. Her smile edged awake, her eyes still closed tightly. Oh how I had missed her touch, that smile, those lips. She was mine and I was hers. Counting down the days and filling them with anything and everything that would keep my mind busy had finally come to an emotional end.

'You don't know how much I have missed you.' As she had a habit of doing, she spoke aloud my thoughts. The tears in her eyes threatened to travel south, her trembling lip too enticing. I took her in my arms and before she could utter another word, before her tears could stain her shirt, I kissed her. Boy, did I kiss her.

I had one arm wrapped firmly around her tiny waist and the other across her cheek, my fingers tousling her hair. Her feet were now clear of the floor, and if I hadn't needed to breathe I would have held her there forever. Her sweet, balmy lips were no longer a happy memory but a deep, all-encompassing yearning. I pushed harder, as did she, my grip on her tightening as the fear of waking up and not having her there in front of me edged into the forefront of

ASCEND   *Billie Jade Kermack*

my mind.

'Hello to you too. So you missed me too, then?' She smiled broadly and my heart lit up in response, its magnetic counterpart now at arm's reach.

'Me, miss you? Maybe just a little bit' I lied, hating that there was now inches of space between us, inches that felt like miles.

'I need you to stay here – right here.' I placed my hands on her waist and pulled her into me, her body cushioned comfortably against mine. The space between us was no longer a problem.

'You look so tired, Gracie' I mused, running my fingers over her cheekbones, silently apologising. She was perfect as she was, and this added weight loss just made her look fragile and doll-like.

'I'm fine, just tired is all. I didn't realise what you going away would do to me.' She smiled, but the deep-rooted pang of guilt that I felt at seeing what my absence had caused her made me want to hug her. More importantly – I wanted to feed her.

THIRTY-ONE
ೞ)cx

GRACE

'If I eat another piece of chicken I think my stomach might explode. So what was with the whole show entrance?' I asked, pushing my feta salad around my paper plate and smiling at the memory of him making his way through the crowd towards me like Moses through the parted Red Sea.

'I wanted to show you how much I missed you. One of my happiest moments was with you in Bournemouth, so the song choice seemed fitting.' He beamed proudly, patting himself on the back for successfully surprising me.

'You don't know how to do anything by halves, do you?'

'Not when it comes to you, Miss Gracie. You send me crazy, and I just can't seem to help myself.'

'You're a right romantic git when you want to be' I chuckled, pushing my plate aside.

ASCEND

Billie Jade Kermack

'I love you, you know' he said, taking me off guard. I knew it to be true, but his unguarded, heartfelt admission made me want to sob all the same. Happy tears, of course.

'Funny thing... I love you too' I beamed, knowing I would never be able to truly explain to Beau just how much he meant to me; even amidst the danger, how much joy he had brought to my life.

ೞಒ

Now locked in Beau's arms as we swayed to the music, women around us still *oohing, aahing* and gossiping animatedly with their friends about his performance, I felt sated. As had been common in my life lately, the warming feeling didn't last long. Amongst the crowd, amongst the happiness, like a rotting weed in a garden filled with blossoming roses – there she hovered.

Not alive, past dead, stuck helplessly somewhere in-between. Her congealed blood dripped from her shaking fingertips onto the dancefloor, pooling around the feet of an unaware nearby couple who smiled widely, kissing and frolicking about the vermilion-bathed floor with absolutely no idea what I could see.

I contained my freak-out, moving Beau around so that he was facing her. I had to know if he could see her. If she was a ghost and not a figment of my imagination, he would see her. It wouldn't be long before I had to tell him everything;

ASCEND

this was it, I had to test his Spidey-senses.

I frowned and solemnly lay my head on his chest with my eyes shut tight. I was devastated that this evening, an out-of-this-world, ripped from a romantic film evening would now be forever ruined, surprisingly not by the gift that he possessed but the damaged spirit that had attached itself to me uninvited. I peeked up at him with bated breath, waiting for his reaction as he looked over my shoulder to where she was hovering.

'So it looks like Amelia and Jack are still going strong' Beau chuckled, tightening his grip around my waist and pulling my hip to fit snugly into the contours of his muscular frame.

Ignoring the obvious twang of desire, my body's natural reaction as we grew closer, I whipped around sharply. Amelia and Jack were embracing lovingly, her face nestled in his chest, his cheek on her forehead. She was still there, next to them, staring wide-eyed at me, beckoning me to acknowledge her. Taunting me silently with the truth of her existence. But then I saw it, in her eyes: *fear*. She didn't look scary to me then, she looked saddened; petrified, forced to watch everyone live life instead of having to endure death, like her.

For the first time since she had visited me I felt sorry for the human she once was, the horrific ordeal that had led to her untimely death and the lonely spirit she had been forced to become. Compelled to spend an eternity as a trapped soul in limbo, forced to watch the world move on around her. The cruelty of it made a solitary breath hitch uncomfortably in my throat.

'You okay, beautiful? Fancy grabbing a cab? I'm beat' Beau asked as he kissed my forehead. The pulling desire to be alone with him briefly shunned any sane thought; or *insane* thought, come to that.

'Sure' I smiled, still unable to take my eyes off of her. It was strange that Beau couldn't see her, wasn't it? Did that mean she wasn't not a ghost? Better question – did that mean I was officially crazy?

ಸಂಡ

BEAU

'Is there something on your mind, something I should know?' My words were heavy as I searched her eyes for something she was holding back from me. Something about her was different; I just had to find out what it was she was hiding. Her silence only fuelled my suspicions. 'I'm serious Grace, are you keeping a secret from me?'

'This isn't the time, for now I would like to just forget it. I haven't seen you for what feels like an unbearable eternity so please, for tonight, can we just be... together?'

ASCEND

Billie Jade Kermack

If ever there was a sentence that held too much confusing weight, this was it. Something was definitely wrong but I knew what she was feeling, that desire to be *together*. I had missed her terribly, and after wrestling with my conscience I decided that whatever was going on, it would still be there tomorrow. For now we were alone, and as my protective guard over Grace fell away for another day, I took her hand in mine.

'Is it another ghost thing?' I pushed, without realising what I was saying.

'I'd rather kiss these lips than talk about ghosts.' She spoke softly, sultrily and a little authoritatively as she ran her thumb over my slightly-parted lips. The noise that came from her next as she closed her eyes and I kissed her thumb was a groan, a yearning sigh of want and desire. I felt compelled to be as close to her as was humanly possible. The intoxication of her smell, her light but determined touch; I wanted to drink her in slowly, savouring every inch of her. I wanted to feel her hands intertwined with mine, then breaking free and exploring my skin.

ASCEND *Billie Jade Kermack*

GRACE

His hands slipped slowly over the creases of my shirt and settled into place – one at the base of my spine, the other wandering hesitantly back up my side to cup my face. As his fingers danced over the bare skin around my collarbone, my neck, each breath I exhaled was laboured. A flash-fire of explosions erupted in the pit of my stomach, every nerve throughout my body alert and waiting as he pushed a strand of my hair behind my ear.

Even such an otherwise ordinary act sent a rippling sensation setting my body alight. I responded to his every move, enjoying the effect my reaction to his touch was having on him; my responses were slaves to his tutelage as my body bowed down to his. My smile knew no bounds as I gazed up into those diamond-blue eyes of his.

'I want to kiss you so much right now' he chuckled, his voice a whisper, his lips just mere inches from my ear. I fought to keep my eyes open, savouring the feeling of his warm breath on my skin, my head dipping back slightly as I stifled a sigh. I knew I had missed Beau, but it wasn't until this moment that I realised just how much.

Without a second thought my lips were on his, sweetly and

ASCEND *Billie Jade Kermack*

reservedly at first, instantly reminding me of our first kiss, but then without warning shifting into bone-shuddering intensity – we grasped each other possibly too tightly as the space between our bodies dwindled. My hands wandered purposefully up into his hair, my knuckles grazing the stubble along his jaw. I didn't want to pull away but my lungs begged for oxygen, and the lightness in my head forced me to buckle under the pressure. I hadn't realised it but Beau had already lifted me up into his arms, my tiptoes every so often touching the floor. He lowered me down slowly back to reality, my body running over his.

I was with him. That was all that mattered, and for once, the darkness wasn't scary.

THIRTY-TWO
∞☙

'I could stay here forever' I whispered, my face nestled into my pillow, my eyes fixed on Beau lying next to me. I wiggled over, snuggling into the crook of his outstretched arm. His eyes were closed but as his lips curled into a smile, I knew he was awake. I traced my index finger agonisingly slowly in circles around his chest, feeling his quickening heartbeat. He ran his free hand through his ruffled bed-hair, stretching his torso beneath me.

'Forever sounds good to me' he said as he leant over me, his fingers exploring my jawline, eyes dancing over my exposed neck. Any and all words were immediately stifled. Teasing me and enjoying it, he slowly made his descent, his lips ready to meet mine and now mere inches from my face.

Knock, knock.

'Beau, when you're up and... decent. A man named Albert has just called for you. I hope you won't mind that I answered it, but you left your phone in the living room. Apparently you're late, I suggest you get a move on! I made you a coffee in the kitchen.' My mum yelled through my

ASCEND *Billie Jade Kermack*

closed bedroom door, her voice muffled by the wood.

My embarrassment caused me to giggle uncontrollably as Beau's face shone a bright crimson. He rushed about the room, grabbing his jeans from the pile on the floor and his crumpled T-shirt from the end of the bed frame.

I cocked my head to one side and questioned, 'Albert?' Beau mirrored my movement with a smile and replied 'lecturer' in that special little way he did to get me well and truly off of a line of questioning.

'Love you always' he whispered into my ear, planting a quick, chaste kiss on my lips. Before I could settle back down into bed and Beau could shut the door behind him my computer pinged, notifying me of a new e-mail. 'Looks like I'm not the only one who has to get up' he teased, pulling the door closed. I heard his hurried footsteps beating against the stairs as he made his way down and out of the front door, my mum practically throwing the beaker of coffee at him as he passed.

10.22AM

Grace,

I've been thinking about everything we discussed and I think you should contact Raoul Martinez. He works at the hospital and is a creative genius, he's the talent that reconstructs unidentifiable patients or DOAs.

ASCEND

Billie Jade Kermack

He can draw a person's likeness just from examining their bone structure, or even from description alone. I'm sure he can help us find out who or what it is we're dealing with. I'm guessing Beau's just left (late as usual) so get your butt out of bed, get dressed and get on it, he's expecting your call. We're one step closer to sorting this all out! 0208 – 516 – 2323.

Love and stuff sweetie,

Gwen xx

Wow – she is good! Beau's side of the bed wasn't even cold, she couldn't have been more right if she had tried. But then, Gwen never ceased to amaze me.

సౌర

With my bed shoddily made (the throw cushions, as usual, the bane of this task) and my jeans and navy baseball T-shirt combo now replacing the Romanesque wrapped white bedsheet, I sat at my computer table and searched for my phone amongst a trolley-load of papers – coursework, university applications and photography notes. I grabbed at a stapled wad of papers aptly entitled *'What Was Lost Is Now Found'*, the first draft of an English essay that was covered in scribbled red notes and Post-its. It had never made it off my table; I had spent a whole twelve hours trying to mould it into an A Level-worthy piece of work, but had

ASCEND *Billie Jade Kermack*

finally accepted how terribly vapid it was and branded it pointless.

With the title jumping off the page and into my reality, there it was: my elusive phone, the piece of touch-screen technology that usually just frustrated me. If I was going to get anything done, this wasn't the place to be. With my phone in one hand, I grabbed a pencil out of desk caddy and wrote a note to my mother:

> *Going to the library – be back soon, got phone!*
>
>   *Grace xx*

ಸಿಠಿ

> *'Yea, when this flesh and heart shall fail,*
> *and mortal life shall cease,*
> *I shall possess, within the veil,*
> *a life of joy and peace.'**

Before I could get up from my swivel chair, the radio kicked to life from across the room. The song was seductive, intensely growing to a crescendo peak as the blue bars signalling the increasing volume continued to climb on the radio screen. I shuddered as the woman's soft but evocative voice tickled over my skin in waves. I didn't know why, but I felt sleepy and alert all at the same time, conflicting

---

*   *'Amazing Grace', John Newton 1779*

ASCEND
Billie Jade Kermack

emotions tugging at my brain. My hands were heavy and stiff, my head light. *Remote!* I thought, realising I had already started my search as I quickly threw things across my desk and out of the way. Suddenly there was another deafening component to fight, the whimsical tinkling of the song's string section.

Ring, ring. Ring, ring.

I pulled open the desk drawer and pushed about its contents in a bid to find the radio remote; *loud* was now an understatement. I pulled a dried wad of bubblegum from the numbered buttons whilst rapidly pushing the volume button, so the song eventually provided a hushed backdrop to the ringing of my mobile. I accepted the call.

'What happened Grace, why didn't you call Raoul?' Gwen sounded impatient and, oddly for her, a little confused – it wasn't common for Gwen not to know what was going on. Her gifts pretty much secured her a permanent position at the table of all-knowing.

'Wait a minute. I only got your email about twenty minutes ago, give me a chance!' I chuckled uneasily, still feeling a little out of whack. My thighs felt stiff and aching as I stretched them out under my desk.

'Grace, I sent that over to you hours ago.' Her impatience cooled as concern flooded her voice.

I looked up at the clock on my wall. *3.28PM* I said almost

ASCEND *Billie Jade Kermack*

internally as I racked my brain for some – ANY – rational explanation. 'I don't understand, I was just writing... and then my phone...' I was confused and a little panicked, which made my head hurt. I still had the pencil gripped tightly in my left hand, the nib now worn down to a messy stub, my fingers a smudged, burnt grey. *I'm not left-handed* I thought, briefly forgetting the extent of the situation.

Was I in a daze, did I blackout? What's happening to me? Then I saw it; I saw where my missing hours had gone, what I had been doing without even realising it.

Droplets of blood, slow and steady at first but becoming an unrelenting flow as my panic grew, hit the sheets of paper on the table in front of me. The bright crimson splatters looked cartoonish, the blood almost too red, but this was not what sent a shiver rushing up my spine or caused the hair on the back of my neck to stand on end.

Her charcoal-grey stare, sad and alight with loss, was burning into me, reaching into my chest and playing a dangerous game with my soul. My hands shook uncontrollably in my fear-fuelled rush of anxiety. *Who did this?*

# THIRTY-THREE
ಸಂ

'Gwen... I have... I have to call you back.' I didn't wait for her response and disconnected the call, my eyes still drawn to my blood. After wiping my nose clean with my sleeve I rubbed at the blood soaking into the crisp white paper, smearing it rather than clearing it from the page. I rearranged the pages on my desk in front of me. There were at least twenty, and all were the same. The drawing was a perfect artist's likeness, skilled lines, contoured shading; it was the woman I had been seeing.

Without the brutality that I had seen when she visited me her face was beautiful, her eyes shining pools, her rosebud lips, although straight and emotionless, defined and perfectly in keeping with the idea of an English rose.

I looked closer at the sketches. Their detail was mesmerising; every strand of her long wavy hair and laugh line around her big eyes was there. Each flicker of an eyelash individually drawn, the uneven bow of her lips marred with a small scar, each stroke steady and sure. This wasn't just strange, it was extraordinary. Me, who got an E in GCSE Art; me, who found it difficult to draw a believable

ASCEND   Billie Jade Kermack

stick-man.

After looking through the top layer of papers, I came to a selection of drawings that weren't so beautiful. I didn't know how I had done it, but the brutality which punctured and tore at her skin in the picture was so believable that if held at arm's reach, it could have been a photograph of the spirit.

Around my feet were more crumpled pieces of paper, drawings that I had discarded. I unravelled one after another; like a puzzle, they all fit together. Part of an eye, a rounded chin, a section of wavy hair. After I was finished and had pieced the drawings together, they covered pretty much every inch of my floor. It was her. She wanted me to know what she had looked like.

Now, I had to listen. She had become increasingly impatient – there was something she was screaming at me that I just wasn't getting, and I didn't want to know what she would put me through when she had finally had enough. The radio played erratically as it searched for a station. Every so often a tune popped to life, only for static to take over again, as if searching for something in particular.

'I once was lost but now am found,
was blind, but now I see.'

With its choice made, the words coming through the speakers were now full of purpose and meaning. The volume once again began to rise on its own though the

ASCEND
Billie Jade Kermack

remote lay untouched on my desk, confirming my fears.

I stood up and edged away from the papers lined up on the floor as though they were toxic, reminders of the world I had fallen into. *I shouldn't be able to do this, it isn't down to me to fix this.* To my surprise, I snapped. I screwed the pieces up into balls and stuffed them into the waste basket, as though this would quiet the raging hysteria in my head. I left the drawings on the table in a chaotic mess. *I have to get out of here, I can't be here right now* I thought as I grabbed my coat, my bag and car-keys from my bed. 'I don't want to see, I don't want to see!' I shouted into my empty room before slamming the door behind me.

'Grace, are you OK?' my mum asked. I had almost bounded into her on the stairs as she struggled under the weight of awashing basket filled with freshly-ironed clothes in her arms. The radio from behind my closed bedroom door spluttered in defeat and switched itself off, the silence not as comforting as I would have hoped.

'Neat trick Grace, hiding the remote in your pocket?' she chuckled. I attempted to follow suit but my laugh was uncomfortable, to say the least. 'Is there something wrong, sweetheart?' she added, her concern clear.

'I'm fine. I'll be back soon. I've really got to go... and see Gwen.' I kissed her urgently on the cheek and kept on rushing down the stairs.

I stopped suddenly, my hand grasping the cold steel of the

ASCEND
Billie Jade Kermack

front-door handle. The long mirror fixed to the wall beside the door held a memory that I hadn't thought about for a while. That night last year when Beau had taken me out for my birthday, the night I had discovered just how much he loved me. The night had been magical and tragic all rolled into one, a heady onslaught of elation, desire, confusion and sheer terror. That night I had been blissfully unaware as to where my life was heading, how events would lead to... all this.

I moved my ruffled chestnut hair from my shoulders with a despondent sigh and it fell down my back, leaving my features exposed. I looked intently at my reflection, seeing how I had changed in such a small amount of time. The romantic notion that my life was my own – that I, Grace O'Callaghan, decided my fate – was now just a mere memory of a childhood fantasy. I had seen things incomprehensible to most normal people.

A pang of jealousy hit me without warning. I wanted Beau in my life; no, *needed* him in my life, but just one day of not knowing about all this, the ghosts, the Shadows, the *evil*. I would have done anything for just one more of those days. My eyes seemed darker than I remembered, the charcoal shading below them revealing my stress and anxiety. My hair was dull and as I curled it around my fingers it draped over my shoulders in rough chocolate waves, lacking life, an extension of my worry. The once giddy, love fuelled glow in my cheeks was now non-existent, washed away by long nights of hauntings, illness and masked feeling of loneliness. I was a shadow of my former self and I was clueless as to

ASCEND   *Billie Jade Kermack*

how to stop the decline.

CRASH! I heard something hit the floor from my room upstairs, the white crystal-draped chandelier above me shuddering, causing its elongated gems to tinker like wind chimes.

'Mum! Mum, are you OK?' I shouted in a fit of panic, dropping my bag at the foot of the stairway and taking the stairs two at a time, my breathing laboured as my foot hit the last step. I could never have anticipated the state I found my mum in, could never have guessed how much my secrets could affect her.

The pile of laundry was now in a jumbled mess on my carpet, the basket on its side next to my mother's feet as she sat on the edge of my bed, a few of the papers grasped tightly in her clenched fist. I edged towards her like I would a frightened puppy, who would react by cowering away if I got too close too quickly.

THIRTY-FOUR

ଚ୍ଚର୍ଷ

'I don't understand. Where did... who... how did you get these?' My mother waved a handful of drawings in front of me, pleading for an answer. There were tears in her eyes, her question confrontational and harsh. The balled-up papers showing the cuts, bruising and burnt flesh were still in the bin. I was pleased my mum hadn't found those – that would have been harder to explain. She stroked her finger lovingly over the paper, across the woman's face. I was unresponsive, trying to think of a plausible answer. *Why had my mum reacted the way she did?*

'You know her?' I asked.

'Linney Rose' she said with a half-smile, a secret that hadn't left her lips for eighteen years still weighing down one side, sadness clearly still present as she stared at the drawing. 'It was only your father that called her Linney, everyone else knew her as...'

'Alison Rose Dwight' I interrupted, taking her off-guard. The horror on her face was evidence enough that I had finally correctly deciphered a puzzle piece in this mystery. I knew that name. A flashback of Gwen's voice as she read out the list of victim's names from the hospital files rang loudly in my head:

'Alison Rose Dwight, 21, murdered 1991'

'How did you know that?' A rogue tear dribbled down my mother's cheek, her eyes alight with fear; a fear of finally speaking the truth? Maybe even just the fear of knowing the truth.

'Nobody called her Alison, she'd hated it ever since she was little. She introduced herself as Lindsay from the moment she called talk. Your father called her Linney; he had done since he was small, he couldn't pronounce the *d* in Lindsay. It sort of stuck, it was a thing they shared.' She chuckled at the memory and at the unguarded thought of my father. The jumbled montage of all the clues I had been given finally started to make sense. It all came down to my family's past.

'Alison Rose Dwight is actually my Aunt Lindsay?' I muttered faintly, secretly fearing that if I spoke the words aloud it would somehow make them more true, that I somehow held the power to make it all go away if I wanted to. How hadn't I seen it before? We had pictures of Aunt Lindsay in photo albums that I had flicked through so many times, and yet I still hadn't put it together.

I always thought Glen had tortured me because of what Beau could see, that his gift was why I had to endure all this

ASCEND *Billie Jade Kermack*

pain. It was now clear that Glen's link to me was a family secret; one which, if I had known about it earlier, could maybe have saved me from all this.

When Glen had tried to inhabit my body last year as he strapped me to a chair and tortured me, he had told me that I resembled one of his victims. He may have been sadistic, but at least he wasn't a liar. *Nothing about that is comforting!* my inner voice bellowed, the panic surging through my body at an alarming speed.

I remembered the words he had carved into my skin, that the *father – my father – could not save them both*. He couldn't save his sister who Glen had brutally murdered, and he couldn't protect me as Glen held me hostage. I was a pawn in a large-scale game of chess that I hadn't even known I was playing, moved around on a whim by a spirit who enjoyed watching me crumble.

'Grace Rose O'Callaghan; I'm guessing I'm named after her?' My mother was quiet, her lips still trembling as she clasped them in her fingers to still her nerves. 'Or my middle name, at least.' How had I not figured it out?

Glen had not only brutally murdered my aunt, he had left a black mark on my family's existence, secrets manifested from pain and lies. As the truth broke free, my world, all that I knew, began to dwindle; a flame was extinguished as the knowledge of what my family had been forced to endure became my only thought.

ASCEND *Billie Jade Kermack*

'She didn't die of cancer, Grace' my mother said solemnly, wiping her blotchy, tear-soaked face with a tissue. Now of course I knew just how big a lie it all was, but I couldn't let my mother know that I knew the truth. It would have meant answering a lot more questions, ones that if I didn't have any believable answers for.

ಸಿಂಧ

After an hour of wandering down the blood-soaked paths of memory lane with my mother, I decided I had to tell Gwen everything; she would know what to do next. I ran all the way there, almost getting run down by a bike messenger in the process. All the while, I was still muddling through all the new information that I now had – or at least the sense I had made from the information we already had.

I still couldn't really believe that my aunt had been one of Glen's victims; that I was in some way connected to the spirit who had been haunting me, who had inflicted such pain on me. I bounded through Gwen's front door without knocking. The sofa stopped me and I leant against it panting, the drawing of my Aunt Lindsay still clasped, folded, in my hand.

Gwen walked into the room down the main stairway, rubbing a flannel over her forehead and behind her neck. She looked awfully pale.

'I had a vision today, I think you know what I'm talking about.' I nodded in response, realising that the speech I had

ASCEND *Billie Jade Kermack*

been practising on my way over wasn't needed. Gwen, as always, was a step ahead.

'Get Beau on the phone. He needs to be here, you need to tell him everything now' she said, shuffling through the archway into the kitchen. Gulping down a fresh glass of water, she added: 'I think it's time we had a chat with Aunt Linney.'

THIRTY-FIVE

For the first time since my hauntings had begun, I was going to be willing the spirit of my dead Aunt Linney to visit me. Safe to say I wasn't keen on the idea, but I knew deep down it was a must in order to set my life back on the straight and narrow path of normalcy. OK, so maybe not *normalcy*, but the less death-inducing end of the scale would be nice.

Telling Beau every little detail of what had been happening to me had been a cause for concern. Once again, I witnessed the downward spiral into guilt that left him with a sombre expression which he tried, and failed, to hide behind an uneasy smile. I soothed his worries as best as I could, and having Gwen on hand to soften the blow had meant that he concentrated on how to fix the problem rather than who was to blame for bringing it into our lives.

Beau dumped Gwen's heavy drawstring bag of tricks onto the dusty floor of the abandoned lot and slowly span around, taking in the vast, decrepit warehouses that stood before us. The strawberry and honey-coloured sky felt oddly prescient and for what felt like too briefly, a smidgen of hope sprang in my stomach.

ASCEND

Billie Jade Kermack

'So, can I ask why we didn't just do this at home?' Beau questioned, kicking a rusted Coke can amongst the light dusting of dirt beneath his feet.

'Beau. Firstly, your tone there didn't go unnoticed, so watch it. Secondly, in order for us to conjure the spirit of Grace's aunt we need to summon her in a place that holds some history for her, a place she's familiar with.'

'Did she work around here or something?' I asked. The worn signs for an old chocolate factory, *Burt's Blacksmiths* and *Denny's Car Garage* were pinned high above the rusting, shuttered doors of the now-abandoned collection of warehouses around us.

'I thought you knew. This is... this is where she... died.'

I hadn't even considered the possibility. Gwen's words were sobering and my surroundings, though bathed in the warmth of the sun, were now eerily unsettling.

'I found a couple of pages shoved into one of the other victim's files – I didn't get to read it all, but they were the ones missing from your aunt's file.' She pulled the papers from her knapsack and handed them to me. Now, I saw them in a whole new light; they weren't just victims on a page any more. All at once I felt overcome with grogginess, like I was nursing a severe hangover. My knees threatened to buckle and the files slipped from my hands, hitting the floor, the papers now spread over the dirt.

ASCEND

Billie Jade Kermack

Beau rushed to my side; holding me with my arm around his neck, he walked me over to the weathered bench outside one of the factories. Once he was sure I could sit there unaided, he went about picking up all the papers before the wind had a chance to whisk them away.

'How about I look after these? You can have a look at them later, when we're done here' he said with a forced half-smile, grabbing my hand to reassure me.

High above me, there stood a carved statue of a nearly wingless angel. Planted firmly in its low, crudely-bricked enclosure, the stained remnants of a fountain mixed with rainwater were still present around her feet. Her form, probably once sleek and flawless, was now crumbling; hacked away at by the elements, each crevice of the rock now covered with mottled green and black growths.

I inquisitively reached out towards her outstretched hand, which seemed to invite my presence. Upon impact, a surge of heat vibrated painfully up my arm, leaving confused receptors in its wake as it continued on down my spine. I was tethered to her, my grip on the steel-cold stone tightening as though my life depended on the connection. A blinding flash of blood-red flooded my mind like oil in water, its surface momentarily impenetrable as it sussed out this foreign intruder. But then access was granted, and *there* – as clear as day, a vision of my previous visitor. Her slender, shaking, vermilion-spotted hand was holding onto the angel tightly, as I was, dirt embedded beneath her

ASCEND

Billie Jade Kermack

broken fingernails...

'Hey, Grace.' The sound of his voice made my heart swell in response, and I was back. I cut the connection, rubbing my palm furiously as the burning heat refused to leave my skin. However much it hurt, I pushed my hand down into my pocket as Beau caught up with me.

'Everything okay Gracie?' he asked, stroking a speck of dirt from my cheek.

'All tickety-boo!' I lied, my smile forced, but masking perfectly the sneaking concern lying behind it.

൫൯

Our only source of light and warmth, the burning wood crackled and hissed in the metal drum, sending golden sparks floating aimlessly up and into the cool night breeze. The sun had made its descent across the acres of dirt-covered wasteland that surrounded us. The murky clouds, bruised purple and blue, almost completely shrouded the crescent moon that hung low in the starless sky. I was now wearing Beau's black leather biker jacket, but even that left me chilly.

'I don't mean to push this, but some of us like having all of our fingers and toes intact, so do you think we might be able to start this soon?' Beau smirked, cupping his hands around his mouth and blowing his sweet, warm breath into them.

ASCEND

Billie Jade Kermack

'Not long now – you could help' Gwen mused, pulling free from her bag four white candles spotted with dried, dripping wax from previous use. With her tools laid out in front of her, Gwen began to set the scene. With every minute that crept by, the realisation of exactly what we were there to do sent a surging gut reaction like nerves fluttering aimlessly around my body.

An engraved ivory-handled blade: check. Four white candles: check. One of those smelly stick things that burn slowly: unfortunately, check. (I wasn't altogether clear on why these had to be used, but I thought twice about asking.) Gwen's star-embossed magic book that had an aversion to having any stranger as a travelling companion.

It was an arcane object that seemed, even though I knew it was impossible, to have a life of its own. It lay on a mauve shawl on the floor next to Gwen with a suspicious and cautious air about it. It couldn't move, I knew that, but from what I could witness out of the corner of my eye, I might have sworn differently. As Gwen walked round, marking a circle in the dirt – first with the dagger, then with the salt – it seemed to move with her, like a loyal puppy-dog following its master.

'It's drawn to her,' Beau whispered from behind me.

'Huh?'

'The book, it senses Gwen's presence. You have to remember that Gwen comes from a long line of witches, her ancestral

ASCEND
Billie Jade Kermack

line makes Houdini look like a crappy £5-an-hour clown at a kid's birthday party. I don't think even I know what she can really do.'

'Na-marouté, Fo-tu-mayacré...' Gwen walked round the circle with a stick made of bound, burning leaves and herbs, repeating her chant over and over again. The thick white smoke from the lit end billowed around us, its musky stench filling my nose, forcing me to gag. At the north, south, east and west points around the circle, as on the face of a compass, Gwen had drawn a selection of symbols that I remembered from the Book of Aurora. I put my hand up to my nose as she passed us, the smell still turning my stomach.

'It's to cleanse the space, not the most fragrant but it gets the job done. I once knew a guy once who lost a leg because he forgot to add wolfsbane,' he whispered. I giggled, not immediately realising how serious he was being.

'Wait, what? Are you pulling my leg?' I knew my mistake the second the words left my mouth.

'That's what he said!' we both said in unison, as I predicted his lame joke. I laughed, he laughed; it was all very *When Harry Met Sally. Boy, I love this man*! I thought with a smile as he moved his hand up to my chin, pushing my hair away from my neck. His fingertips grazing my throat, my breath hitched a little as he moved up towards my ear. 'Oh Beau, I love you' I mused, briefly lost in the moment.

ASCEND
Billie Jade Kermack

'I love...'

'Beau, can you grab me some sage from the bag please?' Gwen said, interrupting Beau mid-sentiment. She lit the final two candles and edged down onto the floor next to me, closing her eyes and taking in a deep, calming breath. I stifled my giggles as Beau poked his tongue out at me. I waved my arms at him to stop as my laugh teetered behind my pursed lips, ready to escape if I let it. Each ridiculous, contorted expression on his face pushed me further.

'I may have my eyes closed but I know exactly what you two are playing at.' Beau and I shared a complicit smile and regained our composure. But something was niggling at me, gnawing like a hungry rodent at my subconscious.

'Grace. I need you to open yourself up to her, welcome her,' Gwen murmured. My reaction to what she had told me was surprising to us all. Suddenly I felt anger boiling up inside of me, as everything I had born witness to, everything I had been forced to endure, bubbled to the surface. The playful exchanges with Beau moments before were now long gone.

'She has to know you want her here with us' Gwen added, realising that she was losing me and my co-operation.

'Welcome her? Why should I? I don't want her here – that's the truth. Even when she's not around, even when I don't see her, she's there, haunting me. I know I'm not meant to, but a part of me hates her. She may be my aunt, but I hate what she has put me through. I hate that this is how I'm

ASCEND   *Billie Jade Kermack*

spending my Friday evening, I hate that sleeping or waking, I have no safe haven.' Beau pulled me into the warmth of his arms and silenced me the only way he knew how, with a kiss that for a second lulled my heartbeat into an uneven but calmer pace.

'That's a hell of a lot of hate, Miss Gracie. I know you think that's how you feel, and if you didn't I would find it strange, but you are a lot stronger than you give yourself credit for. You're meant to be feeling a little crazy right now, it's only natural.' Beau spoke softly, the rhythm of his words soothing. He pulled my hand up to his parted lips, his warm breath grazing my knuckles as the tension in them ebbed away.

'But...' I tried to interrupt, attempting to fight my waning frustration. He clasped my hands tightly in his, his eyes never leaving mine.

'But nothing, Grace. You forget I know about all this, I've lived it for practically all of my life. I know you can do this. You don't see yourself how I see you. That beautiful smile' – his thumb grazed my lips – 'that Nancy Drew desire to shed light on anything that doesn't move fast enough. Your beautiful, big...' he paused with a cheeky grin '... heart' he finished, placing his palm on my chest. 'And the legs. Whoa, the legs!'

'What?' The surprise was evident in my voice.

'Your stunning long legs! They're a welcome distraction,

ASCEND *Billie Jade Kermack*

pretty much always' he chuckled, his eyes wide and inviting. He leaned in close to whisper his last point. 'You are not meant to understand all this,. You don't have a manual, it's not meant to be easy. I *know* how hard all this is and it's my job, as the best boyfriend ever, to guide you through it the best I can. Now let's get on with it and conjure up the spirit of your dead, murdered aunt.' Although the situation called for serious attention, his last words were childish and light-hearted. A smile broke on his lips, those cute dimples gracing his cheeks momentarily.

'What... what if I can't help her?'

'Then you can't help her. For this moment in time, you have to deal with what comes your way, however uneasy it makes you feel. You are about to get a glimpse into the spirit world, you have been given the gift to help her rest in peace. You're only human. Remember, I will be right here holding your hand. This will all be over soon, you will be fine – I promise.' His eyes were wide, the blue in them now a misty grey. Although his words were sincere, I wasn't sure whether he completely believed them.

'Hey, love-bugs. I need silence now, any more interruptions could break the spell' Gwen chirped, a small smile on her face. I giggled, briefly forgetting what we were there to do.

'Earth, air, water and fire, we call on the elements here and all the power they hold. With the protection of Aurora I ask for strength, and the guidance to summon one who no longer walks this earth in solid form, neither breathes the

ASCEND *Billie Jade Kermack*

air, feels the fire nor needs the water. I implore your aid in bringing her to us. I summon thee, Alison Rose Dwight. Come to us so we can learn of your fate. Answer our questions and find agreeable solace in our presence. Aurora the almighty, please protect us from those who may mean us harm. Guide our words and thoughts and channel who we seek.' She placed four clear crystals inside the circle as she spoke; for a second or two as they made contact with the ground they hummed a translucent grass-green, an acceptance of sorts.

I hung on her every word and watched the world bow to her whims. A stream of water from a hose tap on the side of the old car workshop surrounded us with a moat, its boundaries rigid in a perfect circle around us, mirroring Gwen's circle of salt. The ground began to shake around the four ancient symbols that Gwen had marked out, sending conical wisps of dirt up into the air. A light breeze weaved around us and the hairs on the back of my neck stood to attention. The last of the elements to concede was fire as the candle flames rose steadily, higher and higher, at least five inches above the wick.

'Earth, air, water and fire, we thank you. Aurora, we bow to your powers. Empower us now with all your might. Please, help us seek the one we have beckoned and bring her here to us. To us, to us, to us. Bring the one we seek. To us, to us, to us. Alison Rose Dwight, we mean you no harm and invite you into our circle. We beseech you. Join us, join us, join us!'

ASCEND
Billie Jade Kermack

'Why isn't she talking? Can she hear us?' I asked impatiently, drumming my fingers on my knees. 'Maybe she wont answer to that name. Call her Linney, my father always called her Linney.'

'Sometimes it takes time. We have to be patient, she has to know she can trust us. Names aside, if her connection is as strong as we believe it to be, then she is with us. The balls is in her court now, we have to wait and see if she wants to connect with us. I would usually conduct a séance on a familiar date for the spirit, but as you know, that part of the file was missing' Gwen said, dabbing her forehead with her white handkerchief.

From my back pocket, I pulled out the drawing I had done of my aunt whilst in a trance. The fold-lines were now worn and dishevelled, the charcoal lines slowly disappearing. I quickly folded it back up and pushed it down into my pocket for safe keeping.

'We need something more, this isn't enough to will her here.' As she finished her sentence, Gwen removed two photographs of my Aunt Linney from her satchel: one, the photo both the police and Glen had used as a victim reference and the second, a crime-scene shot of the aftermath of Glen's handiwork. The two were polar opposites of her existence. The happy, carefree expression in one was that of a young woman faced with the endless possibilities of what was to come in her life. The other was a canvas smeared black, a soul howling in pain, an expression devoid of any life, loneliness in its most cruel form. 'Is it completely necessary to have that photo there? It creeps me out', I shuddered.

'It wouldn't usually be my first choice but thanks to incompetent police officials, much like most of the other evidence in this case, a usable morgue photo apparently grew legs and wandered off whilst no-one was looking. I need a connection from her passing and unfortunately, without holding the weapon that took her life or invoking the spirit of the sadistic maniac who did this to her, this photo is our best and only option.' She spoke hurriedly, her words lacking their usual compassion as she wiped her sweaty brow with the sleeve of her brown woollen jumper, huffing with frustration as she continued to arrange objects around us. 'I'm sorry, I didn't mean to snap. Let's get on with it' she said, with a steadying breath and an apologetic half-smile.

THIRTY-SIX
ༀ

BEAU

Grace was out of her sitting position and up onto her feet in one swift, sweeping motion, her stare transfixed on the spirit of her aunt who was now levitating in the confines of the makeshift circle in front of us.

'Gwen, something is wrong, shut it down.' I didn't take my eyes off Grace as I spoke. My gut was screaming at me to do something, my body a slave to shock.

'It's OK Beau, she is just acknowledging her presence' Gwen muttered, holding up her hand to stop me bounding after her.

Grace took a step forward and crossed the shiny, almost mirrored, bubble-like barrier that separated us and her aunt. It flickered as it accepted her body into the circle.

'Wait. I don't understand... the circle is bound. She

ASCEND *Billie Jade Kermack*

shouldn't be able to touch it, let alone enter it,' Gwen said in amazement. She flicked her fingers in the air, beckoning to her book which obediently obliged and leapt to her side, exposing its pages. I attempted to follow Grace but was met with the force of the tank-strength field and denied entry.

'Grace, Grace, don't look at her. Grace, come to me.' I held out my hand, pleading for her to look at me, to break whatever hold she was under. I looked to Gwen, her expression perplexed as she assessed the situation, frantically racing through the thick pages of her spell book. The crystals began to throb an intense shade of red, the flames of the candles high and bright, the wick tips now a harsh, blazing blue.

'This is bad, isn't it?' I didn't know whether I was asking myself or Gwen, but I resorted to the only thing I could think of. I pounded my fists over and over against the almost-invisible force field until my knuckles tore at my flesh, charging at her enclosure repeatedly until my body recoiled with pain and I fell to the floor.

I wiped the sweat from my face, the blood from my knuckles now on my cheek. Out of breath and scrambling to my feet, my fear for Grace's safety now uncontrollable, I clenched my teeth and popped my shoulder back into its socket. There was nothing I could do to help her.

Gwen chanted frantically behind me, falling to her knees in a praying position. Her hands caressed the air just shy of the obstacle. and every word from her mouth grew more panicked. Her breathing was laboured, her forehead sweaty, her face getting paler by the second. It seemed the life was draining from her and I didn't know how much longer she could carry on.

'Grace, please, look at me. You can't go with her. You can't go where she is. I love you. Please!' I begged, I pleaded with every inch of my soul. I couldn't lose her, not now, not after everything we had been through. 'Follow my voice, come back to me' I pleaded.

'Beau, if she goes with her, we may never be able to get her back' Gwen warned.

'You have to reverse it, all I need is a second to grab her. Drop the barrier.' I hadn't realised it, but I was stifling tears that had pooled in my eyes.

I watched as Gwen used the double-edged dagger to first carve an ancient symbol into the dirt, then slice open the sweaty pink skin on the palm of her hand. She made a fist and a steady stream of blood droplets hit the dirt within the symbol, causing a reaction that sent up wisps of white smoke. Her chanting melted away distantly as I concentrated on Grace. *Is this the worry she felt when I left her, is this how much it hurt not knowing how to fix it?* I was bombarded by an onslaught of questions that I couldn't possibly answer.

'It's not working. Why isn't it working? I don't know how much longer I can hold on, Beau – Linney has created her

ASCEND   *Billie Jade Kermack*

own chamber in there. I don't know why, but she wants Grace all to herself. I can't seem to stop it.'

'Gwen, I will never ask you for anything else as long as I live. Please, I won't... I can't lose her.'

The spirit of Alison Rose Dwight reached out her hands, beckoning Grace to take another step towards her. If I hadn't seen it for myself, I would never have believed it. As Linney lay her hands upon Grace, I watched her transform: a pale liquid coursed up her transparent hands, warming them to a skin-like consistency. She was using Grace, her life force, stealing her essence. Like a faulty television set, her image flickered between that of a beautiful woman with long, flowing brown locks and crystal blue eyes and a bedraggled corpse, her skin torn and bloody.

'No, you can't have her! Don't you take her away from me' I barked, at a loss, knowing I was powerless to her whims. A glance from Grace and then from Linney, and it happened instantaneously. They were there, and then they weren't. With a flash of imploding energy the bubble separating us had turned into a solid portal and shattered, diamond shards flying everywhere. The crystals were now just grey rocks and the candles smoked, not a flame in sight. Grace had vanished, and the barrier had disappeared. I was now on my hands and knees in the circle, glass embedded in my hands as I pounded at the floor.

'I don't understand. Where is she? I promised her it would be fine.'

GRACE

'What really happened to you? That's why we're here right, you wanted me to know something?' I asked the spirit of my aunt apprehensively, questioning myself whether I really wanted to know the horrific truth. I had witnessed more than I should have, I had experienced a deep, depraved level of horror that I wouldn't have wished on my worst enemy. But I had come out the other side – fortunately, with my life intact. She hadn't been so lucky. At that moment I wanted to run, run away from it all and never look back; the spell she had me under was briefly dispelled. Sensing my desire to flee, she beckoned me towards her with an outstretched hand and a small, lopsided smile.

'You are the only one who can help me. I can't explain it to you, but I can show you.' Her voice was mesmerising and melodic. The words, dripping with intrigue, sounded somehow far away, like listening to a pre-recorded book on tape. I edged backwards again as her voice transported me back to that night on the beach, where I had welcomed my own death with bated breath; the night Linney had shown me what Glen had done to her.

ASCEND　　　　　　　　　　　　　　　*Billie Jade Kermack*

If things couldn't have got any stranger, the walking, talking, transparent image of my dead Aunt Linney was now mere inches away, her arms outstretched to either side of me. My mind was a flurry of manic thoughts and emotions. She clapped her now almost solid, milky-skinned hand round my wrist, my eyes wide and fixed on hers.

I felt almost strangely serene as a bright white light began to emanate from her hand; it tickled as it caressed my skin, the contact calming. My fear and apprehension slowly ebbed away as a feeling of contentment enveloped me. The white light bubbled up through my skin, sparking as its energy rippled through my pulsing veins.

With both her hands gripped around my wrists the skin beneath them began to pucker and blister, shrivelling as though her touch were scarring. Memories of when Glen had me tied down against my will were nothing to the reality of the identical marks around her wrists. I had to go with her – I had to help in any way I could. Didn't I?

'No, you can't have her! Don't you take her away from me.' Beau's voice pulled me back to reality, but only briefly. He looked panic-stricken and furious, his eyes filled with an awaiting flood of tears.

'You must come now. You have to help me', Linney whispered calmly. I didn't have a chance to answer Beau before, without warning, she held me close to her cold, battered body. It felt oddly solid, not at all like I had expected. The overpowering charcoal scent of burnt flesh

ASCEND *Billie Jade Kermack*

that suddenly reminded me of an overcooked spit-roast pig assailed my nostrils. As though hurtling towards the ground at great speed, my body travelling through space, my lungs argued at the foreign invasion of air, making me splutter and wheeze.

The transition made me feel heady and sick and I knew it was more than probable that once we stopped spinning, I would be greeted by my lunch. The wide open space around me quickly constricted, a vibrating mass of energy tightening around me. Beau and Gwen disappeared into the background, a swirl of vivid colours and unidentifiable shapes. Mirrored shards of broken glass seemed to circle us in mid-air, everything around us moving in slow motion, as though we were stuck at the heart of a tornado. Then we were gone.

THIRTY-SEVEN
ෂාෆ

The bright orange sun flooded in through the sparkling clean, floor-to-ceiling shop windows, the warming rays bathing the room in a golden hue. There were four desks in the centre of the large, open-plan room, all facing the windows. It could have been an office, a travel agent's maybe. Posters of beautiful holiday destinations littered the walls; waterfalls, mountains, the pyramids, the Great Wall of China – places that I longed to see, that I maybe would one day see, if I could keep myself alive that long. Four women sat at the desks, each one tapping away at their old-school computer keyboards and nattering, the radio blasting a Blondie tune in the background.

'We're definitely not in Kansas anymore!' I muttered, strangely remembering the entire plot of the *Wizard of Oz* with great clarity. I was clearly stunned as the collection of pictures ended up in my brain, then struggled to add two plus two and not end up with seven.

'I've seen that look on your face on others – things work a little differently here. The most inane memory can be your most poignant. Kind of one of the downsides of all this. As long as you listen to me, you will leave here with your brain functioning.' I felt an odd shiver up my back as she finished her sentence, an out-of-place smile curling only slightly at the corners of her mouth.

'Will Beau be okay? He looked really panicked, I don't want to worry him' I asked, banishing my building fear for a moment I tugged at my necklace. I ran my fingers over the wound silver chain, remembering the panic on his face as I left him standing there without an explanation.

'It will all be fine... soon' she replied, her stare now transfixed ahead of us as she passed me to get a better look at what was going on inside the room.

ಜಯ

My Aunt Linney – deceased – giggled, which made me jump. The soft and otherwise flattering lighting did nothing for her. She was forced to exist with the brutality of what Glen had subjected her to, her appearance a constant reminder of the life he had stolen from her. Spending some quality time with my Aunt Linney, I began to see beyond the bumps, bruises and obvious torture that was clear on her burnt, broken skin. Sensing my eyes on her, she glanced back over her shoulder at me.

'I know how I look, but don't worry, they can't see us' she mused, drinking in the happy-go-lucky atmosphere with a deep breath and a beaming smile. Memories of the fear she had instilled in me all those times she had visited me were

ASCEND *Billie Jade Kermack*

slowly drifting away.

'You haven't visited this memory much, have you?' I asked, my eyes transfixed on her as she eyed the scene dreamily. Even if only for a moment a glint of hope lingered in her eyes, dispelling her usual molten air of fear and sadness.

'More times than I would have you know. I brought your father here once.' Her words flew right out of left field, caught me off guard and threatened to knock me to my knees.

'You've seen my dad?' My voice squeaked with excitement, immediately transforming me back into a scared but intrigued little girl.

'Only that one time, sadly. The moment you die, you travel to whoever rushes through your mind at that exact second. Your last conscious thought. I don't know why, but I was your father's. It took a little while to calm him down – nothing like you, you have your mother's temperament, thankfully. I also had to get used to that hospital gown he was wearing. Do you know how hard it is to have to constantly remember that if you aren't careful, with one wayward glance you could catch a glimpse of your brother's rear end?' She shuddered and smiled at the same time, like I would have done if I was in her position; there are some sides of your siblings that you should never see. After he saw it... my death, he had closure. He had blamed himself for so many years for what happened to me, for not stopping it, not finding my killer.' She wiped a single tear from her cheek as the memory of his face popped into her head. I quickly looked away; fearful that her sadness would most definitely be contagious.

'I miss him so much' I whispered almost internally, swallowing the lump of emotion stuck in my throat.

'Me too. I would give anything for just one more day, any day, with him. He wasn't just a brother, he was my confidant, my protector, my best friend. But like everything else, he was taken away from me. I guess he found what he was looking for – knowing, understanding, peace. Not even death could box in that man. Before I knew it he was gone, and I was alone again... I'm always alone' she pondered, fiddling with the burnt remains of what varnish-coated nails she had left.

'He didn't leave, Beau has seen him! He spoke to me last year. Maybe he can't find you. I don't really know how all this works yet, but we will sort it out, I promise.' As though the possibility of hope had quashed our sadness the scene around us was once again painted a warm orange rather then a dull tan colour. I realised quickly that nothing in Aunt Linneys world shone any other colour then sickly black for her as I peered up into the dark grey pools of her eyes.

'You need to know, I don't want to show you this. But you, like him, have to understand. You have to see what happened to me. There is a reason we met.'

I gulped as the memories of her injuries – the awful damage

ASCEND

Billie Jade Kermack

that had haunted her in this life and the last moments of her previous one, those that Glen had callously been responsible for – flashed through my mind in quick succession. A searing, bright white light seemed to radiate from behind each one like an old-fashioned photography bulb set up on repeat, giving me a headache, the clink of the filament as it blew ringing loudly.

I shook it off and followed her eyeline, trying desperately to dispel the images of her that were now ingrained in my brain, like unwelcome squatters refusing to budge. I rubbed my head furiously and edged out of the darkness behind Linney.

The women, one redhead, one brunette and two blondes were strangely dressed; the redhead wore a mustard, double-breasted, cropped jacket with large lace lapels, her permed tresses pulled up high in a side ponytail. The two blondes both wore dresses, one a soft pink and sky-blue knee-length with shoulder pads that could sink a ship and the other a backless, navy blue and white striped dress with statement red bow and sailor collar. Their hair should have held a safety warning; they had enough hairspray and glittery mousse in their permed, back-combed barnets to blow up a small nation.

'Why does it look like they've shoved their heads into a candyfloss machine?'

My Aunt Linney giggled. 'As long as it wasn't straight! That was the ultimate sin in the 80s.' She then started patting and plumping her own singed, ratty mass of hair, forgetting for a moment that it was half-gone, her bare scalp red, flaking and raw as it wept.

'Wait – the 80s?'

'80s, 90s, it's all a blur... ghosts don't have the best grasp of dates. What year were you born?' she mused, eyeing me quizzically.

'91.'

'1991 it is then' she replied cheerily. She clearly remembered the year fondly but the memory of her murder soon squashed that; her expression sank, her light eyes mottled and tear-soaked.

She died the year I was born? I immediately felt awful for my father. It couldn't have been easy for him, to have found out some maniac slaughtered his sister in the same year he became a father. Was there anything else I didn't know about my family? My past read like a Stephen King novel and however cool that may sound, the reality was far from it.

I glanced back at the women who were now animatedly singing along to a grungy Madonna track. One of the blondes had reached into her purse and after removing her smudged beauty spot with a wet finger and applying a new one with eye-liner, she vigorously applied another coat of

ASCEND

Billie Jade Kermack

bright pink blush – she didn't need it!

Although I only caught glimpses of her as she fiddled with what I thought was a fax machine on a table propped against the far wall, the brunette woman seemed familiar. Her beautiful cobalt eyes shone from behind heavy coal-black eye-liner and turquoise cream eye shadow. Her natural looking curls fell halfway down her back in ribbons of lustrous chocolate and hints of honey gold, as the sun hit them at an angle. She hadn't spared on the hairspray either. She took her seat at a vacant desk, the assortment of neon plastic bangles on her left arm tapping against the wood every time she reached for the keys on the top line of the keyboard.

Oh my God! How had this not occurred to me earlier?

'You haven't just visited this place after you died, have you?' As soon as the question fluttered from my lips, I successfully finished adding two and two together to make four. Everything fell into place – a bemusing and utterly unthinkable place where the obvious was no longer shrouded by the temporary, debilitating brain damage caused by ghostly time travel. *You couldn't make this stuff up,* I thought, still in shock at the revelation.

Aunt Linney's bangles, which beneath the caked-on dirt, burnt plastic and remnants of her own viscously spilt blood were a selection of neon colours, jangled as she pulled her hand up to move some hair from her face. That is, what hair she had left; half her blistered scalp was visible, her once stunning locks singed or missing.

'That's you. The brunette. But how... how are we... ?'

'I've brought you back. To that day, my last. I was happy before... you know. I wanted you to see me like this. You also need to see what really happened to me, how I ended up like... this.' She tugged at her burnt mini-dress, attempting to make this horrendous scene a little more bearable. She hadn't succeeded, but glancing between the ghost of my Aunt Linney and the memory, vision, whatever it was, of a happier Aunt Linney from the past, it became easier to look past her ravaged body, to see who she really was.

'It wasn't the best job. If I had known I was going to end up the way I did so soon, I probably would have chosen a different career. I always wanted to be a dancer.' Her smile was infectious as she stared off dreamily into the distance; without even realising it she stretched out her good leg, her toes pointed, beautifully straight. His entrance pulled her back.

'Dad!' I went to step towards him. Tears welled in my eyes, threatening my composure in a head-straining, perplexing situation.

He was huge, 6-foot-something with broad, muscled shoulders but not Schwarzenegger bulk; he looked healthy, strapping and handsome. His jet-black hair, like Linney's

ASCEND *Billie Jade Kermack*

brown, was naturally curly, slicked back with gel and pulled in at the nape of his neck. He had one ear pierced and a couple of tattoos poking out from his loose green T-shirt. His ¾-length jeans were dusted with sand and were wet around the hems. As the door swung closed behind him I caught a familiar whiff of his aftershave mixed in with the saltiness of the sea water from his clothes.

'I miss you, I miss you, I miss you!' The words clung to my throat, coming out in just spluttering whispers.

'Hey sis, being the fantastically gorgeous brother that I am, I thought I would bring you lunch. No need for any *thank yous,* but if you did have any free tickets for a holiday to somewhere hot lying around, I would happily take them off your hands.' Past Linney still sitting behind her desk smiled at him, obviously used to his cheeky, easygoing demeanour. That same smile, although bloody, was also etched on Spirit Linney's face as she stood silently next to me. My father was a happy memory for her.

'He looks so happy, so much happier than I remember' I said, still transfixed on his every move. I hadn't realised it, but the good memories I had of my father had been drowned out by his condition, his emaciated form as I saw him dying. I had forgotten him like this.

'He was. Your mum was studying hair and beauty at the college just around the corner from here and they were expecting you. Your mum was huge. We used to compare her to a whale, but as the months ticked by that became less

ASCEND *Billie Jade Kermack*

funny to her. *Hormones fuel a woman's belief that they are right, all of the time, no exceptions,* he would say.' She laughed at the memory. The normalcy of everyday life clearly tugged somewhere deep inside at Linney, as the realisation of what we were here to witness unceremoniously hit her again.

'Cat's finishing college early today and she has a serious craving for a Chinese, fancy meeting us at Chong's later? My treat!' My dad spoke, and I savoured every word. I yearned to know him like that. Since my horrific ordeal with Glen when I had battled for my life, my dad's spirit hadn't visited Beau. Beau had skirted around the subject, fearing he would upset me, so I hadn't pushed it. I didn't realise until this moment how much I needed to know where he was.

'I've got this last customer, then I have eight hours working at *Jerry's*.' Past Linney gestured with a fake, plastered-on smile towards her customer, a short, portly, fair-haired man who seemed oddly nervous amongst the women. He sat with his legs crossed, twiddling his thumbs, eyes large behind his thick prescription glasses as he stared briefly up at my father.

My dad raised his eyebrows as the man returned to a brochure of sights in Hawaii on the varnished maple desk in front of him, his attention captivated for the time being by bikini-clad women. Past Linney returned my dad's questioning expression with a brief smile that spoke louder than any words and he responded with an understanding nod and a half-smile.

ASCEND

Billie Jade Kermack

'Little Gracie Rose is coming, and she has a hankering for sweet and sour chicken balls – surely you can put Jerry off, just this once?' he pleaded with a pouty expression.

My dad was talking about me, I was due. It was a strange and unimaginable feeling, travelling back into the past to a date before I was even born. I suddenly had a hankering for a much needed glass of chilled Pinot Grigio to steady my already car-wreck amalgamation of nerves.

Oh, how times have changed I thought, realising immediately that it would have been something my Inner Bitch would have snarkily remarked. Had I lost her, lost a part of myself on this journey? I suddenly felt like a piece of me was missing. I was there, but I wasn't; not entirely, anyway.

'Your dad was so excited about you being born. He would wake up in a panic sometimes and go on random shopping sprees; nappies, cuddly toys, Moses baskets. He had three so far. I really wish I had taken him up on that offer of dinner.' It hadn't gone unnoticed how much this was hurting my aunt. She placed her hand on my shoulder, which sent an uneasy shiver up my spine – this wasn't her fault, it was part and parcel of being dead, so I didn't let her know what I had felt. It would have just been another reminder of what she had been forced to deal with.

'Hey, if it was just once I would totally blow Jerry off but it isn't! Last week it was ice cream, the week before that we

ASCEND *Billie Jade Kermack*

had to travel to Camden to that old-fashioned sweet shop. '

'On that note, enjoy your lunch.' He handed her a Tupperware box with *'Linney's Lunch'* scribbled in black marker on the side.

'Sherbet pips, Skittles, bonbons – James, this isn't lunch. You know sweets aren't one of the main food groups, right?' She teased with a knowing smile.

'Hey be grateful, at least you know I'm thinking about you.' Past Linney grabbed a few Skittles from the box and threw them one by one at my dad, trying but failing to hit him. He caught them in his mouth with ease, ducking and diving as she launched them at him. *So I'm not the only one with a skill for Skittle Dunk* I thought, beaming as I watched this playful, carefree side of my dad that I hadn't seen for such a long time.

My happiness was short-lived. We weren't there for me to visit a time before I was born, a time that held laughter and joy, a time where my father was alive and well. We were there to decipher what had happened, to witness a horrific and unprovoked murder. My Aunt Linney stepped back into the shadows for a brief second – no, *stepped* was wrong. She sort of floated, her feet never making contact with the ground. I could hear her sniffling as my dad left the office. He put on his mirrored aviator sunglasses, adopting a Tom Cruise-like swagger. The sun still beamed down onto the streets outside and with a skip in his step, he was gone.

ASCEND *Billie Jade Kermack*

'He told me to be careful. He hated me working nights, especially with the murders, but as usual I was adamant I could look after myself. Stubborn as a rock, to boot.'

Watching him leave was clearly as painful for her as it was for me. Our faces were a mirror-image of woe and longing.

'If only I had known that would be the last time I would see my brother.' Linney wrapped her arms tightly around herself for comfort, longing to relive that moment, his hug, his touch, just one more time.

Past Linney shook the hand of her final customer and gathered up her stuff. She slung her bleached jean jacket over her shoulder, put on a pair of tortoiseshell-rimmed sunglasses and rested her tasselled brown purse strap on her shoulder. After giving her hair a quick scrunch and pouting those pink, gloss-covered lips in the wall mirror she left, tottering towards the warm, sun-soaked freedom just beyond the office doors.

'That's our cue to follow' Spirit Linney mumbled solemnly, the vision, memory, whatever this was, suddenly doused in a shadowy grey hue that stirred the feeling of dread lying at the pit of my stomach.

I can't do this. How can I watch her die?

THIRTY-EIGHT
೮)ㄸ

'Close your eyes,' Spirit Linney instructed. I did as I was told, not knowing where she was taking me. 'You can open them now' she said, a moment later. With a blink of my eyes we were on the pavement outside the travel agent's, watching Past Linney raise her hand apologetically, holding up a moving car as she ran across the road. 'I don't know if you can pass through things as easily here – could be extremely embarrassing if I walked you straight into a pane of glass,' she chuckled.

'The whole blinky thing works for me' I said, my knees still shaking as my legs got used to the hurried change of placement.

We walked through the middle of town, moving ever closer to Past Linney's death. People were oblivious to us and with the whole walking through objects being a possible problem I stepped around everyone and everything in my way, resembling a frantic salsa dancer.

The fact that we could move amongst this very real-feeling memory was lucky considering what the spirit of my Aunt

ASCEND
Billie Jade Kermack

Linney looked like, with her bruised and battered body. As the sun beamed down on us, the light speckling gold flecks in Past Linney's copper hair, I realised I had started to see beyond the appearance of the spirit beside me. I imagined her more as the beautiful, svelte woman of her past that was strolling along in front of us. Reading my more open and understanding posture, my Aunt Linney the spirit was now visibly more relaxed.

'OK, time for that 'blinky thing' again, as you so aptly put it' she said to me, grasping my hand in hers to solidify the connection.

Out of the sunlight and now in a large, dark, strobe-lit basement bar, we followed Past Linney as she greeted patrons and staff. Although I knew we couldn't be seen I still felt the need to creep carefully through the alcove, down the flight of ramshackle wooden stairs and into the changing rooms, through an open yellow metal door behind Past Linney. As always, the spirit of my Aunt Linney glided through the air making not a peep, the knowledge of what would happen at the day's end clearly weighing heavy on her mind.

She threw her coat on top of the rusting red lockers that were bent out of shape, covered with the black remains of stickers that had once adorned them.

'Hey, you. Did you hear about that last girl? I heard she was almost unrecognisable. Nasty way to go,' a girl said from behind the changing curtain before she swung it open.

ASCEND
Billie Jade Kermack

Holding a dress-bag on a hanger, Past Linney swapped places with the girl, pulling the curtain shut.

'I don't know why you guys even read the papers about that stuff, it's creepy. James has given me three bottles of pepper spray just in case. I had to convince my date the other night that they were deodorant,' Past Linney said. The dark-skinned, brown eyed girl in stone-washed denim shorts and a rainbow boob-tube giggled infectiously, making me smile.

'I wish I had known then what I know now. Puts a new spin on learning things the hard way' Spirit Linney whispered, finding it hard to look at the scene playing out in front of us.

With that Past Linney emerged from behind the curtain, fiddling with the sides of her hair, securing them back above her ears. I stared at her and swallowed hard, clearing the lump in my throat. Ghost Linney tugged nervously at the dishevelled hem of what remained of the black-and-white cocktail dress that was soaked in her dried blood. Past Linney was wearing the exact same outfit, right down to the patent shoes, except hers was immaculately-pressed, a picture of runway beauty.

'At least I got to die in my favourite dress, I guess' she retorted sarcastically, her only means of distracting herself from the saddening reminder of just how close to her end she was.

'Is this your handsome brother James we're talking about?' the girl asked, licking her lips and savouring his name.

ASCEND

Billie Jade Kermack

'Hold your horses Amy, he is happy and soon to be a father! He doesn't need this... or *that*' Past Linney giggled, pointing first at the other girl's face and then her svelte, toned body with a beaming smile.

'What makes you think he could handle all this?' she chuckled, running one hand down her waist and using the other to gently tease her immaculately coiffed, tightly-curled hair. 'I was just making an observation, anyway. I should never have let him go when I had him.' She spoke now only to her reflection as she puckered her lips in her locker mirror.

'Give it a rest? You went out for drinks, once, like three years ago. Let it go, woman!' Past Linney laughed, tossing an orange waist-length apron at Amy and diverting her attention away from her locker. She pulled out another apron blazoned with *Axel's Bar and Grill,* pulling it over her head and secured it around her waist. The spirit of my aunt hovering next to me exhaled a stunted breath, longing swamping her stare.

'You know Amy died two years after this, in a robbery gone wrong. She never saw who shot her. She visited me before she crossed over; she had searched tirelessly for months to find out what had happened to me. She still had that same illuminating tenacity and desire for life, even as a spirit. If I wasn't already dead, I'd think I was cursed – everyone around me dies.' It was clear that the people Aunt Linney held dear when she was alive had all felt the same about her.

ASCEND *Billie Jade Kermack*

Her remark about everyone dying around her hadn't gone unnoticed, but when was my safety ever not an issue? I couldn't help but wonder: why had she been targeted? Was it really a curse, or just bad luck? I had read the files and knew Glen's victim type; young girls, isolated, lonely. He revelled in being something more to them than just their murderer. Why would he choose to murder my aunt and then wait 18 years to hunt down her niece? I was barraged with an onslaught of unanswerable questions, all of which made me cry out for the comforting solace of my bedroom, for the life I had left behind with just a fleeting backwards glance.

'Can I ask why you don't have the same last name as Dad? I think we could have got to this point a lot quicker with that information.' I smiled, remembering why we were here, and that I would have probably given anything to be anywhere else.

'Unfortunately, I was one of those teenagers who believed they knew best. I was married at sixteen to an older man who, true to form, eventually showed his leopard spots. He wasn't exactly Prince Charming material – unless Prince Charming thought giving his Princess a black eye for Valentine's Day meant romance.'

She pondered on the memory that had obviously stuck firmly with her, even in death. Her natural response to her words was to pull her long feathered fringe across her cheekbone, hiding the invisible marks of abuse she had

ASCEND   Billie Jade Kermack

endured. 'But I got my act together and divorced that sorry excuse for a man.' She composed herself with a deep breath, her anger dissipating as she once again pushed her hair behind her ear.

'But you never changed your name?' I asked.

'When I say divorced, I use the term loosely. He was kind of against the idea and after months of fighting him for my freedom, I found myself permanently out of the race. I was murdered before the papers were final.' *Trapped in life, trapped in death; sounds scarily like a curse to me*, I thought, unable to find the words to console her plight.

Completely absorbed by our conversation, I hadn't noticed that we had followed Past Linney back up into the bar. My attention was now tightly focused, everything else around me suddenly mere background noise as his face loomed into view just a metre in front of me. A cautionary breath hitched in my throat and, sensing my growing fear, the spirit of my Aunt Linney reached out for my hand.

Propping up the bar and nursing what looked like a double shot of whisky, or possibly rum, was Glen.

Though he appeared less menacing than when he had visited me last year, it only took one of his disgusting sly smiles – as Past Linney handed him another tumbler full of the brown liquid from off her tray – to drag me back, kicking and screaming, to the torture and depravity he had put me through. That grimace resonated sickly in the air,

ASCEND

Billie Jade Kermack

vibrating goosebumps over the skin on my arms.

He picked at his dirty fingernails, hunching over as he intently read the front cover of a local newspaper. I tried to look away but everything in me was suddenly stilled. I felt separated from my limbs, bound only by an intense feeling of fear that I had come to recognise only too easily.

The excited wails coming from a group of guys in maroon football jerseys in the corner of the bar watching a game on the boxy television made me jump, pulling me from my trance. Their cheers of joy seemed to mock my silent pain. I continued to edge backwards, each step cautiously quiet until my back met with an untreated red-brick pillar.

Glen raised his glass to a lofty, dark-haired, moustached man in his late-20s who was sitting at the end of the bar in a secluded corner booth. His face was partially masked in the shadows as he moved in and out of the green glare from the neon lights behind the bar. His appearance was immaculate; hair side-parted, not a strand out of place, his blue suit buttoned up, a thin black tie centred and tucked into it.

With my nerves almost shot and my brain struggling to contain my fear, Glen turned around, his eyes scanning the room and fixing on me for a brief second or two. *Can he see me? No one else can see me!*

'I can't do this, I don't want to see this. Please, I want to go home' I whispered, in a delirious panic. Imagining my shoes to be ruby red and with the power to transport me there, I

ASCEND *Billie Jade Kermack*

almost clicked the heels together in a last act of desperation.

I closed my eyes tightly and crouched down to the floor, praying that now would be the moment that I would finally awake from this nightmare.

ASCEND *Billie Jade Kermack*

THIRTY-NINE
ఏసఁ

'The blinky thing again?' I asked, desperate to find myself back in Beau's embrace. Linney nodded without looking at me, her stare tethered to something in the distance behind me.

'Wait, I've seen this place before. Where are we?' I wracked my brain for any information on my location but came up with *diddly squat*, as my grandmother would say. We were free of Axel's bar and I was now crouched on a dirt floor, surrounded by newly-abandoned warehouses, seemingly in the middle of nowhere. The balmy evening breeze whistled around me, cooling with every passing second, the sun beginning its descent in the distance.

I got to my feet shakily, flicking the dry dirt from the knees of my jeans. I spun around, looking for an escape, the land surrounding us just a barren sea of brown dirt. The tall buildings circled us, each with freshly boarded-up windows and 'Going Out of Business' signs hung above their doors. Before I could repeat my question, a car pulled up at the rear of *Trucker Joe's Auto Warehouse*. I could just make out the rear tyre as it steadied on the gravel, the reflection of the

ASCEND

Billie Jade Kermack

tail-lights on the wall of the neighbouring building, but that was about it.

'Linney, where are...' I didn't need to finish my sentence. As I turned to my aunt I caught sight of something, something that told me exactly where I was and just how close I was to witnessing my aunt's end.

I took a few steps forward towards the stone angel that stood tall in all its etched beauty, not a crack or flaw in sight. Her wings stretched out to either side, each feather carved delicately into the stone. It was the same statue I had stood in front of only hours previously, Beau by my side, as we set to the task of conjuring the spirit of my murdered aunt. It was cleaner now, still perfectly formed, untouched by the raging elements.

I looked back towards Linney who was silently wrapping her hands around herself. She hurriedly beckoned me to come back to her, hidden out of sight behind a metal support beam. I did as I was instructed, reading the utter fear in her wide eyes.

Safely hidden in the shadows, we listened as heavy footsteps made their way into the back entrance of the warehouse and an overhead bulb inside pinged to life, its light only visible in strobes through slats of wood crudely nailed to the windows and beneath the shuttered entrance.

'They can't see us, right?' I whispered softly, hoping I was correct.

ASCEND

Billie Jade Kermack

'We may not be able to be seen but exposing your soul in this memory, adding yourself to it, will only further haunt you. I told you I would show you the truth, however much I would like to keep it hidden. If I'm being honest, you know too much already. No one can protect you from this any more.'

With the strange desire to see into the warehouse and a flicker of armoured strength I didn't know I had, I took a step forward. I was beckoned by the low hum of an inaudible conversation coming from inside, the click of a radio further disguising the voices. I ignored the whispered pleas of my aunt not to look, to stay back.

I placed my hands on the rough wood to steady myself, still questioning why it was I didn't fall straight through. I peeked in through the crudely-arranged slats and searched the room. Out of the corner of my eye, in a another room with no door, I could see a pair of feet, eerily still, bound to the legs of a metal-framed garden chair. As I moved to the next slat I clasped my hand across my mouth to silence my surprise, as her monochrome, bloodstained dress came into view. I turned to the spirit of my aunt who already knew the question swimming around in my head. She replied with only a nod, her eyes welling up with tears.

I heard his offbeat cackle before I saw him. I shuffled along the wall, looking for a better view inside the warehouse. I stepped up onto an old tin bucket, careful to keep quiet, balancing as I looked through into the cracked window.

ASCEND

Billie Jade Kermack

Using my sleeve to wipe away the dirt meant it was now a lot easier to see into the spacious room; rusting tools of the mechanic's trade hung on every wall, and through the open shutters leading out back I made out the wide boot of a dark blue car. Its engine was still running as the red brake-lights shone brightly onto the dusty floor.

Glen walked into view, a green petrol canister in his hand. I could only see the suited arms of the other man; he was waving them manically, his voice fraught and angry towards Glen, who shrugged off his displeasure with a sly smile. As her legs began to twitch frantically I suddenly didn't care who the other man was, or why he was so annoyed with Glen.

As her polished, broken nails fought to free her from the worn rope that held her hostage, I prayed that she would escape, that this wasn't her end; that maybe, just maybe, Past Linney could break free and set off into the shadows, unseen, to live another day. The reality of what would surely happen whether she was able to intervene or not crept to the forefront of my mind.

'I wish I had died there on that floor.' I turned to see the ghost of my Aunt Linney floating in mid-air beside me, her head bowed, unable to look directly at her own battered but still-living body. 'You need to come over here, away from the windows.' As her hand gently wrapped around my wrist, I felt no pulling pressure from Linney; my legs had begun to obey before I could decline, and I was off the bucket.

ASCEND
Billie Jade Kermack

Once by the safety of the cast-iron support beam, I span round to see Past Linney crawl underneath the partially-open shutter in an attempt to save herself. She hobbled across the dirt as quietly as she could manage, her broken ankle clearly hindering her immensely, any pressure she put on it producing gurgled screams that she tried to silence with her hand.

She eventually gave up and fell to the floor, the pain now too intense to stifle. She pulled her broken body across the dirty floor, her fingernails – what was left of them – digging fruitlessly into the ground. She reached out to the only thing that could steady her and help her to her feet, the angel standing tall above her. I glanced down at my palm, feeling the subtle remnants of the heat that I had felt when I had seen this from my time. I had felt her, sensed her presence. It wouldn't be long before all hope was irreparably dashed and her fate was decidedly set.

We hadn't noticed but Glen had been resting against the shutter, his weapon of choice, selected from the mechanic's wall, gripped tightly in his hands. In a flash he was beside her; towering above her silently, now creeping slowly along beside her, laughing as he watched her ravaged body fight for freedom, for her life. He held the blunt weapon high and effortlessly pitched it through the air, pummelling it into the angel, taking her wings from her in the process. Chips of stone rained down on Linney as she cowered at his feet, her wounds grounding her, forcing her to stare death in the face. Her high-pitched wails resonated in the humid air, reaching far and wide, the vast, deserted land leaving each

ASCEND

Billie Jade Kermack

plea unheard as he dragged her by her hair back into the warehouse. Praying for her silence felt incredibly wrong, but the tears that charged down my face only revealed a fraction of the sorrow I felt for her.

Even from outside the warehouse I could hear his weapons soaring like birds through the air, each blow resounding with a deafening *crack* as its mass met bone. I knew Glen, and he wouldn't let this be it. He had tortured her; he had allowed her to believe, if only briefly, that she could escape, and now he would beat any speck of hope that she had left out of her. He was enjoying this, and would undoubtedly squeeze every last moment out of Linney before her body finally caved to the pressure. Before long, she would stop fighting. She would have to give in to the solace of death.

'I don't want to be here for that, I don't want to see,' I sobbed. For the first time, I secretly damned Beau and his gift. I cursed my lack of gratefulness for the safety of my once-mundane life before Beau had come to Gallows Wood, before my soul became a disposable plaything, before the risk of dying became a weekly occurence. It was hard to believe in the existence of love when death, destruction and depravity haunted me at every turn. Could love really ever be enough? Yes, I had made my choices, and on more than one occasion, I had chosen Beau. I had happily decided on a life with him by my side, and before this moment I would have stood by my choices, head held high; now everything had changed, had slipped through my fingers before I could stop it. Would I ever be back in his arms? Would my life ever be normal again?

FORTY

I hadn't expected the surprise that I was in for. I wiped the tears from my cheeks; without realising it and against my aunt's instruction, I had begun to walk forwards, my feet dragging on the floor as I wandered out from the safety of our hiding place.

'Grace. GRACE!' the spirit of my aunt squealed through gritted teeth. The moonlight shifted just enough for me to identify the stranger standing in the shadows. The orange gleam at the end of his cigarette blazed red as he inhaled the toxins and silently watched on as Linney was butchered. His pressed suit and sleek hair, the tightly-knotted tie around his neck, his stern but appraising expression.

The creepy guy from the bar. What is he...

Before I could finish my train of thought I felt Linney's hand wrap around my wrist, as she hurriedly fought to drag me back into the shadows.

'You can't intervene, this has happened already – we can't

make a difference and I don't think you need to see what's going on in there.'

'But...'

'No buts, Grace' she interrupted sternly, with a steadying exhale of breath and a raised eyebrow which immediately reminded me of my father.

ଽଠ

The silence was soothing, the shadows now a fixture as the warehouse lot faded away, taking its horror and my sadness along with it. For the first time that day I felt calm, as though I could live to fight another day.

'Grace, what is going on? I don't talk just to hear the sound of my own voice. Have you been listening to a word I've said?'

'What do you mean... where are... who was... where's Glen?' I had too many questions, yet apparently I had lost the ability to finish a sentence. Luckily, listening was a skill that took very little effort.

'You need to find my trinket,' she pressed. I gazed at her intently, my body still filled with panic and confusion as it sought to find its bearings. She pulled at a tarnished gold, ruby-studded bracelet on her wrist, hidden beneath the burnt, misshapen bangles.

ASCEND

Billie Jade Kermack

'I remember my mother gave it to me when I got married' she said, gazing longingly at it. 'It is the one thing still tethering me to the human world; I can't crossover until it is found. You probably wouldn't imagine it to be true, but I am so incredibly tired. On the brink of flat-out cosmic exhaustion, actually.' Her face dipped and a rush of anguish tugged at her shoulders, making her posture slumped and contorted. She was giving up. 'I can't look at this brutality any more.' She pulled at the burnt dress that was caked in her now dried, brownish blood. 'I can see the sun but never feel it, hear laughter but never experience it. I can't relive this nightmare over and over again – I just can't.' Her words were sobering, her eyes laden with indecision.

If you can exist but still be haunted by your death, is that really any existence at all?

'Can't we cross you over without your trinket, by using a spell or something? I've heard that chicken's blood vamps up a spell's potency and I'm pretty sure there's a KFC factory just off the M11. You wouldn't believe what I've seen Beau and Gwen do.' I attempted to lighten the mood and for a brief and fleeting moment it worked, as her bruised lips curled into a tiny smile. It was strange how being away from the warehouse lot, from the scene of her murder, could alter the mood around us, successfully – if only momentarily – sparking an instance of hope free of fear. The moment came and went in a heartbeat.

'Look, Grace. My soul bears the Shadowed Curse.' Her face was taut and solemn now.

ASCEND

Billie Jade Kermack

'Shadowed Curse?' It was evident that around every corner there was something new to learn with all this gift and magic malarkey.

'Glen's evil and torturous actions, his lack of humanity or remorse, his blackened heart and soul... all of these things, amongst others, mean that he has imprinted part of himself on me. My body, my memories, my choice of an afterlife are no longer mine. He sort of... what's the word...' she rubbed her head furiously, urging the right word to step forward: '... *stained* me. I have seen my end. I have seen what I just showed you over a hundred times, maybe even over a thousand. I've lost count. I may be a ghost, but there's only so much even I can take. I am stuck in a loop, forced to watch on and relive my murder. He ripped my bracelet from my body as a memento as I lay in a pool of my own spilt blood and I wasn't the first, or the last. He had accumulated a little collection of hunting trophies. They may have been more inconspicuous than a boar's head strapped to the hood of a pick up truck, but death was blindingly clear all the same. Whatever goodness I had left after the brutality he put me through, clung to this.' She was on the brink of tears as she tugged again at the gold reminder wrapped around her charred wrist. 'Not only was my life taken, but my soul as well. He watched on with a smile as the life trickled out of me, until there was nothing left. I cannot continue to belong to him!'

Hanging on her every word, I hadn't realised it, but I was the one who had started crying. Sobbing, actually, with the

ASCEND *Billie Jade Kermack*

realisation of the weight of what she had gone through, the level of agonising fear she had been forced to experience and come to terms with. Watching on as family, friends, everyday civilians moved on with their lives, taking for granted the simplest of things. I suddenly felt an overwhelming pang of selfishness as she walked towards me, reaching out to comfort me. Her hand was there but it wasn't, in front of me but just a white, translucent shadow. It felt like a breeze dancing over my skin as our bodies connected, all the little hairs standing to attention as a buzzing shot vibrated down my spine, her energy now growing and travelling through me. My senses were heightened, my brain nearing combustion at the overload.

'How am I meant to find it?' I was clueless, dumbfounded as I attempted to process all the information she was giving me.

'I don't know, Grace. I am so sorry to burden you with all this, but I found you for a reason. You were the only one able to see me, after all this time – please, I need your help. I see his other victims, you know. They're always around, women like me, who went through what I did. The darkness on this side breeds, growing in numbers every day, stealing the souls of the damaged to use for their own sick and twisted means. Like zombies they wander, slowly losing the ability to remember; who they are, how they died. I think that because of you, I have been able to hold on to who I was. You need to find my bracelet and the trophies of Glen's other victims – nobody deserves to wander for an eternity in this world.'

ASCEND *Billie Jade Kermack*

'It's not like I can walk up to Glen and ask him where he hid some jewellery. He's dead, remember!' I stressed. Linney rolled her eyes, again immediately reminding me of my father.

'You have very little faith in yourself, you know. Glen may be dead – and thank the Lord for that – but he's never truly gone, not for good anyway.'

'The Shadows, right?' I remembered Gwen's warnings that spirits as evil as Glen's could only ever be destroyed forever from both worlds once the Shadows decided they had no use for them. Apparently Glen wasn't yet a useless entity and the future of his existence was cloudy, which gave me the creeps.

'You know a lot more about all this stuff than you let on, don't you?' she mused, reading my expression. Her lips curled up slightly at the edges as though she now had proof that what she had first believed was actually a carved-in-stone fact.

'I'm a fast learner. You have to tell me how I'm going to help you, because at the moment the words *needle* and *haystack* are jumping about like bunnies in my head.'

'There is someone who can help you, but...' she fiddled with her nails, another trait my father had possessed when he was handling a tricky subject. It took him a whole two hours to tell me our dog Scooby had run away to live on a farm (it had taken me another three years to realise 'farm' meant a hole in our back garden). Her fiddling with her fingers was not a good sign and I winced, bracing myself for her next words.

'But what?' I questioned, not sure I wanted to know the answer but aware that we may not have much time left to chat.

'It's not going to be easy.'

Without warning, I snapped. My emotions were in a whirlwind, my brain unable to take in anything else, and her words sent me spiralling. The months of torture I had been forced to endure, the happy existence I had said goodbye to as I accepted Beau's gift.

'Does it look to you like any of this so far has been *easy*? My dad died and then came back, I'm stalked by a raving lunatic spirit who liked to hunt and murder pretty young women on his days off work, I find out there's a whole world of ghosts, witches and God only knows what else, and then to top it off – not even touching on all the other stuff by the way – I have spent this year being haunted by my dead aunt whose grand idea of a family reunion is the equivalent of handing a bunch of Chucky dolls and a filleting-knife gift set around a children's nursery. I am so tired, mentally exhausted, and I think my psyche has been battered about as much as it can bear! If you remember rightly, the first time I met you, you were battering the life out of me. Vision or not, that hurt!'

ASCEND

Billie Jade Kermack

I took in a deep, much-needed breath, very aware that I may have crossed over into the realm of insanity. I had allowed months' worth of pent-up anger, fear, sadness and hate to flood out of my mouth like vomit, all mixed in with my usual determination to fight. Like a deserted and lonely island floating in a sea of messed up emotions I was lost, stranded and confused. I had been lost for a while, I suspected, without even realising it. I hadn't let it all hit me; until now, that is.

'I wish I could hug you. Properly, I mean.' Her remark, filled in equal measure with love and sadness, snapped me out of my train of thought. I was being selfish. She hadn't asked for any of this to happen to her, and anything I had been through didn't really come close. She was dead; I was lucky to be alive.

'I'm sorry I snapped at you, it's kind of been a rough year. I don't think I could ever truly understand what you went through, what you are still going through, but I can't help you. I want to help you, but I'm not the right person for the job. Beau is the special one, he's the one who can help you, he's got...' she interrupted me as the tickling sensation from her fingertips caressed my arm.

'You have so much more power than you know, Grace. I believe in you but until you believe in yourself, you're right, you can't help me.' I was silent, watching her wide eyes silently plead with my conscience.

'OK, what do I do?' I have to help her. *About bloody time*

ASCEND *Billie Jade Kermack*

squealed my Inner Bitch, mopping up her tears with a Kleenex; my Inner Bitch, who I thought had abandoned me when I had crossed over into Aunt Linney's world!

'You have to find Edward. He can help you find me, find my soul. Restore what has been broken for us all.'

'Edward who? I don't know an Edward.' Our surroundings had been changing as our emotions grew without us noticing; they were now hazy, swirling psychedelic colours, taking on liquid form around us like a lava lamp, drowning out the now misty formation of my Aunt Linney's spirit. She was fading, and fast, faster than either of us could have anticipated.

'Who's Edward?' I pressed. Time was slipping away, and we both knew it.

'I haven't got much time, but I want you to know Grace, you were my last thought. You were who I visited after I died – your birth was the greatest moment I could ever have wished for.' Her voice was delicate, a hushed, faraway whisper, dancing dust in the wind. The realisation that this could very well be the last time I spoke to the spirit of my aunt made me shudder, a bursting fit of all-encompassing despondency brimming up inside me.

'Who was the man with Glen, where is your trinket hidden, who is Edward?' I had nothing but unanswered questions and a looming feeling of apprehension piggy-backing itself into the darkness with me.

ASCEND

Billie Jade Kermack

'Edward... Edward... Langley. I think that's it, but I'm not sure.' Linney struggled to remember, rubbing her temples in frustration, willing her brain to search out the right memory to help her. 'I see fire, all I see is the bright, golden orange of burning flames. My vision is distorted, it's right there on the cusp but I just can't reach it.'

Realising she had missed what I had asked her, she stopped worrying about *Mr-Edward-possibly-last-name-Langley* and turned to me. 'Wait, go back, what man with Glen?' She was confused, her words an ethereal whisper, barely audible. She hadn't seen the man, and I wouldn't have the time to describe him. Her form took on an almost completely transparent shimmer as she began to fade away.

'Don't leave me, please, Aunt Linney, you can't go! I need to know more, I don't know what to do. You can't leave me again!' I screamed, tears rolling down my cheeks as every fleeting second that passed cruelly ripped another part of my aunt along with it.

She was gone. A coarse and violent wind of emotion, fear and the unknown swept me into nothingness. Without light there is no dark, without sound there is no silence. I couldn't centre myself, my senses a jumbled mess, my insides in a panicked rush to feel normal.

A light drumming began to vibrate around me. I could feel it beneath my feet, on my bare arms, the sensation alone forcing my hair out of my face. With a *thud* I felt as though

ASCEND

Billie Jade Kermack

an invisible brick wall had suddenly been erected mere inches from my face, the powdery dust causing me to sneeze. Claustrophobia set in with a sweeping, unexpected rush, low in my stomach. I felt as though something or someone was smothering me; my airways tightened and contracted and I fell to my knees, coughing and spluttering in the surrounding blackness, the silent but oddly not-so-silent space that sent vibrations coursing over every inch of my body, working their way into a frenzy until my head began to pound in frustrated argument. My eyes grew heavy, exhaustion swallowing me as my face met with the floor.

FORTY-ONE
ಸಿಂಲ

BEAU

I had watched her, day and night, as her still body offered up no signs of life. It had been countless weeks since the spirit of her aunt had dragged Grace over the threshold of the circle and into her world. Each day of no response had swept into another, and her 19th birthday was now mere days away. When I slipped in and out of sleep, the memory of better times was my only comfort; the vision of her beautiful face, happiness brightening her cheeks as we sat beneath the tree in Gwen's garden, embracing. That was now only a memory and the fear that I would be left with only that, forever more, tugged painfully in my chest.

The drip that fed her was never empty, yet her face, once bright with life, was now gaunt and deprived. Her skin was almost a translucent grey, as though malnourished and dehydrated to the point of onset decay. Where once her beautiful full, pink lips would have parted for a laugh or a smile, they were now permanently forced open by the

ASCEND   *Billie Jade Kermack*

intrusion of a thick, clear tube that was strapped to her face. Air from the life-support machine that travelled into her lungs was keeping her alive, but only served to remind me that this was a natural reflex she could not manage alone. Her chest rose and fell to the squishing beat of the pumps, and I lived with the constant knowledge that if we had a power-cut, I could lose her forever.

She was alone, sick, and in an undetermined coma that neither we nor the doctors had any idea how long would hold her hostage. Passing time ran her body dry, on the brink of life but constantly edging closer to death. I felt helpless, forced to watch her slip away from me.

I sat by her side everyday, only taking time to go home to wash and change my clothes. I held her hand and told her stories, each time praying that today would be the day she would come back to me. Roses, daisies, lilies, chrysanthemums – as each bunch of flowers wilted and succumbed to their fate, a new vase filled with fresh ones was centred in their place. They only reminded me of the passing time I had to endure without her, and the possibility that one day these flowers could be arranged around her grave. I couldn't think like that, didn't want to even imagine it as a possible outcome. Since the day she had been taken from me I had felt lost, like a piece of me was missing, my heart splintered and disconnected. My soulmate lay there unresponsive to my touch and my words.

Before I could wallow further in my pool of self-destructive thinking, I was ripped back into the real world by Grace's

ASCEND   *Billie Jade Kermack*

doctor entering the room.

'I'm sorry, but nothing has changed. Although there is some brain activity present, it is dwindling fast. We need to consider our options.' He spoke slowly and with little compassion, as though he was reading a pre-prepared speech. Catherine, Grace's mother, was speechless; she stopped arranging the bunch of pink geraniums and attempted to understand the doctor's callous outburst.

'What *options*, other than getting a doctor who knows what he's talking about? This conversation is over' I retorted angrily, invading his personal space and poking him forcefully in the chest. At roughly six foot we were evenly matched, but I think the fury in my voice gave me the upper hand. The doctor ran his hand down his shirt and adjusted his tie, trying to fathom what I was going to do next. Seeing how it would probably play out before it did, I felt Gwen's hand on my arm, I understood without making eye contact with her, turned away from the doctor and wrapped Catherine up in my arms.

ஐஓ

With the doctor's words rattling around in my head I fell in and out of sleep, with little regard to the time. Catherine had to go home for Cary and I promised I wouldn't leave; his words were clearly also playing heavily on her mind.

Gwen was snoring on the day bed under the window, her big black book of spells clutched tightly in her arms, a pentagram charm necklace wrapped around her fingers. She had tried everything she could think of to bring Grace out of her coma, out of that place, but nothing seemed to work. Wherever Grace was, we couldn't reach her.

'Gwen, Gwen, you need to wake up! GWEN!' I shouted in a panic, not taking my eyes off of Grace.

I was by Grace's side instantly, clutching her cold, limp hand in mine. Her body shook violently as I attempted to hold her still.

'She's Ascending' Gwen said sombrely, as she got to her feet.

'No, what do you mean? She can't Ascend, she isn't a witch. You have to stop it!'

'I can't now, she's seen too much. Beau, she's been through too much. There's nothing I can do for her now, the final stage is approaching. I'm sorry sweetheart, I had no idea it would come to this.' Gwen pointed toward Grace's arm, her other hand stifling her sobs.

The pasty pink flesh on Grace's wrist started to bubble and swell. Inch by inch, line by line, out of nowhere, the Star of Aurora was branded onto her wrist. I turned to Gwen who pulled up her jumper sleeve, silently answering my unspoken question as she brandished the star that, like Grace's, had appeared on her skin to signal the next chapter in her Ascent.

ASCEND

Billie Jade Kermack

'Even with the decades of witches in my bloodline, I barely survived it. I couldn't stop this, even if I wanted to.'

'It was a trap – me coming back to her, walking back into her life, thinking I could save her from some invisible force. Someone wanted her dead and they have used me to help them.'

'None of this is your fault, Beau! You could never have guessed that this would happen. Any instance could have led her down this path, to this conclusion. Her starting work at the hospital, her dabbling in my books, her missing a bus because I was too unwell to take her. We cannot know where or when this all went wrong for her, where fate stepped in. She wanted you with her, she loved you so very much, can you not see that?' she yelled, shaking me by my shirt collar until I looked away from Grace and into her eyes, pleading with me to hear her.

All I could see was Grace slipping further and further away, all I could hear was the furious bleeping of her machines as technology failed her, as I had failed her.

FORTY-TWO

ঞ‌ca

'She's going to die if you don't stop it!' I knew what was coming, deep down I knew there was nothing Gwen could do. I had read the books, done the research, but I couldn't let her go, not without a fight. 'Please, stay with me, you are going to be fine, I just need you to breathe now, Miss Gracie... please.' But before I could open my mouth to beg, pray, challenge a higher power further, she had crossed over to the point of no return.

She floated like an angel, slow and steadily up into the air, her hospital gown trailing over the cotton sheets in the void between Grace and the bed. Her arms moved out, extended on either side of her body, perfectly straight, her legs together, toes pointed. A visible current raged through her and her body reacted violently, crashing back down onto the hospital bed, the metal frame buckling and bending beneath the force. From the sleeve of her hospital gown, my mother's necklace fell onto the bed. With one final pulse Grace's body contorted, her body twisting, back arching. Finally, her body gave itself over to the torture and relaxed.

'She's gone.' Gwen was by my side, her words a whisper. As the realisation of what she had said hit me, the life support machine beside Grace flat-lined; the continuous high-

ASCEND

pitched squeal was deafening.

I grabbed the necklace and decided to fight like there was no tomorrow, determination, deliriousness, or possibly denial fuelling me. 'No, Grace, no. CPR, I can do that.' I could feel it breaking, the dull and smiting bite as the stabbing pain travelled from my heart outwards, infecting my body with devastation, with loss. Even though it wasn't her choice, she was leaving me.

'Breathe Grace, please baby, please don't leave me, I can't be here without you.' I pushed on her chest, frantically willing her heart to react, praying for a spike on the screen. My lips touched hers but there was nothing; her warmth, her life had been swallowed whole, stolen from her. Her chest rose and fell like a balloon as I tried with all my might to breathe some life into her. I couldn't do it, I wasn't doing it right. *What if I never again kiss those beautiful lips, never again hear her tell me she loves me, just once more, please, just once more...*

'I should have seen the signs, but I was so distracted. She could see the spirit of her aunt because she had begun her journey as a Channelling Empath the night Glen tried to kill her. That bond between our world and hers was fused thanks to her death-induced intervention. I've read the Book of Aurora more than a thousand times, why didn't I see this?' Gwen panicked, suddenly piecing together all of the inconsistencies that she should have picked up on and hadn't. I had no time for any of this. I had to wake her up and pull her back and I had to do it now, before it was too

ASCEND   *Billie Jade Kermack*

late.

Breathe, please Gracie, breathe. For me. I pressed my forehead against hers, willing her to telepathically receive my message from wherever she was. She had to be in there somewhere, she had to hear me. I wished for the sound of her breathing, the shallow dip of her chest, the twitch of her fingers as her soul rejoined her body. Anything, any sign of life.

'Gwen, get help, she needs help' I sobbed, still frantically pressing on Grace's chest to no avail.

'Beau, she's gone.' Gwen held her hands over mine on Grace's chest to stop me pushing. 'She's gone, sweetheart. I am so sorry.'

'No, no, no she can't be gone – we need to get a doctor. Someone needs to help her, it's only been a minute. Wake up, please, wake up!' I cried, shaking Grace, but she was unresponsive. I pulled her face to mine, my hands gripped in her hair and around her neck to steady her, her arms slumping down onto the bed behind her. 'This can't be it, I haven't had long enough. You can't leave me here alone.' I laid her back down carefully, pacing the floor, thinking of my next move.

'You need to help her Gwen, please, I know you can do it.' I fell to my knees on the freshly-waxed blue linoleum, clasping my hands together in prayer. 'I'm begging you Gwen, a spell, a potion, anything. You can't just let her die!'

ASCEND *Billie Jade Kermack*

Gwen ran her hand through my hair and bent down to kiss my forehead, a loving move a mother might make to console her child.

'She's at peace now.' The finality in Gwen's voice was devastating.

I returned the necklace to around Grace's throat. She should have it, even if I couldn't have her.

I sat on the floor of that hospital room and watched on as it filled with doctors, nurses and interns rushing about manically, assessing the situation, checking her statistics, rushing through the machine printouts, all the while knowing that I had failed her. I had let this happen. I cried harder than I ever had before as with every passing second the distance between us grew. Cary and Catherine had been and gone, Catherine's shock and upset flooding out in waves as she cradled the lifeless body of her daughter in her arms, only to be pulled away by a doctor when her body caved to the pressure of her heartbreak.

'Beau, where did you get that necklace? Where did you find it?' I could read Gwen's lips and I knew exactly what she was saying, but I couldn't hear her. I didn't want to hear anything. Blocking it all out I waited, until one by one, everyone left.

෩෨

Calm and contemplation now filled the dark room, the

ASCEND *Billie Jade Kermack*

monotonous *tick tock* of the wall clock echoing around me. I was alone with her finally, with my love, my soulmate; or her body, anyway. I lay there next to her for what seemed like hours with just the dim lamp clipped onto the bed-frame above us for light, clutching onto any last remnants of warmth, of life, of *her,* as they slowly dwindled away. I needed to remember her, the smell of her hair, her soft skin, her beautiful lips. I trailed my fingers up her arms, across her collarbone, around her jaw line, willing my brain to remember it all, every single inch of the woman I loved. Why wasn't she coming to me? Why couldn't I see her spirit? I dealt with death everyday, I touched it, I saw it, I sensed it. I was tainted with the deaths of so many, hundreds possibly, but only one death would stick with me forever more.

'It wasn't supposed to end like this' I breathed, pushing a rogue strand of her hair behind her ear. Suddenly, I realised the poignancy of my words; the weight that, just maybe, they had always held.

ಸಃ

⁐ SIX MONTHS PREVIOUSLY ⁐

BOOK OF AURORA

THE SHADOWED VEIL
Seeing the Truth

ASCENDING

An amalgamation of unexplainable events will show the universe's selection of a Gifted one set for Ascension. It is imperative that the soul Ascending be of pure magical bloodline. If this is not the case, a cleansing ritual is necessary to bind any and all wayward powers. A gift from birth is preordained and set, but a near-death experience will taint a soul and allow for the possibility of gift placement with an otherwise normal soul; in some, but not all cases, this is acceptable.

Those of single vision (the *Ungifted*) may be exposed to the supernatural world and if a greater understanding beyond their usual comprehension is reached, the scales will be tipped. Signs to look for to determine whether a soul bears the potential to Ascend are:

> Communing with spirits, sensing the veil, an influx of otherworldly phenomena, emphatic channelling, inherited memory or visions passed down from the spirit world.

But heed a warning: if the Star of Aurora appears on the skin of someone with single vision, inevitable wrath will ensue. Death will be near once the final point is branded, and their soul will be forever stripped from their body.

&&

OK, so new resolution for this year – don't Ascend! I giggled to myself as I shoved the book back onto the shelf. I hopped excitedly down the stairs and fell into the comfort of Beau's waiting arms, the scent of his body intoxicating as I nuzzled into his neck and wrapped my arms around him.

&&

Billie Jade Kermack lives in London, England with her family. She currently works as a makeup artist for TV and film. *Ascend* is the second novel in the *Shadowed Veil Series,* book three *Hallowed* is due for release later on this year.

Follow up to date news on this bestselling series at :

Www.facebook.com/BJKAwoken

Printed in Great Britain
by Amazon.co.uk, Ltd.,
Marston Gate.